The Rampart

Barlow felt proud of the men of 39th, proud of the uniform he wore, and of the country he served: one built on fundamentals such as freedom, justice, and opportunity for all. No enemy could defeat such a nation, nor would any future foe. Not so long as men such as those who marched with him this morning into the valley of the shadow were willing to fight and die for her survival.

And then they were in range of the Creek rifles. A soldier fell. Then another, and another. The soldier immediately to Barlow's right suddenly fell, shot through the head. Barlow called on his company to be steadfast, even though he saw none who faltered.

Now he could hear less of the din of battle—the gunfire, the drumbeat, the shouts, the cries of anguish—and all he could see was the color guard in front of him. . . .

THE LONG HUNTERS

Jason Manning

A SIGNET BOOK

SIGNET
Published by New American Library, a division of
Penguin Putnam Inc., 375 Hudson Street,
New York, New York 10014, U.S.A.
Penguin Books Ltd, 80 Strand,
London WC2R 0RL, England
Penguin Books Australia Ltd, Ringwood,
Victoria, Australia
Penguin Books Canada Ltd, 10 Alcorn Avenue,
Toronto, Ontario, Canada M4V 3B2
Penguin Books (N.Z.) Ltd, 182–190 Wairau Road,
Auckland 10, New Zealand

Penguin Books Ltd, Registered Offices:
Harmondsworth, Middlesex, England

First published by Signet, an imprint of New American Library,
a division of Penguin Putnam Inc.

First Printing, October 2002
10 9 8 7 6 5 4 3 2 1

PUBLISHER'S NOTE
This is a work of fiction. Names, characters, places, and incidents either
are the product of the author's imagination or are used fictitiously,
and any resemblance to actual persons, living or dead, business
establishments, events, or locales is entirely coincidental.

To Rebel Dog and Double Naught,
young American warriors

PART I

—————◆—————

March–April, 1814

Chapter One

The concern foremost in Lieutenant Timothy Barlow's mind as he rode along the road that had been cut through the wilderness between the Coosa and Tallapoosa rivers was that he would be too late to participate in the battle he felt sure was imminent.

The scouts' reports that had reached Fort William, and which indicated that the Red Stick Creeks had fortified a position along the Tallapoosa, Barlow believed to be accurate. Creek medicine men said the fortifications were impregnable, so the Red Sticks were waiting, supremely confident of victory. All Andy Jackson had to do was make his way from Fort William to the Indian stronghold at Horseshoe Bend and engage the enemy.

General Jackson was not one to drag his feet when a fight was in the offing. Though Barlow, as a lieutenant with the 39th United States Infantry Regiment, had only been around the general for a couple of months, he knew this from experience.

The men he traveled with knew it, too. Like Jackson, they were all from Tennessee, and they knew Ol' Andy by reputation.

"Those Red Sticks don't stand a chance in hell," declared Luther Wayne, who rode alongside Barlow, and who was, as Barlow understood it, the chosen leader of the band of eleven backwoods volunteers who were accompanying him from Fort William. Wayne was a brawny, bearded, buckskin-clad man.

His companions looked no less rough hewn. And they were all eager to catch up with Jackson and his army—every bit as eager as Barlow. "Cap'n Andy will teach them heathens a lesson they won't never forget," continued Wayne. "If they think they can get away with burnin' our farms and stealin' our children and molestin' our women, they're gonna find out otherwise here right soon."

Barlow just nodded. He, too, thought the Creeks had made a grave mistake. Most people blamed the fact that they had gone to war against the United States on the word of the Shawnee prophet, Tecumseh. It was known that Tecumseh had urged the Creek Nation, back in 1811, to join a confederacy of tribes that would rise up together and halt the westward tide of white settlers. It was said that Tecumseh was a great orator, and that he had persuaded a great many of the Creeks—and Choctaws, too—that their only hope for survival, and for holding on to their lands, was to fight the white long hunters who were coming by the thousands, chopping down the forests, plowing up the earth, and killing the game.

Barlow, though, was convinced that Tecumseh was not solely to blame. The United States was at war with Great Britain, and rumor had it that British secret agents had gone among the tribes in the south, trying to recruit the Creeks, the Choctaws, the Chickasaws, and even the Cherokees as allies. Barlow was fairly confident that the blandishments of these redcoat spies had had an effect on the Creeks.

Whatever the cause, a large number of Creek warriors had joined a fraternity called the Red Sticks. They were moved to violence against Americans by the visions and predictions of a mystic order of prophets who said they could do all manner of amazing things, such as stop an enemy bullet in midair, or start fires and earthquakes, or make all the water in a river disappear.

It had begun a little over a year ago, in February of 1813, when a party of Red Sticks, returning from a visit to the Shawnees, destroyed seven white frontier families. An Indian agent by the name of Benjamin Hawkins had prevailed on the tribal council to punish the warriors, and eight of the Red Sticks were put to death. But the other Red Sticks rose up and slaughtered the braves who had carried out the orders of the council.

Then, that summer, a group of Red Sticks bound for Pensacola to purchase arms and ammunition from the Spanish governor who presided there stopped off at another frontier farm and carried away the wife of one Jim Cornell, a woman they sold off at a Pensacola slave auction. On their return, with a hundred horses and mules laden with guns, powder, and shot, they were set upon by a band of frontiersmen at Burnt Corn Creek. Though they had the element of surprise on their side, the backwoodsmen were ultimately thrown back. Georgia and the Mississippi Territory launched armed forays against the Red Sticks. These were beaten back. The Red Sticks grew bolder, more confident. Their prophets, it seemed, were right. They were unbeatable.

"They should've known," declared Luther Wayne, at one point during the journey, "that if they needed a job done right they'd have to depend on us Tennessee boys."

In essence, "they" had done just that, as Barlow well knew.

Late in the summer just past, Major General Andrew Jackson, commanding the militia of the state of Tennessee, had issued orders to his brigadiers that every brigade be made ready to march at a moment's notice. It was clear to Jackson, as it was to most others who lived on the frontier, that the Red Sticks had to be crushed. Their continued success would only serve to inspire other tribes presently in an uneasy peace with the whites to take up arms against the settlers. If that happened, there was no guarantee that the settlers could hold out. They might be driven back across the mountains. And then Tecumseh's dream would come true, even as the dreams of thousands of frontiersmen and women—people who had risked all to make a new beginning in the virgin wilderness—would be shattered.

Men like Andrew Jackson and Luther Wayne were not going to allow that.

"Ain't no redskin gonna drive me out of my home," said Wayne. "Not while there's breath left in my body." He glanced at Barlow then. "But don't you fret none. Andy By-God Jackson will teach them red niggers a lesson they won't soon forget."

"I'm not fretting," Barlow assured him.

That wasn't exactly true. There was one aspect of the entire affair that did worry him. From what he understood, this man Jackson had never commanded men in battle until this Red Stick campaign. Barlow couldn't fathom how a fellow with no real military experience could end up commanding the entire Tennessee state militia in the first place. He couldn't name any names, but he was confident that Tennessee could produce a good many ex-soldiers. And yet Jackson had been given the commission of major general. Barlow suspected this must be favoritism at work, or some undue influence that Jackson wielded in the state government. As Barlow knew all too well after two years of service in the United States Army, the ablest men were not always the ones who were placed in positions of authority. He feared that Andrew Jackson was a case in point.

Of course, Barlow was far too circumspect to give voice to his suspicions in the presence of Luther Wayne and his fellow Tennessee long hunters. For some reason, these backwoodsmen idolized Jackson. Why this was so had thus far escaped Barlow. Jackson was an attorney and planter who liked to wager on his racing thoroughbreds. Apparently, he had fought a duel or two. Barlow felt sure that neither Wayne nor any of the others actually knew Jackson, other than by reputation or, perhaps, by sight. And yet they were fiercely loyal to the man. And, as Barlow's experience had been that frontiersmen were usually quick to take offense, he saw no point in provoking a quarrel regarding the fitness of Andrew Jackson for the command he now held.

Facts, though, usually spoke for themselves—and the facts seemed to demonstrate that Barlow had good reason to hold Jackson's military abilities suspect. Shortly after Jackson had alerted his brigadiers to prepare their men, the Red Sticks attacked Fort Mims in the Mississippi Territory. The small stockade, filled with fearful settlers seeking protection from the Creek menace and held by a token militia garrison, was easy prey for the hostiles. Up to a thousand Red Sticks, led, it was believed, by William Weatherford and Jim Boy, had attacked the fort, killing most of the whites within and carrying off the rest. Nearly two hundred and fifty mutilated bodies were found when a column of reinforcements arrived three weeks later—and many of the bodies were those of women and children.

News of the Fort Mims massacre spread like wildfire throughout the entire nation. It was the event that had brought Barlow's 39th Infantry marching into Creek country. And it had also brought Jackson with his Tennessee militia. Luther Wayne had shown Barlow an advertisement Jackson had placed in a Nashville newspaper.

> The horrid butcheries perpetrated on our defenseless fellow citizens cannot fail to excite in every bosom a spirit of revenge. I indulge the grateful hope of sharing with you the dangers and glory of prostrating these hell-hounds who are capable of such barbarities.

No sooner had the Tennessee legislature convened to authorize Governor William Blount to call 3,500 militia into service than Jackson was calling his volunteer army, including a brigade of cavalry under the command of Colonel John Coffee, to rendezvous.

In a matter of days, Jackson was on the march, cutting a road through the wilderness to the Coosa River, where Fort William was constructed. He sent Coffee's mounted riflemen to attack a Red Stick village at Tallushatchee. Coffee's men killed nearly two hundred Creeks and took over eighty women and children prisoner, balanced against a loss of only five of their own. Then, receiving news that friendly Creeks at the village of Talladega were being besieged by a large force of Red Sticks, Jackson struck again. Marching two thousand men thirty miles through the wilderness in a single day, Jackson attacked the Red Sticks and broke the siege. Over three hundred Red Sticks were slain. The problem Barlow had with all this was that nearly a thousand of the hostiles managed to slip away.

"Damn it to hell!" That had been the reaction of the 39th Infantry's commanding officer, Colonel John Williams, upon news of Jackson's "victory" at Talladega. "The uprising could have been crushed right then and there. If only this fellow Jackson had waited for our arrival. We might have trapped the entire Red Stick army and done away with them."

"I hear that Jackson is an impatient sort," remarked Captain Donovan. "And not inclined to share any glory that might be had."

Though Jackson was a major general, he was not regular army, so Donovan knew he could criticize the man without fear of repercussions.

"He may have thought it prudent to save the friendly Creeks," said another of the officers at the meeting. It was customary for Williams to allow all those with commissions to attend. "Had the Red Sticks taken Talladega, other friendly villages might have gone over to their cause, fearing the same fate if they did not. And we're still at least a fortnight away from Jackson."

"There may be some truth in that," conceded Williams. "But I doubt that it was a factor in Jackson's thinking. He is unschooled in tactics, and his men, while no doubt zealous in their desire to take Indian scalps to hang as trophies over their fireplaces, are an undisciplined lot. A golden opportunity was squandered, and I fear Jackson will find his adversaries doubly hard to catch from this point on."

Williams's words turned out to be prophetic. Although a force of three thousand volunteers from East Tennessee—along with a contingent of Cherokee warriors, eager for any chance to strike a blow against their perennial foes, the Creeks—were within a few miles of Fort William, its commanding officer, Major General John Cocke, chose not to coordinate with Jackson and ordered an attack on the villages of Indians who had just signed a treaty of peace. Since Cocke and Jackson were not on speaking terms, the latter had no way of knowing this. The villages were destroyed, women and children were killed. Believing the destruction to be the product of blackhearted betrayal by Jackson, the surviving warriors vowed vengeance and joined the Red Sticks. All this thanks to the petty rivalry between the Tennessee commanders.

As the 39th marched to reach Fort William, Jackson had found his troubles mounting. With winter coming on and their period of enlistment expired, many of Jackson's Tennessee volunteers headed for home. Neither cajolery nor threats from their general could stop them. Jackson considered their actions mutinous, but the long hunters had whipped the Red Sticks, not once but twice, and many felt as though Fort Mims had been avenged. For a while, Jackson was left with less than a hundred men and, worse still, he was desperately short on supplies. Yet he was not about to go home himself until the Creeks were conquered.

Fortunately, other volunteers soon arrived to take the place of those who had gone home, so that before long Jackson could put almost a thousand men into the field—counting several hundred Cherokees. Meanwhile, Georgian militia and friendly Indians under the command of General John Floyd attacked the Creek village of Autossee. Two hundred Creeks were killed, and Autossee was put to the torch. Floyd also destroyed Tallassee—then took his men home. Then General Ferdinand Claiborne and his Mississippians attacked the Creek Holy Ground, Ecunchate, the day before Christmas Eve. Jackson could not tolerate being stuck behind the walls of a fort while battles were being fought and won. He set out with his nine hundred long hunters and Cherokee warriors and struck out south along the Coosa. The Red Sticks struck at Emuckfau Creek, and after a fierce, daylong battle, withdrew. But they struck again two days later at Enotochopco, and while the battle was a draw, Jackson saw the wisdom of returning to Fort William.

It was at this point that the 39th Infantry arrived, on January 14. In the weeks to come, fresh volunteers streamed in by the hundreds, so that by the end of February, Jackson commanded an army of five thousand. He was ready to march again, more determined than ever to crush the Red Sticks. Scouts had reported that at least a thousand warriors had fortified a position in a bend of the Tallapoosa River, a place called Horseshoe Bend. Their prophets had told him that the position was impregnable, and if the long hunters dared attack it they would discover that the Red Sticks were impervious to their bullets. It was there that the Indians would make their stand—and it was there that Barlow was bound, in the company of Luther Wayne and the other backwoodsmen.

"Reckon we're close now," said Wayne, out of the blue, and wincing as he flexed his saddle-weary body.

"I hope so," replied Barlow.

Wayne grinned at him. "Can't wait to get your hands on them redskins, eh?"

Barlow answered with a noncommittal shrug.

"You ever fought Injuns before, Lieutenant?"

"No," said Barlow, both annoyed and dismayed that the subject had come up, as he'd feared it would, eventually.

"Where'd you say you were from? I know you told me, but I forget."

"Philadelphia."

"Well, then," said Wayne, with a sardonic smile creasing his leathery face. "I reckon you ain't had a whole lot of experience with redskins, you being from the city and all. Way I see it, you soldier boys just got to keep one thing in mind. Injuns don't fight accordin' to the book. And if you try to fight them that way, you might not live long enough to regret it."

Barlow grimaced. It seemed as though these back-woodsmen liked nothing better than to lecture any soldier wearing the uniform of the United States Army on how to fight. Implicit in Wayne's remarks was skepticism about the regulars and doubts about how effective they would prove to be in a scrape. Barlow was sure that, if given a chance, Wayne would freely disparage everything he had learned in his years of study at the military academy recently established at West Point.

"I'll keep that in mind," he said. He was also keeping in mind Colonel Williams's admonishment on the eve of their departure for Creek country.

"You will instruct your troops to avoid conflict with the militia," Williams told his officers. "And you will lead by example. This won't be easy for you. These southern frontiersmen will hold us suspect until we prove ourselves under fire, for the mere fact that we are not as they are. And they will give us no respect simply because we wear this uniform." Seeing some of his subordinates bristling at this notion, Williams had indulged in a tolerant smile. "You have your or-ders—and my complete confidence that you will carry them out in a satisfactory manner."

So Barlow bit his tongue and didn't bother challenging Luther Wayne's contention that he, and the 39th, were ill-prepared to fight the Red Sticks.

Barlow was of medium height, and more than a bit on the thin side. Luther Wayne outweighed him by fifty pounds of brawn. But Barlow wasn't afraid of the backwoodsman, or of getting into a physical alterca-tion with the Tennessean. There had been more than one upperclassman at the academy who'd misjudged

Barlow's grit and physical strength—and his fierce determination to prevail in anything he set out to do, whether it was his studies or a bout of fisticuffs. Within the slight and soft-spoken lieutenant lurked an indomitable will. One could see it in the stubborn set of the square jaw, and in the dark blue eyes that were sometimes partly obscured by the unruly curl of jet-black hair that fell across his forehead. He was the son of a merchant, from a prosperous family, and there were some who made the mistake of concluding from this that he was not a scrapper. But they were mistaken.

It was late in the day, and Barlow was beginning to wonder if their reckoning had been off—he and Wayne both had agreed that by today they should reach Horseshoe Bend. And then he heard a faint sound, faint but quite familiar to him. There could be no mistaking it for anything except what it was. Gunfire. He glanced at Wayne, and could tell by the expression on the backwoodsman's face that he, too, had heard and correctly identified the sound. Wayne looked at him—and without a word they kicked their trail-weary horses into a gallop down the road Andy Jackson's army had recently hacked out of the wilderness.

They had not gone far before a man stepped out of a thicket adjacent to the road, not fifty yards ahead. Barlow and the Tennesseans checked their mounts sharply. The man who stood before them was an Indian, clad in a beaded buckskin hunting shirt that hung down to his knees, leggings and moccasins. He carried a long rifle cradled in his arm. Alarmed, Luther Wayne yanked a pistol from his belt and brought it to bear. But before he could fire, Barlow knocked his arm aside.

Wayne's temper flared. "What the hell . . . !" Rage

made him choke on the rest of the sentence, and for an instant Barlow thought the man was going to turn the pistol on him.

"He's not a Red Stick," said Barlow tersely. "He's Cherokee. Which means he's probably a friendly. Maybe even one of General Jackson's scouts."

"You know a lot about Injuns for someone from Philadelphia," growled Wayne.

"I know what I see, and I saw plenty of your general's Cherokee allies at the fort."

Luther Wayne gave the Indian on the road another look—and put the pistol away, ashamed of his reaction to the man's sudden appearance. Barlow was right. The Indian was obviously a Cherokee, and easily distinguished from a Red Stick Creek, if for no other reasons than the pattern of beadwork on his buckskins and his hair; in the latter case, the Red Sticks sported heads that were shaved but for a scalp lock. This Cherokee's hair, as was customary among warriors of his tribe, was full and shoulder length, with braids, adorned with feathers, on either side of the head.

As Wayne belted the pistol, the Cherokee began to walk toward them, and Barlow detected a certain disdain in the Indian's expression and posture.

"You are Sharp Knife's long hunters," said the Cherokee. That he spoke English so well surprised Barlow.

"Sharp Knife?" asked Barlow.

"He means Ol' Andy," said Wayne. "It's what the Cherokees took to calling him. Now the Red Sticks, they're inclined to call him Old Mad, from what I hear." He turned to the Indian. "You scout for Sharp Knife?"

The Cherokee nodded. "I am Mondegah."

"Luther Wayne, from Clarksville, Tennessee, as are these boys." He aimed a thumb over his shoulder to indicate the other backwoodsmen. Then he tilted his head in Barlow's direction. "This here is Lieutenant Barlow, of the 39th Infantry."

Mondegah gave Barlow a head-to-toe appraisal. His gaze came to rest on the saber that dangled in its scabbard from the pommel of Barlow's saddle. "Did the other long knives leave you behind?"

Barlow reddened. "I fell sick at Fort William, and was ordered to remain behind until I was well enough to travel."

"We heard some shooting way off yonder," said Wayne.

"Sharp Knife has sent some of his men across the river. They shoot into Tohopeka, the Red Stick village. The battle has not yet begun."

"Good," said Wayne, immensely relieved. "I would have purely hated to miss it."

"It will happen soon enough." Mondegah exhibited none of the enthusiasm for battle that Wayne did. It wasn't that he was afraid—this, Barlow knew instinctively. Clearly, Mondegah was no stranger to battle, and he knew how high was the price of glory.

"Come," said the Cherokee. "I will take you through the pickets to Sharp Knife's camp."

"Sounds good," replied Wayne. "Wouldn't want to have come all this way just to get shot by my own people, and I reckon them pickets can get pretty quick with the trigger."

Mondegah was inscrutable. "That seems to be so with many long hunters."

Barlow suppressed a smile. He detected a note of sarcasm in the Cherokee's voice, and assumed Mondegah was referring to Luther Wayne's precipitous brandishing of his pistol only moments before.

Mondegah turned and began loping down the road. Barlow and the Tennesseans put their horses in motion and followed his lead.

Chapter Two

They passed through the pickets without being shot at, which Barlow would later learn was no small feat. In Jackson's army nerves were on edge. Tension filled the air. He felt it right away. He assumed that it stemmed from the situation the army found itself in. The enemy—the Red Sticks—had backed themselves into a corner, and made preparations for a set-piece battle from behind fortifications. It was not just a win-or-lose proposition for the Indians, but rather a win-or-die one. There was no retreat for them. The Tallapoosa River encircled their stronghold on three sides. A log rampart, in places eight logs high and pierced with gun ports, ran the length of the fourth—the northern—side. If Jackson managed to breach that wall, the Red Sticks would be doomed. It was as simple as that. There was nowhere for them to run, especially as Jackson had sent Colonel Coffee and a large force across the river to take up positions there. If the Red Sticks tried to escape downriver by canoe, they would be caught in a devastating crossfire. If they tried to swim the river and reach the other side, Coffee's sharpshooters would pick them off in the water.

And that was what made every man in Jackson's army nervous. This was not the way Indians usually fought their battles. They preferred hit-and-run tactics. They always had one or two escape routes worked out in case the tide of battle turned against them. They didn't usually dig in and make a stand. The Red Sticks were ably led by brilliant war chiefs. They were clever and elusive. Yet here they were, doing everything they weren't supposed to be doing, everything that went against their nature. Was it a trap? Were the Red Sticks behind that stout log breastwork decoys? Put there to hold Jackson's attention while other hostiles slipped up from behind and caught the long hunters—and the "long knives" from the 39th Infantry—in a trap? Such a possibility had apparently crossed Jackson's mind. He had stationed a ring of pickets behind his position, and kept a screen of Cherokee scouts like Mondegah out to keep an eye peeled for a Red Stick flanking movement.

All this Barlow learned as, upon his arrival, he reported to Colonel Williams. The 39th's commanding officer welcomed him warmly, and spread a map out on a field table that stood in front of his tent. Williams told him about Coffee's crossing of the Tallapoosa, pointed out the deployment of each element of the army, and informed Barlow that reports were indicating at least a thousand warriors waited behind the log breastwork, with half as many women and children in the village of Tohopeka.

"You got here just in time, Lieutenant," said Williams. "General Jackson has called a meeting that will include myself and the commanders of the East and West Tennessee brigades. I'll want to see all regimental officers immediately after. It is my understanding that the general intends to launch an attack on the enemy position tomorrow."

"I'd like to get the lay of the land, sir, if you don't mind."

"By all means. But it isn't wise to venture too close to the enemy fortifications, especially after sundown. The Red Sticks have been making forays almost nightly. Nothing much to them, really. Just a handful of young bucks aching to test their mettle—and maybe harvest a few of our scalps. We've killed some of them, yet they seem to persist in their ridiculous belief that our bullets can do them no harm. Their prophets hold sway over them, no question about that. But then, what can you expect from heathens?"

"Not that much different from Christian warriors of another time, sir, who thought they could not be killed in battles against infidels if their faith was strong."

Williams chuckled. "I forget, Barlow, that you are a serious student of history. But go take a look at what we're up against, if you're so inclined. Just make certain you came back with all your hair. And be sure to take someone along with you." The colonel looked around. Several young ensigns stood conversing nearby. "Houston!"

One of the ensigns broke away from the others and came over, saluting briskly.

"Yes, sir!"

"At ease, Ensign. Do you know Lieutenant Barlow?"

"We haven't been formally introduced, sir. We're in different companies."

Barlow realized that he knew Houston by sight, but had not until this moment known his name. Despite his boyish good looks, the ensign appeared somehow older than his years. This was due, decided Barlow, to the perpetual scowl on the young man's earnest face.

"Take the lieutenant as close to the enemy breastwork as you can and still come back alive," said Williams. "He would like to see what we're up against."

"Yes, sir." Houston looked gravely at Barlow. "I'm at your disposal, Lieutenant."

"I'm ready," said Barlow. "There's no time like the present."

Houston nodded. "I suggest you leave your horse

behind, sir. You'll make too fine a target for the Red Sticks if you're in the saddle."

They headed for the front lines. Barlow noticed that the Red Sticks had built their wall across the most narrow spot on the neck of the horseshoe-shaped peninsula encircled by the river's looping bend. Several hundred yards to the north lay the army's front line. Between the two the ground rose steadily, so that from any vantage point along Jackson's line one could see the heavily timbered tongue of land behind the Red Sticks' fortifications. From those trees rose a haze of wood smoke that, said Houston, marked the location of the Creek village of Tohopeka. What interested Barlow more than this was the fact that the slope between the army and the Red Sticks' breastwork was cleared—a wide strip of open ground flanked by thick stands of timber. No doubt this had been a factor in the decision of the hostiles to make their stand here; they had a clear field of fire and there was no natural cover whatsoever for attackers.

Ensign Houston led the way into the timber to the west of the open slope. They climbed to the top of a hill and found Jackson's battery of two cannon—a three-pounder and a six-pounder. Seeing that Houston and Barlow were proceeding down the other side of the hill, toward the enemy position, an officer called out to them.

"I wouldn't venture much further, gentlemen. The Indians are prone to shoot into these trees on a regular basis."

"We'll keep our heads down, sir," replied Houston with a wave, and they continued on, down the timbered slope. The trees were mostly pine, so the underbrush was sparse—Barlow could see that they were within two hundred yards of the Red Sticks' breastwork. He wondered just how close the ensign planned to get, and was about to swallow his pride and say something on that subject—perhaps to remind Houston that Colonel Williams had ordered them to come back alive—when Houston stopped and produced a spyglass, which he proffered to Barlow.

"This is about as far as we should go, sir," he said.

"Well, if you say so," said Barlow nonchalantly. He took the spyglass and surveyed the log wall. It appeared to be from six to eight logs high, with two ranges of loopholes, and erected in a zigzag pattern so that attackers would be enfiladed. Here and there Barlow spotted the head and shoulders of a Red Stick warrior above the top of the wall. The breastwork itself, he decided, was not that much of an impediment; it could be scaled with relative ease. But reaching it alive—now that would prove to be the trick. He scanned the entire field, and then studied the river that was visible about a hundred yards to his right.

"Is there no ford to cross the river?" he asked Houston.

"None. She runs deep all the way around the bend. And the current is quite strong."

Barlow lowered the spyglass, realizing there was nothing more to see—nothing that would make him feel any better about the daunting task that lay ahead of the 39th.

"So the only approach is from the north. Across that open ground."

Houston nodded. "So it would seem, sir," he said, phlegmatic. "And from what I've heard of the man, General Jackson will not hesitate to send us straight on against that wall."

Barlow handed the spyglass back to the ensign, but kept his gaze fastened on the wall. "I hear there are a thousand Red Stick warriors behind that breastwork."

"That's what I hear, too, sir. And we've got about

two thousand men on this side of the river. Colonel Coffee is on the other side with seven hundred militia and several hundred Cherokees. To cut off the Red Sticks in case they try to escape across the river."

"Do they have canoes?"

"We've seen some, sir, on the banks not far from Tohopeka. But not nearly enough to carry a thousand warriors and half as many women and children."

"My understanding is that the Red Sticks have no intentions of trying to escape."

Barlow heard, even as he spoke, what sounded like an angry hornet buzzing through the tree limbs directly overhead. An instant later he heard the crack of a long rifle. Houston raised the spyglass, searching for a telltale puff of powder smoke along the breastwork that would indicate the position of the Indian who was shooting at them.

"You think they've seen us?" asked Barlow, trying to keep his tone of voice casual.

"Possibly."

Barlow said nothing, expecting Houston to suggest a withdrawal out of rifle range. Instead, the ensign lowered the spyglass with a shrug—he'd seen no smoke—and continued their conversation as though they were sitting in the safety of a parlor and not standing within range of a thousand Creek rifles.

"I've heard the same about them, sir. They're convinced that they can't be beaten here. That this will be the site of a great victory for them. Their prophets have told them so."

"Let's hope their prophets are wrong."

Houston looked at him—and then a quick smile softened his stern countenance. "Indeed, Lieutenant, let's hope!"

Several more bullets whined overhead, followed by the reports of several rifles from somewhere along the breastwork. Barlow forced himself to stand straight, even while his first impulse was to throw himself to the ground.

"First time I've been shot at," mused Houston. "At least, while wearing this uniform."

"You joined the regiment a few months ago, did you not?"

"The first of the year, sir. How long have you been with the 39th?"

"Nearly two years. And until now I've not been under fire, either."

Houston smiled again. "A shame, isn't it, Lieutenant? Especially since we're supposed to be at war with the British at the present time."

Barlow ruefully shook his head. "The War Department fears an invasion from the sea. That's why we've been stationed so close to the capitol. Why we haven't been sent north, where all the action seems to be."

"You attended the military academy?"

Barlow nodded. The U.S. Army's academy at West Point had opened for business several years earlier. He had been the eighty-ninth man to graduate from it. Unfortunately, that seemed to be an accomplishment that impressed precious few at the present time. Still, *he* was proud of it, and supposed that that was what really mattered. Then, too, he felt that what he had learned there would stand him in good stead.

"Well," said Houston, "we'll be seeing action soon enough, sir. On the morrow, if I've guessed correctly."

Someone was shouting at them from behind, higher up on the hill, where the battery was located. Barlow looked over his shoulder. The artillery officer and several of his men were hurrying down the slope.

"It appears we're being rescued," said Barlow wryly. "I think we should go back, Ensign. One of them might be hit, and we'd have that on our conscience."

"Yes, sir. You're right."

Houston turned and headed up the hill. Barlow followed, the cold finger of dread running down his spine every time a Red Stick rifle spoke. The range was long, and shooting upslope at a target required a certain expertise. Were the Creeks poor shots, as a rule? He could only pray that it was so. If not, the attack "Old Mad" Jackson was sure to launch against the hostiles would be a bloodbath.

Back at the 39th Infantry's encampment, Barlow was greeted warmly by Lieutenant Michael Moulton, with whom he shared a tent. After assuring his friend that he was completely recovered from the fever that had overtaken him at Fort William, Barlow commented on how subdued the camp was. As usual, the men were gathered round their campfires, but there wasn't much loud talking or laughter, as would normally be the case. A camaraderie developed among men who marched and drilled and fought together, and it was difficult to stifle. But Barlow sensed that tonight the men were keeping much to themselves, and he noticed that quite a few of them were tending to their weapons.

"Everyone expects we'll be going into battle tomorrow," said Moulton. "For many of them this will be the first action they've seen."

"For us, as well," said Barlow.

Moulton smiled. "Yes, I'm a bit nervous, I freely confess. Can you tell?"

"Not in the least." That was a lie. Barlow knew Moulton well enough to have already detected the anxiety in his friend's voice.

"In fact," said Moulton, a little sheepishly, "I'm just finishing up a letter to Anne."

"Oh, I see." Anne was Moulton's young wife. Barlow had met her once, on the day Moulton had wed her, as he had stood as his friend's best man. Until this moment he had envied Moulton for finding a bride of such beauty and refinement as Anne Sedgwick. But he didn't envy Moulton at this moment, and was glad that he didn't have someone like Anne, someone he would have to be afraid he might never see again.

"What about you?" asked Moulton. "Shouldn't you write a letter to your family? You know—just in case."

"Later," said Barlow. He had no intention of writing any such letter. Mark it down to superstition, but he thought writing a letter on the eve of a battle—a letter to be sent to one's home and loved ones in the event of one's death—to be bad luck, a preparation for death that could well become self-fulfilling prophesy. Besides, he couldn't imagine what he would say to his father and mother, his younger brother and twin sisters back in Philadelphia. Yet he would tell Moulton none of this, as his friend obviously was not of the same opinion where letter writing was concerned, and now was hardly the time to debate the issue.

A corporal approached them, saluting. "Colonel Williams wants to see all commissioned officers at once, sir," he informed Barlow.

Barlow nodded. "Thank you, Corporal."

The corporal moved on, and Barlow glanced at Moulton.

"I suppose it's time we find out whether I need to finish that letter," said Moulton.

He ducked into the tent to retrieve his shako and saber, and then they made their way to the colonel's tent. Williams stood with his staff under a tarpaulin elevated on poles that were lashed in place by taut ropes staked to the ground. Several lanterns provided ample illumination. A map was laid out on a field table, held down on one side by a saber and on the other by an empty scabbard. As Williams told his subordinates to gather round, Barlow got his first look at the map—and recognized it as Horseshoe Bend, the ground he had just surveyed for himself that very afternoon.

"At dawn tomorrow morning," said the colonel solemnly, "we will advance on the enemy breastwork. The 39th has been afforded the honor of holding the center of the line. The Tennesseans will take their positions on either flank. It is General Jackson's intent to commence an artillery barrage upon the enemy position, after which, upon his signal, we will advance. The general entertains the hope that the cannon may breach the wall." Barlow thought he detected a degree of skepticism in the colonel's tone of voice. "Whether a breach results, we will take the breastwork and proceed with the advance until the enemy has been driven into the Tallapoosa River."

Williams paused and took a moment to survey the faces of the officers collected around the field table.

"The honor of the 39th must always remain foremost in your minds, gentlemen. There are, by all accounts, hundreds of Creek women and children in Tohopeka village. Unless they are armed and resisting, I want no soldier in this regiment to be the agent of any harm that may come to them."

"What about the Tennesseans, sir?" asked Captain Harding. "Are they under a similar restraint?"

"I cannot say what the Tennesseans will do," said Williams.

Barlow thought about Luther Wayne and the other backwoodsmen with whom he had recently traveled. Were they the kind who could refrain from taking the lives—and the scalps—of Red Stick women and children, especially in the heat of battle? He seriously doubted it. They wanted Creek scalps to take home as mementos of the campaign, and he had to wonder if they would be particular about the age or gender of the Creeks whose hair they might lift.

"One last thing," said the colonel. "General Jackson has issued a general order. That, and I quote, 'Any officer or soldier who flies before the enemy without being compelled to do so by superior force shall suffer death.' Needless to say, at least where the 39th Infantry is concerned, such an admonition is unnecessary."

Barlow nodded, along with most of the others. He understood the colonel perfectly. No one in the regiment would take a single step back on the morrow—and if he or any other officer saw a soldier do so, he would be obliged to strike the man down. All for the honor of the 39th.

"Are there any questions?" asked Williams.

There were none.

"Then you gentlemen are dismissed."

Barlow returned to his company, Moulton at his side, and neither man spoke. The soldiers, who were gathered round the campfires or in front of their tents, watched them walk by, sensing that they were the bearers of news that would, inevitably, mean that some of those who lived and breathed in the regimental camp tonight would lie dead on the field of battle tomorrow. *I am a messenger of death for some of these men,* mused Barlow as he glanced at the grim faces, illumined by the firelight, that were turned toward him. He tried to banish the thought from his mind, and any others like it. But he couldn't stop seeing, in his mind's eye, that vast open killing ground, that long slope down which, in a few short hours, they would march, into range of a thousand Red Stick rifles.

He and Moulton reached the tent that they shared.

"Well," said Moulton, subdued in voice and manner, "I believe I should finish my letter."

"Go ahead. I'm staying out here for a while."

Moulton nodded silent gratitude. He understood that Barlow was giving him some privacy, crucial for the all-important and extremely difficult task at hand—saying good-bye to the woman he loved with every fiber of his being.

Barlow glanced skyward at the stars, thinking of home, wondering what his family was doing at this very moment. It would be cold tonight in Philadelphia. They would probably be gathered in the front parlor, his father assiduously reading a newspaper, his mother knitting perhaps, or reading from the Bible, which was the only book she ever read. His younger brother, Thomas, might be playing with the lead soldiers Barlow had given him Christmas last, and wishing he was with his older brother on a glorious campaign against the redskins. And the twins—the twins would, like as not, be at the piano. Jennie would be playing, and Angie would be singing with that voice of hers, the voice angels would envy.

Feeling suddenly homesick, Barlow swallowed the lump in his throat as Sergeant Meriwether approached.

"Begging your pardon, Lieutenant, but the men, they be wondering . . ."

"We attack in the morning."

Meriwether nodded. "Good. Good. That'll be a damn sight better than sitting around here another day, sir."

"Yes, much better," agreed Barlow.

Meriwether started to turn away, then turned back with a grin on his face. "We'll show those Creeks a thing or two, won't we, Lieutenant?"

"They'll wish they'd never heard of the 39th, Sergeant."

Meriwether chuckled and headed for the nearest campfire, where a dozen men stood waiting.

Chapter Three

Rook stood beneath the trees at the edge of the firelight, watching the goings-on around the great fire. Hundreds of Creek warriors stood around the blaze, listening to the words of the war leaders, Menawa chief among them. The Great Warrior was a half-blood. In his younger years he had been called Hothlepoya, "Crazy War Hunter," because of his fighting prowess, demonstrated during numerous raids against the Tennessee settlements. Three years ago, when Tecumseh had come to the Oakfusbee villages, Menawa had been one of his most ardent converts. Menawa truly believed that Tecumseh had been chosen by the Great Spirit to lead all the tribes to victory against the white interlopers. He preached Tecumseh's vision with the fervor of a true disciple. He was preaching it again tonight. Like the other Red Sticks, Rook had heard the sermon many times before. Unlike his brothers, he was tired of hearing it. The other warriors wanted to hear it from Menawa again, though. They needed to hear how the great victory they would achieve on this ground against Old Mad Jackson's long hunters would be just the beginning. They would then drive all the whites from Creek land forever. And they would kill so many of the long hunters that years would pass before the whites recovered.

Listening to Menawa's words from a distance, Rook shook his head. He wished that what the Great Warrior was saying were true. He knew, however, that it would not come to pass. Unlike most of the Red Sticks who heard Menawa's words this night, Rook had lived for a time, as a boy, among the white people. During those years he had kept his eyes and ears open. He had watched and listened. And he had learned a great deal. He knew that even if a great victory was won here at Cholocco Litabixee—Horseshoe Bend—it would not make any difference in the long run. Because there were simply too many whites and too few Creeks.

When Menawa was finished inspiring his followers, the prophet Monahee spoke. Monahee assured the warriors that the bullets of the long hunters could cause no harm to those who truly believed that the Great Spirit had chosen this time and place for the triumph of the Creeks against their enemies. As Monahee spoke, Rook was struck by how much his words, his flamboyant gestures, his loud exhortations, resembled those of the Reverend Bigsbee, the preacher at whose school Rook had learned the white man's language and his history and his religion. Bigsbee believed it his solemn duty to endow the students at the Indian School with a healthy dread of God Almighty. His message was the same, really, as that of Monahee. Those that had faith would be saved. According to Bigsbee, one demonstrated his faith by obedience to the will of God—and it just so happened that God had chosen Artemus Bigsbee as His messenger, charged with conveying His will to those who would be saved. Monahee had visions, sent to him by the Great Spirit, and so he, too, knew the will of the Creek God, and to obey him was to heed the wishes of the Great Spirit.

And the Red Sticks believed. Their presence here, behind the log breastwork, trapped in the Horseshoe Bend, surrounded on three sides by the river and on the fourth by the army of Old Mad, was proof enough that they were staunch believers. As was the fact that they had built the big fire—a perfect target for the cannon of Jackson. A few salvos into the congregation of Red Sticks would put his brothers' faith to the test, mused Rook. Yet Old Mad's cannon remained silent. Ominously so, in Rook's opinion.

When Monahee was done, other shamen spoke, as did leaders of the Newyaucau towns, the Oakchays, the Hillabee and the Eufala. Rook listened for a little while, but his thoughts wandered. He felt suddenly compelled to return to his lodge, to be with Amara and his two sons. He could not shake the feeling that he was wasting precious moments here, and he was about to turn away when his friend Toquay broke from the crowd and walked over to him.

"There are some who wonder why you never join us in these gatherings, Rook," said Toquay, with a faint smile. "They do not know, as I do, that you always stand alone."

"I can hear everything I need to from here."

Toquay looked around to make sure no one was within earshot. "Do you not believe the things Monahee and the Great Warrior tell us?"

"Do you believe Monahee when he says the bullets of the long hunters cannot harm you?" asked Rook. "Do you believe it strongly enough to stand on top of the wall instead of behind it when the whites attack?"

"I believe that the whites will attack tomorrow, and if not tomorrow, then the next day. When they do, we will win a great victory, one that will long be remembered, and we will be honored by our children, and our children's children, for saving the Creek Nation, and stopping the whites from stealing the land our ancestors walked."

Rook put a hand on his friend's shoulder. "I hope you're right."

"But you think I'm wrong. You think Monahee and the Great Warrior are wrong. Since this is so, I am confused. Why are you here, Rook? Why have you fought with us all these months?"

"Because I know Tecumseh and Menawa are right about the white man. They will take our land away from us. They will take all of it, and give us nothing but misery and death in return, so that one day our people will have no place to hunt or to build their villages. Whether we win a great victory or suffer a great defeat will not change that. And I am here because once the Great Warrior chose to go on the war-path against the whites, I had no choice but to fight. The villages that remained at peace are not safe now. The long hunters do not bother to distinguish between Red Stick and peaceful Creek."

Toquay stared at him. "You think we will all die here, don't you?"

Rook gravely shook his head. "No, not all of us. My life is not important. But the lives of my wife and children are. They will not perish here at Cholocco Litabixee."

"How can you be so sure?"

"Toquay, my friend, if the battle turns against us, and you see that all is lost, come to the river where the sycamore lies down upon the water. You know the place."

Toquay nodded.

"I will be at your side when the battle begins," promised Rook. "But if Old Mad's long hunters come over the wall, I am taking my family away from here. I want you to come with us."

"You want . . . to run away?"

Rook sighed. "Do not let pride be the death of you."

"Why run, though? Where would we go? If we fail

here, the cause is lost. The villages who remained at peace with the whites will not take us in. We have made enemies of them by attacking Talladega."

Rook nodded. He had always thought that to have been a grave error of judgment on the part of William Weatherford, who had led the Red Stick attack against the village of the peaceful Creeks. It had been an attempt to frighten the other villages that had not joined the Red Stick uprising into doing so. Instead, it had pitted Creek against Creek, something that was painful for Rook to see. Some chiefs firmly believed that the only hope for the survival of the Creek Nation was to be friends with the whites. Even though he knew the Red Stick approach to dealing with the long hunters was doomed to fail, Rook thought those who took the path of peace were just as misguided. In short, there was no future either in friendship with the whites or in war against them.

"No, we cannot go to the villages that are friendly to the long hunters," agreed Rook. "There is only one place left to go. Florida."

"To live among the Seminoles?" asked Toquay.

"Yes." Rook could hear the contempt in his friend's voice. The Seminoles were an offshoot of what the white man called the Lower Creeks, those who claimed the valleys of the Chattahoochee and Flint rivers as their homeland. Like Rook, Toquay was Oakchay, one of several tribes the white man classified as Upper Creek. Toquay was not himself familiar with these labels placed on the various tribes of the Creek Nation by the whites. All he knew was that the Creeks who lived in the south were very different from his own people. Many of their customs were alien, and considered inferior by the Upper Creeks. There were many years of prejudice that stood like a wall between the northern and the southern Creeks—and it was a wall Toquay had never even considered scaling. He couldn't believe that Rook was suggesting that he scale it now and go live among the Seminoles. As bad as the southern Creeks were, the Seminoles were infinitely worse, in Toquay's mind. They were mongrels, who freely interbred with fugitive slaves and outcast Spaniards.

Toquay shook his head. "I would rather die here," he said.

"I hope you will change your mind," said Rook. He was disappointed but not surprised. Toquay was his closest friend, and Rook had never been one to make friends easily. His father had taken him into the world of the white man at an early age, and when he had returned to his people—he had been twelve years old by that time—most of the Oakchays had shunned his father because of his association, his friendship, with the whites, just as most of the Oakchay children had shunned Rook, as though somehow he had become contaminated because of his education in the white man's school. For this reason Rook had learned that it was less painful to keep to himself. Toquay, though, had befriended him, had breached Rook's childhood defenses, and had never let Rook's natural reserve interfere with their friendship from that point on.

"I know why you are doing this," said Toquay. "For Amara and your sons. Perhaps I would do the same thing if I had a family. I do not blame you for wanting to take them away from this. But you will never be able to return to your own people if you do."

Rook wondered, briefly, if he should tell his friend that, as far as he was concerned, there would one day be nothing left of the Creek Nation to return to. But he could see that Toquay earnestly believed that victory against the long hunters was possible. Maybe it was better that his friend thought that way when tomorrow came. Would it not be better to enter into the fight thinking that you had a chance of winning it, rather than knowing that your cause was hopeless?

"I must go," said Rook. "Sleep well, my friend."

"I will be thinking about what tomorrow will bring, so I will not get much sleep," predicted Toquay.

Rook passed through the night-shrouded woods, coming soon to the village of Tohopeka. He entered his lodge to find Amara waiting up for him. She sat cross-legged near a small fire ringed with stones. The night was cool, but the fire kept the interior of the lodge warm. Rook glanced at his two sons. They slept soundly in their blankets along one wall. Aged thirteen and ten years respectively, Tookla and Korak were old enough to comprehend the perilous situation that they were in. And yet they slept soundly, because they trusted their father to protect them. And their mother. Rook looked at Amara. She was very tired, and very worried, he could tell. Worried not for herself but for her children. In spite of this she smiled at him, a warm and genuine smile. Amara had endured many hardships on the Red Stick warpath. But never once had she complained, or so much as hinted that she wished she could go home, or that they had never embarked on this campaign against the whites. She had thought—as had Rook—that being with him was safer than remaining in the Oakchay village which, since so many warriors had joined the Red Stick cause, would be left virtually undefended. Word that the long hunters had attacked villages of peaceful Creeks had only confirmed their fears. Yet, of late, Rook had been plagued by second thoughts. Any place would be safer than Cholocco Litabixee. He wondered if Amara was having second thoughts of her own, regrets for having following her man onto the warpath. If so, she would never give voice to them. It was not her way.

"Did you speak to Toquay?" she asked.

"Yes."

"He said he would not come with us."

Rook nodded. She could always read him like that. Everyone else found him inscrutable. He had learned as a child to mask his true feelings, back when he had been spurned by both white and Creek children. It was a habit he could not overcome, nor had he ever wanted to. And with Amara he had no need to.

"He will change his mind," she said.

Rook shook his head. "I don't think so."

She rose—and he marveled at how lithe and graceful she was in every movement. Taking his hand between hers, she raised it to her cheek and brushed the tips of his fingers against her warm, soft skin. She knew he was hurting; knew, as well, that there was nothing she could say to ease the pain. But touching her did bring him solace, as she had known it would.

"When will the long hunters come?" she asked.

"Tomorrow."

"How can you be sure?"

Rook's smile was rueful. "I know what kind of men we are dealing with. I lived among them, remember? They are impatient, and so is the one who leads them. They cannot wait. And there is no reason for them to."

Amara glanced at their sleeping sons. "We will be ready."

"I will go to the wall in the morning."

She nodded, knowing that he would have to, and there was nothing to be gained by expressing her wish that he wouldn't.

"If the long hunters get over the wall, you will know of it right away," he said. "Go to the old sycamore and take the children into the river."

"No, we will wait for you."

"You will *not* wait for me. The river runs strong. It will take you quickly past the guns of the long hunters and the Cherokees who wait on the other side."

"We could not make it to Florida without you."

He took her by the arms. "Yes, you can. The lives of your sons will depend on it."

Amara nodded.

Rook could see that she was frightened—as afraid as he had ever seen her. Yet he knew she had the strength and courage and resolve to do what had to be done. He didn't need to ask her to promise him that she would. Wrapping his arms around her, he pulled her close to him. She was trembling, and he embraced her tightly. If he managed to escape with his family, the Red Sticks would call him a coward, a traitor. This he knew—but it wasn't important. What he held in his arms, and what slept beneath the blankets over there—*that* was more important to him than his tribe, the land of his ancestors—and certainly more important than his good name.

Amara led him to their blankets, and they lay with their bodies entwined, and eventually, safe in his arms, she fell asleep. Sleep, however, eluded him. He thought about what the future might hold for them if they did, by some miracle, escape from Cholocco Litabixee. There was no way of knowing. They would travel to a strange land, a land of many Creek legends, and they would live among strangers. That part didn't bother him much. Rook had always felt like a stranger, an outcast, no matter where he found himself. But it would be different for Amara, and for his sons. He had to stay alive, had to be there for them. Because Amara was his life, and Tookla and Korak were his future.

Chapter Four

Barlow awoke well before sunrise. He had slept only a few hours. After completing his letter to Anne, Moulton had wanted to stay up and talk for a while. Though exhausted, Barlow had felt obliged to sit there and patiently lend an ear. For the most part Moulton talked about his wife, reminiscing about the good times they'd had, and the future they had planned together. It made Barlow uncomfortable to hear such intimate details, but he endured, as it was apparent that Moulton badly needed to talk about these things. That in itself was unusual; though long and steadfast friends, the two men usually avoided topics of a personal nature. This was largely because of Barlow; he could discuss tactics or military history or politics and go on and on, because his knowledge of these subjects was quite deep, and he had developed strong and informed opinions. But when it came to affairs of the heart, he was a complete novice, and knew next to nothing except what he had read in Shakespeare or Spenser. Moulton understood this, and out of deference to his friend had never spoken of the things he talked about that night. Barlow was just glad he wasn't expected to participate in the conversation; all Moulton wanted was his ear.

Eventually, Moulton lapsed into a moody silence, and then stretched out on his blankets and went to sleep. Barlow managed to keep his eyes open long enough to confirm that his was friend was, indeed, going to be able to rest. Then he turned down the lantern that illuminated the interior of the tent and gratefully stretched out on his own bedding. He was asleep the moment his eyes closed.

Awakening, he noticed that Moulton still slept, so he did not turn up the lantern, and dressed as quietly as he could. He had worn his white linen shirt and cotton trousers through the night. They were wrinkled and soiled from much campaigning, but there was no help for that. He donned his regulation blue, woolen, single-breasted coatee, adorned with a lieutenant's shoulder straps, a meager piece of once-white worsted lace on the standing collar, and pewter buttons, stamped with the cipher "U.S." in black letters, on cuffs and tail. He pulled on his boots and wrapped black-canvas gaiters on his legs, then tied a red sash around his waist before strapping on belt and saber. Thrusting a pistol under the sash, he retrieved his black leather shako and stepped outside.

A thread of pewter-gray light stained the eastern sky, a hint that day was coming. Sergeant Meriwether and several soldiers were sitting or standing around a nearby campfire. Barlow glanced along the orderly rows of tents and saw that other men had gathered around other fires. Many of them, he assumed, had stayed up all night, unable to sleep for thinking of what the morrow might bring, and finding solace in comradeship with their brothers in arms.

"There's a chill in the air," said Barlow, moving closer to the fire, keenly aware of the fact that his appearance had cut short a conversation Meriwether and the men had been having. He was an officer, and quite apart from the deference that enlisted men were expected to show him on account of this, theirs was a clique that did not include men with commissions. Barlow sometimes found himself wishing this great divide between officer and common soldier did not exist. He liked these men, as a whole. They were solid, stalwart souls. And he believed that they respected him well enough. He had demonstrated that he could be firm and fair at the same time, and he did not lord his rank over them, the way some other officers did. He walked a fine line—he didn't want to appear snobbish, an officer who felt the enlisted man occupied a lower station in life; nor could he be their friend and confidante, no matter how much he might want to be.

"Spare some of that coffee, Sergeant?"

"Yes, sir," said Meriwether readily. He looked for another tin cup, realized there wasn't another one, and dumped the grounds out of his own before filling it up again with the contents of the pot that was balanced on the ring of stones encircling the fire. He handed Barlow the cup, and offered him a biscuit as well.

Barlow thanked him, took a sip of the coffee. It was strong and bitter, the way he had learned to like it since joining the army. Then he dropped the hardtack into the cup. Soaking a biscuit in liquid to soften it was, in his opinion, the only way to make it edible. He didn't have much of an appetite, but told himself that he needed to take some nourishment, considering what lay ahead. Besides, he couldn't let the enlisted men think he was too nervous to eat.

They were watching him, looking for any clue that he was short on nerve. Barlow didn't blame them. Their scrutiny was completely understandable; after all, they were being asked to follow him into battle, to obey his orders without question, even if it meant their deaths. They wanted to be sure he had his wits about him. Their lives might depend on it. He had to appear calm, composed.

"So," he said, pleasantly, "today we'll dispose of

the Red Sticks. Then maybe they'll send us north and let us have a go at the redcoats in Canada."

"That would suit me," said one of the enlisted men. "At least the British are obliging enough to line up in nice neat rows when we shoot at 'em."

Barlow laughed.

"Suits me, too," announced a second man. "I don't care for this southern country. Thickets and bogs and mosquitoes the size of horseflies. I'm told it gets so hot down here in the summertime you can't even breathe."

"We'll be long gone by the time summer arrives," said Barlow confidently.

"Lieutenant," said the first soldier, brows knit, "can I ask you a question?"

"Of course."

"The Tennesseans say these Indians are poor shots with the rifle. Do you think that's true?"

Barlow smiled. "It doesn't matter if they are or not. We're going to drive them into the river, put an end to this uprising, and march north."

"And let General Jackson and his Tennessee boys take all the credit," added Meriwether dryly.

They were laughing at this when Moulton emerged from the tent. Barlow offered him the cup of coffee, still half full and still containing the biscuit. Moulton accepted the cup, looked into it, and winced, handing it back to Barlow.

"I don't think so, thanks all the same."

"You should put something in your belly," suggested Barlow. "There's no telling when we'll have an opportunity to eat again."

Moulton just shook his head and took a look around. Captain Oliver Hatcher, their company commander, could be seen in front of his tent some thirty yards away, accepting a cup of coffee from his servant, a young Negro named Joshua, and speaking to one of Colonel Williams's aides. When the aide took his leave, Hatcher dispatched a corporal on the run through the camp. The corporal came to a halt in front of Barlow and Moulton and snapped off a quick salute.

"Captain's compliments, and he would see all officers at once."

With that the corporal took off at a lope, in search of the rest of the company's officers.

Before Barlow and Moulton reached Captain Hatcher's tent, they heard a bugler blow reveille. Soldiers bolted out of their tents. Hatcher was finishing his coffee as his subordinates arrived.

"Gentlemen, today is the day." He handed Joshua the empty cup, and the servant disappeared into the tent. "The colonel wants us on the march immediately. The 39th will take the center of the line, and our company has been afforded the honor of occupying the middle of the regimental line, with the colors."

Moulton glanced at Barlow, who knew exactly what his friend was thinking. It was an honor to stand with the colors because the men who did so were expected to be particularly steadfast; the regimental and national flags could be expected to draw heavy fire from an enemy.

"Inspect your men," said Hatcher, "and be quick about it. Good luck, gentlemen."

Another corporal arrived with Hatcher's horse, and Joshua emerged from the tent with the captain's sword. Barlow and Moulton returned to the vicinity of the tent, where Meriwether and a few other non-commissioned officers were getting the company into line. The 39th consisted of twelve companies in all, each of which, on paper at least, contained one hundred officers and men. In truth, though, a company was seldom at full strength, due to illness, desertion and detachments. The regiment had marched with only eight companies, four having been previously detached to garrison duty. Hatcher's command, Company B, had started the campaign with eighty-eight men at arms. But only seventy-nine would fight today, and Barlow, doing a quick head count, confirmed that all were present and accounted for. He and Moulton and the company's two other lieutenants, Pryor and Easton, had time to make a quick inspection before the drums began to roll. The companies took their place in a column of twos behind Colonel Williams and the regimental colors.

As they stood there awaiting the command to march, Barlow was struck by how quiet seven-hundred-odd men could be. Usually there was talking in the ranks that had to be squelched by the officers. But this time there was none. Most eyes were glued to the regimental colors—it was all many of the men in the column could see of the 39th's vanguard, which included the colonel, his aides, the bugler and the color guard. All but the latter were mounted. Most of the company commanders were in the saddle as well. Barlow thought they made especially fine targets, and for once was glad he was just a lowly lieutenant. In fact, he was the third-ranking lieutenant in the company. If Hatcher fell, both Pryor and Moulton would also have to fall before command devolved to him.

The drumbeat changed, and Barlow's pulse quickened. The column began to move. An instant later, General Jackson's artillery—the two cannon on the forested hill south of the encampment—began to speak. Barlow wondered with what effect. Could they breach the Red Stick breastwork? He doubted it. But for the moment he could not see the enemy's position, thanks to the contours of the terrain.

The 39th marched over a rise and onto the open slope down which the attack would be made. Now, to his right, Barlow could see the Horseshoe Bend—and the log breastwork that stretched across its most narrow point—about a half mile away. Smoke drifted through the trees where the battery was located; the cannon were being fired steadily, yet Barlow could not see that the barrage was having any effect on the wall behind which the enemy waited. To his left, he could see a wave of buckskin and homespun-clad militia moving down the slope from their camp. The long hunters did not march in formation—this was simply a mass of men coming down the hill to take their positions on either flank of the 39th. They, like Barlow's comrades, were silent. There was no cheering, no shouting. But there was a kind of grim determination about them as they advanced into battle, and Barlow suddenly realized how glad he was that they were here. Men like Luther Wayne were not his kind, and he didn't really understand them, having spent his entire life in the north, in a part of the country where there hadn't been a wild frontier to speak of for a generation or two. But there was some comfort in having such men fighting with him.

It took some time, but Rook eventually found Toquay among the hundreds of Red Stick warriors who swarmed behind the log breastwork. There was a good deal of noise, as the warriors shouted encouragement to one another, or hurled taunts and insults at the oncoming whites. Some were already shooting through the gun ports, though the range was far too great for this to have any effect. It was a waste of ammunition, and Rook knew that shot was in short supply. His powder horn was nearly full, but he had only a handful of cartridges in his shot pouch. He doubted that very many of his brothers could have much more than he.

And then there were the cannon adding to the din. They were hidden in the trees to the northwest of the open slope down which the blue-coated regulars and the buckskin-clad Tennesseans were coming. Rook had heard cannon before, but many of the other Red Sticks had not, and they were momentarily unnerved. Not that Jackson's artillery was doing any damage. A few cannonballs ripped through the trees overhead, felling branches, and a few more bounced off the breastwork. No, the real threat was out there on the slope—the soldiers in their neat columns with flags flying, flanked by the undisciplined but no less dangerous mass of militia.

When he found Toquay, his friend just looked at him and smiled grimly. Rook could think of no words to say. Shoulder to shoulder, jostled by other Red Sticks seeking access to the gun ports, they watched through spaces between the logs the enemy advancing. At about four hundred yards, the bluecoats formed a line, two soldiers deep. Their officers rode up and down the line on prancing chargers, shouting orders. The militia tried to form a line on either side of the regulars. A few of them were shooting back at the Red Sticks who were wasting their ammunition. Rook took a cartridge from the shot pouch at his side and placed it between his teeth. His rifle was loaded, but doing this would shave precious seconds off the time it would take him to reload.

Suddenly the cannon ceased to roar, and it was as though their silence was a contagion that spread through the mass of Red Sticks behind the breastwork, as well as through the soldiers and militia out there on the long green slope. For a breathless moment, time froze, and scarcely a sound could be heard save

for a rifle shot or two from back along the river—
shots that Rook assumed came from enemy positions
located on the other side of the Tallapoosa. The sun
chose this moment to rise above the wooded heights
to the east, just as the bluecoats, in brisk unison, fixed
bayonets, and the sunlight glimmered off steel all
along the line. Rook glanced at Toquay's profile, then
at the faces of other braves who stood beyond his
friend, tightly packed around the gun ports—and he
wondered if some of them were beginning to realize
that they were doomed.

All Barlow could think about at first, as they began
to advance to the measured cadence of the drums, was
what a magnificent fool Captain Hatcher had turned
out to be. The captain had decided to remain
mounted, riding in front of the line, saber in hand, the
color guard a bit to his right and almost directly in
front of Barlow. Most of the other company commanders were leading their men into battle on foot.
Barlow wasn't sure if Captain Hatcher was being vain-
glorious or heroic. He did not know the man all that
well, as Hatcher had joined the regiment only six
months ago. The other lieutenants had not much good
to say about him behind his back, but Barlow put this
down to an effect of Hatcher's preference for avoiding
any socializing with his subordinates. Certainly he was
ambitious. His father had distinguished himself as a
high-ranking officer in the Continental Army during
the Revolution—which was why Hatcher held the
rank he did so quickly after graduating from the academy at West Point. Barlow suspected that Oliver
Hatcher felt he had to live up to family expectations
that were set exceedingly high.

The Red Sticks were shooting at them now. The
range was still too long, but every step the 39th took

brought them that much closer to death. Barlow watched with morbid fascination as the bullets fired by the enemy struck the ground, sometimes throwing up little geysers of dirt. It was, therefore, quite possible to determine at exactly what point they would come within range. Barlow had often wondered how he would react in his first battle. He had heard that some men simply could not handle it; they fled in terror under enemy fire. Naturally, Barlow worried that he might turn out to be one of those men. Yet a profound calm came over him, and he marveled at it. His heart was racing, his mouth was dry—and yet he was quite steady. And collected. He had his wits about him. He was also immensely proud; it was a pride so strong that he felt elated even while he was afraid. Proud of the men of the 39th, proud of the uniform he wore, and of the country he served. A country built on certain admirable fundamentals, like freedom and justice and opportunity for all. No enemy would defeat such a nation, or deny it its destiny, as long as those principles were adhered to. Not the Red Sticks. Not the British. And not any future foe. Not so long as men such as those who marched with him this morning into this valley of the shadow were willing to fight and die for her survival.

And then they were in range of the Creek rifles. A soldier fell. Then another, and another. The soldier immediately to Barlow's right suddenly fell backward, shot through the head and dying on his feet. Others began to fall, just a few at first, and then more than a few, and Barlow called on the men in his company to be steadfast, even though he saw none who faltered. Hatcher reappeared, tall aboard his charger, exhorting his men onward, waving his saber. Barlow could not hear the captain's words over the din of battle. But he did see Hatcher go down as his horse was shot,

not once but several times. The animal shuddered and
staggered sideways before falling, giving the captain
time to free his feet from the stirrups and roll clear.
Barlow rushed to his aid, as did Pryor. Hatcher, un-
harmed, got to his feet, brushed himself off, and accepted his saber—which he had dropped—from Pryor.

"Thank you, gentlemen," he said calmly. "Now be
so kind as to return to your duties."

Barlow had barely made it back to his post at the
far left flank of the company when both wings of the
advancing army—the Tennessee militia—surged forward with a lusty roar. He wasn't sure if they had
been ordered to charge the Red Sticks or had simply
had enough of strolling through a hail of lead. In any
event, they were off and running, so the 39th had to
go, too. Colonel Williams galloped along the line, followed by his aides, and the drummers, behind the line,
changed their tempo. The command came rippling
down the line and the soldiers broke into a run toward
the breastwork a couple of hundred yards away.

Barlow's world suddenly seemed to shrink dramatically. He could hear less of the din of battle—the gunfire, the drumbeat, the shouts, the cries of anguish—
and all he could see was the color guard in front of
him, and the breastworks beyond, shrouded in powder
smoke. He realized he was shouting at the top of his
lungs, as were many others in the regiment, an incoherent sound welling up from hundreds of parched
throats. Realized, too, that he was getting ahead of
the company, closing in on the color guard, so close
that when the corporal carrying the Stars and Stripes
reeled, hit by a Creek bullet, blood spewing from the
mortal wound in his throat, Barlow collided with him.
The corporal went down, dying as he fell. Blinking the
man's hot blood out of his eyes, Barlow saw the flag
falling, too, saw it as though it were falling in slow

motion. He caught it and kept running, flag staff in his left hand, saber grasped in his right.

Then he found himself at the breastwork, and it fairly bristled with rifle barrels protruding from gun ports and between the logs. He thrust his saber blindly through the nearest port, into the mass of Red Stick warriors pressed together on the other side, and felt the blade slash through flesh. An enemy rifle went off right next to his head; the report deafened him, and burning powder scorched his cheek. Again, he thrust with the saber—just as the rest of the company reached the wall, swarming around him. Soldiers slid their rifle barrels through the gun ports, firing into the Red Sticks or impaling them on their bayonets, all the while taking point-blank fire themselves. Barlow's saber was wrenched from his grasp as he plunged it into a Red Stick on the other side of the wall and the warrior fell, clutching at the blade and taking it with him. One hand free, Barlow began to clamber to the top of the breastwork, finding purchase between the stout logs that were stacked, one on top of the next, notched and fitted together at regular intervals. On both sides of him, other soldiers were climbing as well. Balanced on the top, he brandished his pistol and fired down into the press of Creek warriors without bothering to pick a target—it was impossible not to hit the enemy, so tightly packed were the Red Sticks. An enlisted man who reached the top of the wall right alongside him was hurled backward by the impact of a bullet. Barlow threw the empty pistol into the mass of warriors below, saw one swing his rifle round to take aim at him. The only weapon left to Barlow was the flag staff; he thrust the bottom of the staff with all his might into the Indian's upturned face. The Creek warrior spun away, dazed and bloodied. His brethren were beginning to abandon the breastwork, fleeing through the trees toward the river. Barlow found a space where two top logs were fitted together and rammed the staff into it, securing the flag atop the enemy breastwork. The flag itself, whipped by a sudden wind, curled partially round his body like a red, white and blue shroud as he gestured for the soldiers still at the foot of the wall to follow him.

"Come on, 39th!" he shouted hoarsely. "We've got them on the run!"

An instant later, he felt a terrible impact in his side, and found himself falling, falling, falling off the wall and into a black and apparently bottomless pit. . . .

At that moment, near the eastern end of the breastwork—some distance from where Barlow fell—Toquay fired upward into the snarling face of a Tennessee backwoodsman coming over the wall. The Tennessean's snarl dissolved in a spray of blood and he fell at Toquay's feet. Nearby, Rook was trying to fend off several rifle barrels thrust through a gun port by the militiamen on the other side. He was only partially successful. One of the rifles spit flame, and Toquay went down. Rook knelt beside him. Several other Red Sticks leaped forward to take their place, fighting for their lives as more frontiersmen began to pour over the wall.

"Time for you to go," said Toquay, through teeth clenched against the pain from his wounds.

Rook looked around. The long hunters were coming over the breastwork all along the line. Fierce hand-to-hand combat raged on all sides. Some of the warriors were falling back—planning, Rook assumed, to make their last stand defending the women and children in Tohopeka.

"You're coming with me," Rook told his friend.

"No, I want to stay here. Go, save your family."

Rook could see that Toquay had been hit high and to the side above the clavicle. This was not usually a mortal wound. But if Toquay remained here a moment longer, he *would* die. So Rook wasted no more time with words. He hooked his arms under Toquay's and lifted him to his feet, and before his friend could fall again, he ducked under him and bore Toquay's weight upon one broad shoulder. Carrying Toquay and his rifle, he ran into the woods, leaving the breast-work—and the carnage surrounding it—behind.

Chapter Five

Once over the breastwork, the Tennesseans and the soldiers of the 39th Infantry pressed onward relentlessly toward the village of Tohopeka. The Red Sticks fought ferociously, but their cause was hopeless now, and they were steadily pushed back. Meanwhile, Colonel Coffee and his force of long hunters and Cherokees positioned on the other side of the river kept up a steady fire, catching the Red Sticks in a brutal crossfire. Trapped, Creek men, women and children took to the river, hoping it would carry them to safety. Some resorted to hidden canoes, but they were quickly picked off. Coffee's riflemen lined the bank of the river, shooting at the Creeks in the water, and not bothering to discriminate between warrior and noncombatant.

The old sycamore had once stood grandly at the river's edge. A long-ago flood had undermined its root system, though, and the tree had fallen, perhaps on that occasion, or sometime later. But it had not become completely uprooted, so that now the sycamore survived, extended precariously over the surface of the Tallapoosa, branches on one side buried deep into the shallows and holding the main trunk just above the surface. The branches that were partially submerged had collected a great deal of river debris over time, so that the tree, with the accumulated debris, now screened part of the bank from the view of anyone on the other side of the river. This was why Rook had chosen the spot as a rendezvous point. He had anticipated everything that was now transpiring.

To his great relief, Amara and his sons were where they were supposed to be, huddled behind the massive exposed roots of the sycamore. Rook ran to them, knelt, and slid Toquay as gently as he could off his shoulder.

"Is he . . . dead?" asked Korak, wide-eyed.

"No," said Rook. "But he's hurt."

"I am afraid, Father," said Tookla.

Rook was, too—afraid for his family. But he could not tell his son the truth about that. Not this time.

"Do not fear," he replied, with a tight smile. "Come, help me with the log. Let's leave this place."

It was the trunk of a pine tree that had fallen nearby; Rook had trimmed some of the branches away, leaving only stubs here and there, that he and his family could hold on to once the log was in the river. The needles had turned from green to brown, but they remained on the branches, thicker in some places than others, yet providing cover along two-thirds of the log's length. In all, the log was more than thirty feet long and at least two feet in diameter. It was still green and would be quite buoyant. The only question in Rook's mind was whether it would provide his family sufficient protection from the enemy rifles across the river.

As he prepared to push the log into the shallows, aided in the effort by his sons, Amara touched his arm.

"What are we going to do with Toquay?" she whispered.

"What can we do? Should I leave him here to die?"

Amara shook her head. She could tell by Rook's curt tone that her husband was fully aware of the risks involved, aware that trying to rescue Toquay put his family in even greater jeopardy than they were in already. Yet Toquay was his only real friend, and she realized that he was right: What else could they do? The only alternative to taking Toquay with them was unacceptable.

"I will bind his wound," she said, and set to work immediately, using a knife to cut away Toquay's bloodied war shirt, and cutting two long strips from it with which she could dress the wound. Rook nodded to his sons, and the three of them strained to haul the pine log partially into the river—not too far, though, lest the current capture it and carry it away before they were ready. In the time it took them to do this, Amara had done all she could for Toquay. As planned, Amara had brought several blankets, rolled up and tied with lengths of rawhide. Rook untied one, discarded the blanket, and used the rawhide to rig a harness for his unconscious friend, tying the rawhide under Toquay's arms and knotting the two pieces together behind his back. He then carried Toquay into the shallows and, with the help of his sons, secured the rawhide to one of the branch stubs. This done, Rook nodded to Amara, who took her place at the front end of the log. Korak and Tookla clung to the log near the center. Rook would be at the rear of the log; there he could keep his eye on his family, and on Toquay. His rifle and the rolled branches rested atop the log, concealed from view—or so he hoped—by branches.

They were about to cast off when a commotion turned Rook's head. A Red Stick warrior emerged from the brush. In that instant there was a gunshot, and the warrior fell, sprawling facedown not twenty feet away. A long hunter appeared, pouncing on the fallen Creek, laying aside his rifle and brandishing a knife. With relish, the frontiersman grabbed the dead man's scalp lock, lifted his head, and was preparing to harvest a scalp as a memento when he glanced up and saw Rook and his family. For a second or two no one moved. Then the long hunter charged forward, yanking a pistol from his belt.

Rook made a snap decision. With all his might, he shoved the log away from the bank, into the river, letting go as he felt the current catch it. Then he whirled to face the frontiersman's attack. Realizing that her husband intended to stay behind to battle the long hunter—and buy her and her children time enough to escape—Amara cried out his name in despair. But Rook's attention was focused on the Tennessean.

Confronted by Rook, the backwoodsman abruptly halted and took stock of the situation. He saw that Rook had a knife and a tomahawk. The resolution of this confrontation was, therefore, obvious. With a grin, the Tennessean raised his pistol.

Rook realized that the long hunter had the advantage, but he was willing to take the bullet that, otherwise, might have been fired at his family or his friend. Without hesitation, he was ready to make that sacrifice. At the same time, he wasn't willing to die without putting up a fight. He drew back the tomahawk, preparing to hurl it at the backwoodsman, even as the latter pulled the trigger of the flintlock pistol. The pistol discharged, spitting flame, just as Rook let fly with the tomahawk. Even as he experienced a searing pain on the left side of his face, Rook saw the tomahawk hit its mark dead on. The Tennessean staggered, gasping as he clutched at the haft of the tomahawk jutting from his chest. The weapon had been thrown with such force, such accuracy, that the sharp heavy head of the weapon had crushed ribs and sternum and punctured a lung. His beard was suddenly stained with bright red blood that he coughed up with one violent convulsion, and then another. He stared in disbelief at Rook, a disbelief replaced by a flicker of fear, before he toppled backward.

A wave of dizziness swept over Rook. He turned, and then his legs gave way beneath him, and he heard Amara cry out to him as though from a faint distance. He summoned up the last reserve of strength left in him and stumbled, dazed, into the river. His confrontation with the Tennessean had drawn unwanted attention. Some of the enemy rifles across the Tallapoosa were now turned on him; the air around him was suddenly thick with bullets, buzzing like a host of angry hornets. He plunged into the water. Submerged in the cold river, he regained his senses and began to swim, surfacing once to get his bearings. Amara called out to him as soon as he broke the surface. The current was carrying the pine log away. It was rapidly picking up speed. Rook put everything he had into swimming for it. His strength was just about to fail him when he felt hands on him, pulling him in. Tookla and Korak had hold of him, and a moment later he was clinging for his life to a stub as the pine log rushed downstream, pursued for a moment by the bullets of the enemy before they were out of range.

Barlow drifted in and out of consciousness. He came to long enough to see a man standing over him, looking very solemn. The man was wearing a blood-splattered canvas apron. Barlow thought he recognized the man, but he couldn't remember his name. There was a lot of shouting, moaning and cries of agony in the background. This noise seemed to be coming from far away, but the voice of the man in the bloody apron, when he spoke, was very loud, so loud that it exploded inside Barlow's skull and made him wince in pain. It was difficult to believe that he had the capacity to feel any more pain—his entire body was on fire with it, on fire and yet, paradoxically, extremely cold, so that he was shivering uncontrollably.

"The bullet didn't pass through," said the man looming over Barlow. "I had to dig it out. You should survive." He turned his head and spoke to someone Barlow could not see. "Slap hot iron on the wounds and put him somewhere out of the way. We'll dress the wound when we have the time. You there! Bring that man over here now. We'll have to take his leg if there's to be any hope of saving him. Be quick about it."

Barlow was picked up by two men, one taking his legs, the other his arms, and they lifted him off a table. Gasping at a swarm of fresh pain, he discovered that he couldn't draw sufficient air into his lungs. Panic began to overtake him. He slipped, mercifully, into unconsciousness.

Searing pain brought him round the second time—pain that was unimaginable, unbearable. The stench of burning flesh filled his nostrils. Someone was screaming, a guttural, inhuman sound wrought by the purest agony. Belatedly, Barlow realized that the sound was coming from his own throat. He tried to stifle it, but then the searing pain coursed through his body again, so intense that he thought death would be preferable to another moment of such torture—and then he passed out.

When next he regained consciousness, he was lying on a narrow field cot, gazing up at the dirty white canvas of a tent roof. With every breath a stabbing pain made him gasp. He was intensely uncomfortable, but the slightest movement made him even more so.

He discovered that by breathing shallowly he could minimize the discomfort. A deep breath, as much as he wanted to take one, was out of the question. Lieutenant Pryor was bending over him.

"Ah there you are, Barlow," said Pryor. "I was wondering if I could wake you. They told me you'd been given quite a bit of laudanum."

"Not enough," muttered Barlow. His voice was a croaking travesty of its former self.

"Just feel fortunate that you're a commissioned officer, or you'd have got none. There wasn't enough to go around."

Barlow nodded. "In that case I won't complain. But God I'm thirsty. Water. I could drink the Tallapoosa dry."

Pryor grimaced. "You'd want no part of that. The river yet runs red with blood, even now."

"Where am I? What is the day?"

"The twenty-ninth of March."

The twenty-ninth! Two days had passed since the battle. All Barlow could remember was standing on the Red Sticks' breastwork, flag wrapped around him, exhorting his men to follow him over the wall. Then . . . nothing. He drew a complete blank.

"What happened?"

"It was a decisive victory," said Pryor, but he said it in a very noncommittal way, his voice devoid of elation. "They say we killed eight hundred of the Red Sticks. About two hundred escaped somehow. Including their chief, the one named Menawa, unfortunately."

"And our losses?"

"Fifty dead, so far. Three times as many wounded. Many of them will not recover, I fear."

Barlow gingerly felt of the tight dressing wrapped

round his midsection. "What do they say is my prognosis?"

"The surgeon dug the bullet out of you. They cauterized the wound with a hot iron. So far there seems to be no infection, or so they tell me. If that remains the case, you should live."

Barlow raised his head—it took considerable effort to do so—and looked about him. He lay in a large tent—several army-issue tents sewn together—which accommodated about two dozen cots, a dozen on either side, and all occupied by wounded men, like himself.

"What of Lieutenant Moulton?"

Pryor did not answer promptly. Barlow looked at him, alarmed—and felt a sinking feeling, a hollowness in the pit of his stomach, as he read the truth on Pryor's face.

"My God, no."

Pryor laid a comforting hand on his shoulder. But Barlow derived no comfort from it.

"He was killed before we reached the wall. Lieutenant Somerville, Captain Hatcher and Major Montgomery also perished. They all died valiantly."

"Of course." Barlow was in no mood to hear words like valor, honor and duty, words he thought Pryor was prone to utter at such a time, because for men like Pryor they were words that defined purpose and provided solace. Barlow knew he would find no solace in platitudes. All he could think about was poor Anne Moulton, his good friend's widow, a young woman whose life would be forever changed by Moulton's death, whose own wounds would last long, would never cease to bleed, and would not be mended by the news that her beloved had died valiantly in the service of her country.

"If only it could have been me, instead," murmured Barlow.

"It wasn't your time to die," said Pryor. "In fact, it's your time to be a hero."

"A hero?" Barlow would have laughed, but dared not, for fear it would trigger an onslaught of fresh pain. "I hardly think so."

Pryor shrugged. "You may not think of yourself in that light, Timothy, but a certain general does. And, since he's a general and you're just a lowly lieutenant, his opinion matters quite a bit more than yours, I would venture to say."

Barlow could find no legitimate argument with which to counter such purely military logic.

"He's on his way here now, as a matter of fact," said Pryor. "I'll just go mention that you're accepting visitors."

"Wait," said Barlow. He assumed that the general Pryor had mentioned was Andrew Jackson, but he was not, under the circumstances, unduly flattered— or even very much interested—in the attention Sharp Knife wished to lavish upon him. There were far more pressing and vital matters at hand.

"How many others did we lose?"

"In the company, you mean?" Pryor grimaced. "We were certainly in the thick of it; no one will ever be able to deny that. Twelve dead, nearly forty with wounds of some sort. Oh, and the captain's slave has disappeared, as well. As far as I know he didn't go into battle, so I suspect he's a runaway."

"With the captain dead," said Barlow, "you're in command of the company."

"That I am. And my first order to you, Lieutenant, is to recover completely. We need officers like you. Hell, if you're not around when the next battle occurs, who's going to leap astride the enemy's ramparts and get his backside shot off?" Pryor grinned, and with that departed the tent.

Barlow had only a few moments to brood over the death of his friend Moulton before Andrew Jackson strode into the hospital tent, flanked by several aides, Pryor, and the man Barlow remembered seeing during a brief period of consciousness—the surgeon who had been wearing the blood-soaked canvas apron. The apron had been discarded, but the doctor still wore that solemn, haggard expression. He looked like a man who had had no rest for a week.

"Where is this Barlow fellow?" asked Jackson impatiently, scanning the wounded arrayed on the rows of narrow cots.

"Right this way, General," said Pryor.

As Jackson approached, Barlow had time to take the measure of the man. He'd been under Jackson's command for weeks, and had seen him occasionally, but only at a distance. He was quite tall, well over six feet, and very thin. There wasn't an ounce of fat on him. His face was long and lantern jawed, and there was a prominent scar on one cheek. His features resembled those of a bird of prey, Barlow thought; the hawkish nose, long and bent, over tight, stern lips, and piercing blue eyes under bushy brows. He wore white dungarees and a plain blue coatee, both of which were ill-fitting on his gaunt, lanky frame. Barlow suspected that the finest tailors in Philadelphia would be hard-pressed to fashion garments that would sit well on Jackson. The general had narrow shoulders, and a large head adorned with prematurely gray and unruly hair. There was nothing soft about him whatsoever, be it in body or soul. One look at him and you could tell that all the stories they told about this man were true—here was an individual possessed of a ferocious will, relentless stamina, dauntless personal courage, a man who did not brook weakness in himself or others, as elemental a force as a hurricane, and as likely to be diverted from his path by anything short of divine intervention. For the first time in his life, Barlow recognized that he was in the presence of true greatness.

"So you're the fellow who carried Old Glory to the top of that breastwork, eh?" asked Jackson, peering so intently at Barlow that the latter thought he could actually feel the heat of those blazing eyes. "I was watching through a spyglass, Lieutenant, and wondering if the line would falter at the wall under the terrible fire from the enemy."

"The 39th does not falter, sir."

Jackson nodded. "Not with officers such as yourself to lead the way. When I saw you there, atop the breastwork, shrouded in our glorious standard, I knew we had those heathens whipped. And when you fell, I turned to Mr. Reynolds"—Jackson gestured at one of his aides—"and told him to go forward and retrieve your body, the risks be damned, as no hero such as you, sir, should be made to lie long upon the cold earth."

"Thank you, sir," said Barlow. "But every man who fell is a hero. My best friend, Lieutenant Moulton, most of all. Because I think he knew, somehow, that he was not going to live through the day."

Jackson nodded gravely. "Many brave men died that day. But the cause was a noble one. Women and children in their homes the length and breadth of the frontier will rest easier now that the Red Stick uprising has been crushed. We have put an end to them, Lieutenant. Perhaps a handful escaped, and perhaps there will be a few more skirmishes with small bands of them, but the war is, for all practical purposes, over. Now we can turn our full attention to the damned redcoats."

"I'm told it was a British cavalryman who gave you that scar, sir."

Jackson smiled coldly. "Aye. One of Bonastre Tarleton's raiders, when I was but a boy, insisted that I wipe the mud from his boots. When I refused, he took a saber to me. That's the British for you. They think they're better than we are. We showed them the error of their ways once before. I suppose the lesson didn't take. They're back for more. This time, when they run home to Mother England, they'll be better educated." Jackson turned abruptly to the doctor. "I trust this man will live."

The doctor started to shrug, then thought better of it, realizing that what he had initially mistaken for a query was actually an order.

"Yes, sir. I'll see to it."

"Good." Jackson turned his attention back to Barlow. "Where are you from, son?"

"Philadelphia, sir."

"I won't hold that against you." Jackson's lips curled in a taut smile. "Is there any favor I can do for you? Just name it."

"Yes, sir, as a matter of fact there is one thing. The friend I mentioned, Lieutenant Moulton. He wrote a letter to his wife the night before the battle. I would like to be sure that the letter is recovered, and that she receives it."

"Consider it done." Jackson bent his long frame to lay a bony hand very gently on Barlow's shoulder. "Heal quickly, my boy. We have need still of brave men such as yourself."

"I will, sir. Thank you."

Jackson nodded, straightened, and surveyed the wounded on the other cots. "That goes for the rest of you men, as well," he said. "By the Eternal, with soldiers like this, the republic will forever endure."

As Jackson left the hospital tent with aides in tow, Barlow couldn't help but feel a stirring of pride within—pride in the uniform he wore, in the nation he served, and in the fact that he had been afforded the great honor of serving under a man like Andrew Jackson. Too bad, he thought, that the general was not regular army. Had he been, Barlow would have moved heaven and earth to join his command.

Chapter Six

They remained in the river for more than an hour, carried quickly out of range of the guns of the long hunters and their Cherokee allies, putting Cholocco Litabixee miles behind them. Half-conscious, weak and disoriented, Rook was of little use in getting the pine log to shore. But Amara and his sons managed. They laid him out upon the muddy bank, alongside the still unconscious Toquay, and Rook just lay there, gazing up through the treetops at a sky rapidly growing dark as the long, bloody, tragic day drew finally to a close. He felt Amara's cool touch on his cheek, shifted his gaze to see her lovely face above him. She was smiling bravely, a smile that failed to disguise her deep concern for his condition.

"We are safe," she said. "Rest now."

"Toquay?"

"His heart still beats. I will tend to your wound."

"See to him first. Mine is not serious."

The bullet had merely grazed his skull; a fraction of an inch to the right and he would be dead. Rook knew that even minor head wounds bled profusely, making them appear much more serious than was usually the case. The river had washed much of the blood away, so Amara was able to see that he was right to direct her to care first for Toquay. This was asking a lot, Rook knew. He was her husband, not Toquay, so naturally she was inclined to care for him first. But she would do as he asked.

"You must build a fire," said Rook. "The river was very cold, and the night will be colder still. We need the warmth of a fire."

"Will they not come after us?" asked Tookla. "Will they not see the fire?"

There was a risk, of course. But all of them needed the warmth a fire could provide, especially Toquay. Rook thought the chances of Toquay surviving the night were slim. There was not much they could do for him except to cauterize his wound and keep him as warm as possible.

And if Toquay did survive, then what? He was in no condition to travel. And yet travel they must. Amara had said they were safe, but she knew better. She'd said it just to ease his mind, and those of her children. Rook could not even begin to guess how many Red Sticks may have escaped Cholocco Litabixee. Probably not many. But the long hunters and the Cherokees would try to hunt down and kill any who had. This being the case, Rook felt he had to get his family as far away as possible—and do it quickly. His own condition aside, Toquay would slow them down. And yet how could he leave his friend behind? He would not, unless it was the only way to prevent his wife and sons from coming to harm.

Amara took charge of the camp, giving Tookla and Korak the task of building a fire, and reloading Rook's rifle, respectively. She herself attended to Toquay. The bloodied, makeshift dressing was removed. She put gunpowder on both the bullet's entry and exit wounds and then ignited it with a burning brand from the fire. As soon as the fire was hot enough, she heated the blade of Rook's knife and laid the hot steel on the blackened wounds, as well. When she was done there was no more bleeding. But Toquay had already lost a lot of blood, perhaps too much. If he lived, Rook decided it would be because he had spent some time immersed in the cold water of the Tallapoosa, which would have slowed the rate at which the blood pumped through his veins.

Still dazed, Rook allowed his sons to help him closer to the fire. He watched helplessly as Amara and their two boys carried Toquay nearer the fire, as well, and he was angry at himself for being so helpless. He was accustomed to taking care of his own, and he didn't like the feeling of not being able to. It was a debilitation he would have to overcome quickly, or they were all doomed.

Amara made them all shed their wet clothes, and she did the same. The blankets they had brought were soaked by their time in the river. They propped long branches one against another over the fire and draped their clothing and the blankets on the frame of branches so that they would dry in the heat rising from the fire. Amara set the rifle beside Rook and then sat down on the other side of him, her body against his, her arm around him. Korak and Tookla huddled together for warmth, too.

Rook tried not to think about what the future might hold for them, concentrating instead on the fact that they had survived the deathtrap of Cholocco Litabixee. So many others had not. There was no doubt in his mind that the Red Stick uprising was crushed. And the Creek Nation would never be the same. Even those who had not raised a hand in anger against the whites would suffer.

Because he had spent years among the whites, many of Rook's people had spurned him. But he felt no less sad for what had befallen them—and what would befall them in the years to come. Whether they had accepted him fully or not, they were still his people.

Oddly, he found that he did not blame the whites

for what had happened so much as he blamed Tecumseh—and Menawa, the Great Warrior—for leading the Creeks to disaster. He felt particularly strong contempt for Menawa. Great warrior, indeed! The man who had led his followers into the deathtrap at Horseshoe Bend was as responsible as Old Mad Jackson and his long hunters for the mortal blow that had struck the Creek Nation. Rook hoped that Menawa had died at Cholocco Litabixee. Monahee, the shaman, too. It would be fitting if they had died among all the brave young men that had been led to their deaths.

Ordinarily, Rook would have kept watch all night, letting his family sleep. But he knew, as did Amara, that he was in no condition to do so tonight. She told him to rest, that she would stand guard, and wake him if anything happened. Rook had his pride; in this case, though, he swallowed it. To insist that he watch over his family tonight would put them in even greater jeopardy than they were already in. Amara gingerly cleansed his wound, brought him water from the river. He would not drink it, thinking of the many Red Sticks who had no doubt perished in the Tallapoosa. He lay down, and she covered him with a blanket that was still damp in places. Then she laid his rifle across her lap and sat close beside him. Rook closed his eyes and immediately went to sleep.

When she shook him awake he noticed immediately that the fire had died down to orange embers. His sons slept soundly nearby. Amara was peering into the trees that stood thick along the river.

"Someone is out there," she whispered.

Rook didn't ask her if she was certain, but took the rifle from her and kicked dirt over the embers of the fire to extinguish them and plunge their camp into darkness. The night was clear, but the moon was only a thin sliver in the sky, and the night shadows were deep beneath the trees.

"Hold up there," came a deep, drawling voice from somewhere in the trees. "Don't you go shootin' me 'fore I get a chance to prove I mean you folks no harm."

Rook got to his feet, rifle held at the ready. He was dizzy, and swayed unsteadily, but Amara was there to give him the support he needed.

"Come closer," Rook called out, "so that we can see you."

There was a rustling in the brush, and then the shape of a man detached itself from the darkness and approached slowly, arms held away from his sides. When he was ten paces away, he stopped.

"You speak passable good English for an Injun," said the stranger.

Rook could make out enough of the man to tell that he was black, and that he had seen at least thirty winters. He was stocky in build, his clothing plain but in good condition. If he was a runaway slave, he had not been one for long.

"You look to me to be one of them Red Sticks," said the black man. "Was you at Horseshoe Bend, by any chance?"

"I was. But I am Red Stick no longer. I am nothing. I have no tribe. No home."

The black man nodded. "I know how you feel. I'm an outcast myself. Name's Joshua. I run away from my master. If they catch me they might hang me. My master was in the 39th Infantry. Captain Hatcher. He was your enemy, but I ain't. So you can put that long rifle down now."

"No," said Rook. "Not just yet."

"I don't even know if the cap'n is still alive. Soon as he rode off to battle, I slipped away. Figured it to be the best time, what with everybody all wrapped up in the big scrape. Even got me a pack mule. Just found it wanderin' loose. Got an army brand on it, so if they catch me they'll figure I stole it. And that'll give 'em another reason to hang me."

"Why did you run away?"

Joshua cocked his head to one side, a smirk on his smooth, round face. "Now why do you think? I was born a slave. But somehow I never did get used to bein' somebody else's property. They called me a troublemaker even as a child. My mama's master tol' her I'd come to a bad end. She tried to talk some sense into me, but me, I was too mule headed to listen. See, she knew what was likely to happen if I kept on bein' uppity. Me, I was too blind to see. Until, that is, the day the master sold me off to Captain Hatcher's father. That was fifteen years back, and I ain't never seen nor heard from my mama since."

Joshua paused and Rook thought that perhaps the runaway was expecting an expression of sympathy.

"Where are you going?" asked Rook.

"Florida, I reckon. I heard tell there be other runaways down there. Way I see it, Florida is my only choice. How about you folks? Where you bound?"

Rook glanced at Amara, and there was a warning in the glance that she did not fail to heed. It wasn't that Rook found anything about Joshua or his story that was particularly untrustworthy. But he didn't feel as though he was in a position to trust any stranger.

Joshua, though, was no fool. "Thing is, you being a Red Stick warrior, you got to be headin' south, too. That's the only safe direction for you. Seems to me we ought to travel together." He glanced at the unconscious Toquay. "In fact, it's a lucky break I come along when I did. That feller ain't in no condition to travel. But I got the mule, remember?"

Rook nodded. "I remember. What makes you think I won't just shoot you and take the mule?"

Joshua smiled and pointed at Amara. "Her." His smile broadened as he appreciated the perplexed look on Rook's face. "I take it she's your wife. Now, aside from her bein' pretty as a picture, she's got kind eyes. You can look at her and tell she's a nice woman. And a woman like that would not be married to a man who would murder an unarmed feller just to steal his mule."

"You could be wrong," said Rook.

"I could be. But I ain't."

Again Rook looked at Amara. This time there was a question in his eyes. He could not decide whether letting Joshua join them was a good idea or not. The larger the party, the greater the chance of discovery. Rook knew that he and his family could travel without leaving a trace. He could not be sure of the same where Joshua was concerned. But there was the mule to consider. The mule could be the solution to the problem of transporting Toquay, the dilemma he had been wrestling with only hours earlier. He felt as though Amara had a say in this. Her life was at stake, after all, not to mention the lives of their children.

As usual, she knew what he was thinking without a word having to pass between them. And she nodded.

"You may come with us," said Rook. "But if you slow us down, I will leave you behind. And if you betray us, I will kill you."

Joshua nodded. "Fair enough. I'll just mosey on back a ways and fetch the mule."

He disappeared into the night shadow from whence he had come.

"You do not trust him," Amara said, studying her husband's face.

"No. And I do not like the way he looks at you. Put your clothes back on."

Amara smiled. "You are jealous," she said, teasing him, but pulled the blanket that she wore over her shoulders closer around her.

"I have every right to be," replied Rook. "I am married to the most beautiful woman in the forest."

Amara blushed. "I am not worried. I know you will protect me. You will protect us all. You have always done so."

Rook wished he could be as confident of that as she seemed to be.

Barlow's tolerance for lying on the cot in the hospital tent proved to be very low, and as soon as he was able, he began to move about, ignoring the stern warnings of the doctor that he risked further complications that could slow his recovery or even perhaps kill him. Barlow disagreed. The aura of death and disease was strong in the tent. It was not a healthy place to be. So he frequently escaped, aided and abetted by Ensign Sam Houston.

Houston had been hit first by an arrow in the thigh during the attack on the Red Stick fortifications, and then had taken two rifle balls in the shoulder. Only his youth, vigor and stubborn will to survive had prevented these wounds from being mortal ones. While he remained an invalid, unable to remove himself from the cot which would be his prison for many days to come, Houston encouraged Barlow to venture forth and bring back news of what was happening in the aftermath of the battle. Houston had struck up friendships with several of the Cherokee warriors who'd fought alongside the long hunters. One of these happened to be Mondegah, the brave Barlow had first met on the road from Fort Williams. Mondegah made Barlow a crutch from the forked trunk of an elm sapling; Barlow was still too weak to walk upright on his own accord, and found the makeshift crutch, which was lightweight but incredibly sturdy, a tremendous asset.

He found he could wander at will once he was free of the hospital tent's confines. Jackson was lingering upon the field his men had won, letting units gather and bury their dead and search for the missing, as well as for any of the enemy that might be in hiding, and waiting for his scouts to return with the information he had to have before he made his next move.

The first report Barlow made to the insatiably curious Houston concerned details of the battle itself. It seemed that while the 39th Infantry and the Tennessee militia were assailing the Red Sticks' breastwork, some of the Cherokee warriors who were part of Colonel Coffee's command on the other side of the Tallapoosa River had taken it upon themselves to plunge into the river and swim across. They seized Creek canoes and used these to ferry several hundred of their number across to the peninsula held by the enemy. Meanwhile, Coffee had ordered Lieutenant Jesse Bean with forty Rangers to seize a small island located almost directly across from the western end of the Red Stick fortifications. William Russell and his company of spies, along with Major John Walker and thirty Tennesseans, joined the Cherokees who had so boldly plunged into the heart of the enemy stronghold. The fighting was fierce, yet the Cherokees reached the Creek village and set it ablaze, scattering the Red Stick women and children, causing chaos among the enemy and contributing to his demoralization. Still, though, the Red Sticks fought—fought with a ferocity stemming from the sure and certain knowledge that there was nothing left to do except die bravely. There was no escape, and there would be surrender.

Soon the Cherokees found themselves surrounded by Red Sticks fighting to the death. They might have been doomed, except that the 39th and the Tennesseans breached the enemy breastwork—and the rout was on. Unobstructed by the Red Stick defenses, the soldiers and militia swept across the peninsula. The Red Sticks refused to quit—save for several hundred of them, who tried to escape in the river. Coffee's marksmen killed many of them.

The battle raged throughout the day, the gunfire finally dwindling only when night began to descend on the scene. The prophet Monahee was found dead, the lower part of his face blown away by grapeshot; he had been standing atop the breastwork as Jackson's army began its advance, taunting the whites, showing his people that what he had said was true—the bullets of the enemy could not harm those who truly believed.

"Apparently the deluded old fool actually believed his own nonsense," said Houston. "What about Menawa, the Great Warrior, as they call him?"

"Rumor is he was hit six or seven times. They thought him dead. But as the sun set, they went back to where he had fallen, and he was gone."

"Maybe some of his followers carried his body away, fearing we would mutilate the great man's mortal remains."

"Or maybe he crawled off into the brush," said Barlow. "At any rate, the search continues."

Besides Monahee, three other Red Stick prophets had been slain, along with five hundred and fifty warriors on the peninsula and at least one hundred more in the river. Several Creek women and children had also been killed. The rest—some three hundred and fifty of them in all—were captured. Only three Creek warriors were taken alive.

"What will become of the Creek women and children?" asked Houston.

"It seems a good many have been carried off by your Cherokee friends."

Houston nodded grimly. "Turning the vanquished into slaves is a long tradition among the tribes in these parts."

"General Jackson has ordered the rest taken, under guard, to Huntsville. He's made it clear he expects them to be treated humanely."

Houston smirked. "I would expect an attempt will be made to 'civilize' them. I suppose that's humane, depending on your point of view."

Barlow looked at him, curious. "I take it you don't share in the general opinion that Indians are savages that need to be converted to Christianity."

"No, sir, I do not. In some ways they are far more civilized than many whites I've known. Where do you stand on the matter, Lieutenant?"

Barlow shook his head. "I don't know enough to have an opinion."

"Better make up your mind one way or the other, sir. Soon enough this land will be filling up with settlers, especially now that the Red Stick menace has been dealt with. And eventually the army will be required to move the rest of the tribes out. Even our friends the Cherokees, I'd wager. The very braves who fought so valiantly beside us on this field will be transformed into enemies."

There was some question, though, as Barlow soon discovered, whether the Red Stick menace really was over. Scouts brought word that men from the war towns had gathered at Hothewalee in the Hickory Ground. Hearing this, Jackson sent for additional supplies from Fort William and wrote Tennessee Governor Blount that his army was sufficiently strong to proceed to the Hickory Ground and challenge the Red Sticks there where the Tallapoosa and Coosa Rivers joined.

Two weeks later, Jackson gave the orders to march. Barlow wanted to rejoin his company but Prior, now acting as captain, denied his request, deeming Barlow as yet not fully recovered sufficiently to resume active duty. Barlow knew in his heart that Pryor was right, but that didn't ease his disappointment.

Fortunately, Jackson decided to carry his wounded, which numbered nearly one hundred, with him. As the enlistment period for many of the Tennessee militiamen had expired, a lot of them had gone home, concerned about spring planting and believing that the war had been won. The general felt he could not spare a detachment large enough to guarantee the safety of the wounded if they were left behind so deep in Creek country. So it was that Timothy Barlow was on hand to witness the Red Stick surrender.

Reaching the juncture of the Coosa and Tallapoosa, Jackson made camp and ordered another fort built. Crews set to work felling trees. Axes rang out through the wilderness from dawn to dusk. The palisades went up. Buildings were erected. Barlow noticed that the Tennesseans were as adept with the axe as they were with the long rifle.

The expectation was that yet another battle might have to be fought. Instead, the Red Sticks began to disperse. Jackson's scouts informed him that the enemy's numbers were dwindling. Then the leaders came to surrender. One day, William Weatherford, considered the supreme chief of the Red Stick cause, walked boldly into the fort. Barlow fully expected Jackson to order Weatherford hung on the spot. After all, Weatherford had been the leader of the Red Stick party that attacked Fort Mims and murdered all those within. Instead, to Barlow's amazement—and the consternation of many of the Tennesseans—Jackson was sharing a bottle of brandy with Weatherford before the afternoon was over. Barlow was as perplexed by this turn of events as the next man. But he would soon learn more of the details, for several days later Pryor told him that the general wished to see him.

"What does he want with me, sir?" asked Barlow.

Pryor shrugged. "I have no idea. I have, however, heard that Jackson is being given command of the Seventh Military District, with the rank of brigadier general, brevetted to major general."

Barlow was astonished. The Seventh Military District consisted of all the lands south of the Ohio River that lay between the Appalachian Mountains and the Mississippi River.

Proceeding to Jackson's just-finished quarters, Barlow was allowed immediate entry by the sentry posted at the door. He found the general at a rough-hewn table, bent over several maps, peering intently at them through spectacles perched at the tip of his hawkish nose. He spared Barlow the most cursory of glances before resuming his perusal of the charts, pushing the spectacles back up to the bridge of his nose.

"Lieutenant, I was pleased to hear you've been recuperating quite nicely from your wound. How do you feel?"

"Fine, sir. Ready to return to active duty."

Jackson chuckled, and glanced up again, cold blue eyes twinkling with uncommon warmth. "You're bored, aren't you? Well, I have a surefire cure for that. And you're worried about missing the next battle with the Creeks, too, I'll warrant. There won't be one."

Barlow was surprised. "You mean it's over, sir? The Red Stick campaign is finished?"

Jackson nodded. "But the war with the British continues, and it's coming to the frontier. I've been given the great honor of commanding the Seventh Military District. And I am in need of an aide who is familiar with the regular army. I have you in mind, Lieutenant. I have spoken to your commanding officer, and he has recommended you most highly. I could have had you seconded to me without consulting with you, of course. But I want you to join my staff only if you wish to. I need men like you, sir. Your country needs men like you. Brave, intelligent, born to lead. The war with the British will be won or lost *here*." He stabbed the maps on the table with a long, bony forefinger. "In the South. So I require your answer now. Will you help me to save the republic?"

Chapter Seven

Barlow was immediately torn. Torn between his loyalty to the 39th Infantry Regiment and his ambition. For he knew that to be associated with a man of Andrew Jackson's caliber would open many doors for him. He had long since realized that his first assessment of Jackson—the one he had rashly made prior to the Battle of Horseshoe Bend—had been an erroneous one. Jackson might be a man who lacked the advantage of formal military training, but he more than made up for that shortcoming with his many other attributes. He was a born leader of men. Like George Washington, Napoleon Bonaparte, Alexander the Great, he could inspire those who followed him to tremendous feats of courage and to make the ultimate sacrifice. And Jackson had a natural cunning, an indomitable will, an aggressive nature. He had the unique ability, which he shared with all great commanders, of genuinely caring for the welfare of the men under his command, even while he possessed the utter ruthlessness required to send them to their deaths for a cause he could make them believe in to the point where they would gladly surrender their very lives for it. The risks of hitching his career to Andrew Jackson were no doubt great, yet Barlow was betting that the potential benefits were even greater.

And yet—and yet the 39th had been his home for two years. The officers and men, especially those of Company B, were his brothers. Together they had endured many hardships, and this created a special bond between soldiers that was not easy to sever. As a counterbalance to ambition, Barlow was endowed with a healthy dose of conservatism. He was a cautious, methodical man in many ways, and supposed that this trait was due to his being the son of a merchant. If he stayed with the 39th, he would progress through the ranks; he would achieve the higher rank he sought, albeit slowly. But it would be done in the traditional manner, and there was something to be said for doing things that way. The safe way.

Jackson could look at Barlow and see the debate that raged within the lieutenant. So he played another card.

"You are aware, I presume, of my conference with William Weatherford, Lieutenant?"

"Yes, sir. And, if you'll forgive me for saying so, General, the men can't understand why you let him go free. He led the attack on Fort Mims, after all."

"Yes, yes." Jackson made an impatient gesture. "Weatherford is a savage. But he is also a man of his word. An honest man. I can spot them a country mile away. He swears he tried to prevent the slaughter of the civilians who had sought refuge within the walls of Fort Mims. But his braves—and the Negroes who fought with them—had a fever for blood that he was powerless to cure."

"That may be so, sir," said Barlow, emboldened by his own outrage at the thought of Weatherford escaping the justice he deserved. "But I'm still surprised by your generosity toward him."

"Ha!" Jackson shot to his feet and began to pace back and forth behind the map-laden desk. "Generosity? It was nothing of the kind. I received Weatherford's solemn vow that he would never again raise a hand in anger against the United States and its citizens. It is a vow he will keep, or else he'll be without honor, and to be without honor is anathema to the Indian. What if I had ordered him shot? What good would have come of that? Apart from making us all feel better. No, I would have made a martyr of him. Alive, he will always remind his people of the defeat I have inflicted upon the Creek Nation. He is a great man, a great warrior. And yet we vanquished him. You wish him to suffer for what transpired at Fort Mims? Consider it done! He will suffer every day for the rest of his life from the knowledge that he was whipped. He will take the shame of it to his grave."

Barlow was impressed. Jackson was a man of action, but he was also a thoughtful man, someone who obviously considered the consequences of his acts with a sophistication that was almost Machiavellian.

"At any rate," said Jackson, stopping to lean forward over the table, knuckles planted on the maps, "Weatherford gave me some very useful intelligence. He confirmed my suspicions that the British have sent agents among the southern tribes. These provocateurs have been most active in Florida, inciting the Seminoles to raid our most isolated settlements and, perhaps worse, urging runaway Negroes to return to the United States for the purpose of encouraging slaves to rise up and slay their masters. Should the British succeed in this nefarious enterprise, the entire South will be engulfed in blood and fire, sir! We must not allow that to happen."

"Yet how do we stop them? Florida is in Spanish hands."

"The dons be damned," growled Jackson. "They hold Florida in name only. They exercise little control over matters there. They permit the Seminoles to conduct their raids, and even profit by them, selling the guns and powder to the renegades."

"General, I seriously doubt that our government would countenance a campaign against the Seminoles in Florida. We are fighting for our very existence as a nation against the British Empire. Were we to march into Florida, the Spanish would surely declare war against us, too. That is an event our government would want to avoid at all costs."

Jackson's cold blue eyes were so intense that Barlow felt as though they were boring right through him, and the lieutenant braced himself for an explosion. The general had a notoriously bad temper. But then, to Barlow's great relief, a smile curled the corners of Andrew Jackson's taut mouth.

"You speak your mind. That's good. That's what I want. Don't ever be hesitant to do so. We may not always agree. But I want to know your opinions. In this case, you are quite right. Our government would not want to risk war with Spain at this point in time. The president would not sanction a campaign into Spanish Florida. On the other hand, if Florida was handed to him, he would not turn it down, now would he?"

"I'm afraid I don't follow you, sir."

"Are you a gambling man, Lieutenant?"

"Well, I . . . I've been known to make a wager from time to time."

"Then I'll make you a wager, sir. That one day soon we will march south to deal with the Seminole threat once and for all—and in the process we shall take Florida from the dons, and they won't make too much of a fuss about it."

It came to Barlow in a flash what Jackson meant to do. With or without the blessings of the War Department he was going to find some excuse to march into Florida. He would do to the Seminoles what he had just finished doing to the Red Sticks. And in the process he would try to wrest Florida from Spanish control. If he succeeded, he would be hailed as a hero. If he failed, or if he started a war with Spain, he would be condemned as a reckless adventurer. The government would disavow his actions. It would claim he had acted on his own. It was daring, dangerous, grandiose, outrageous—just the sort of thing one would expect from Andrew Jackson.

Right then and there Barlow made up his mind—all too aware that it would probably prove to be the most momentous decision of his life.

"I would be honored to serve as your aide, General."

Weatherford had buried the war hatchet, as had most of the other Red Stick leaders. The Red Stick warriors had dispersed. Some had gone to Florida. There was even a rumor that Menawa, the Great Warrior, was still alive, had escaped Horseshoe Bend, and had gone south, but most people didn't believe it. Still, Jackson proceeded to build a fort at the confluence of the Tallapoosa and Coosa rivers, a fort his Tennesseans insisted be named after him. He dispatched messengers to the Creek villages, calling upon all chiefs to come and confer with him regarding a new treaty of peace. This summons was sent to friendly villages, as well as those that had supported the Red Stick uprising. Some of the chiefs were leery; why, they asked, were they required to sign a treaty of peace when they had not made war against the United States in the first place? An Indian agent named Benjamin Hawkins played a key role in reassuring the Creeks. The Indians trusted Hawkins—in years past he had demonstrated his genuine concern for their well-being. Barlow took a liking to the man. He was tall and ungainly, bookish and soft-spoken. He scarcely looked like a person who could long survive the rigors and dangers of the frontier. But he was living proof that it was a mistake to judge a book by its cover. Hawkins was impervious to hardship, unfazed by peril. And he was a man of immense personal integrity. His word was his bond. When he told the chiefs that signing a treaty with the United States would result in no injury to them, he believed every word, and so did the chiefs.

So it was that, on a hot and humid June day, Hawkins appeared at Fort Jackson to inform the general that the chiefs were coming in. All the tribes of the Creek Confederation would be represented—the Oakchays, the Hillabees, the Newyaucaus and the rest. On this occasion Barlow had not accompanied Hawkins on his journey among the Creeks, though he had done so a time or two previously. Having spent many days on the trail with the Indian agent, Barlow had come to know him well, and found he enjoyed the man's company. They shared several interests—books, whist and history. And Barlow was impressed by the fact that Hawkins was committed to his job, and did it to the best of his abilities. Barlow was, therefore, glad to see Hawkins return safely to Fort Jackson, and was waiting for the agent when the latter emerged from a meeting with the general. But Barlow's smile of greeting faded when he saw the look on the Indian agent's face.

"What's the matter with you?" asked Barlow.

"It's black-hearted betrayal, that's what it is!" railed Hawkins. "By God, I won't allow it!" He stood there for a moment, fairly trembling with fury, and then stalked away with long, angry strides.

Stunned, Barlow hastened to catch up with him. "What's gotten into you, Benjamin? You won't allow what?"

"That . . . that *hero* of yours," sputtered Hawkins, with an angry gesture in the direction of Jackson's quarters. "He and Armstrong—peas in a pod, those two! No better than conniving thieves, the both of them!"

"Have a care," said Barlow gravely, with a quick look around the fort. "This place is filled with Tennessee boys who'd cut you from gizzard to gonads for speaking ill of General Jackson."

Hawkins snorted his contempt for Jackson and his Tennessee boys. "And what about you? You worship the ground that man walks on, same as the Tennesseans."

"I wouldn't go that far."

"Well, maybe you'll have second thoughts about it when you hear the truth of this so-called treaty."

"Then why don't you stand still for a minute and tell me what the truth is?" asked Barlow, exasperated.

Hawkins stopped and whirled. "Your general has orders from Secretary of War Armstrong to steal most of the land belonging to the Creek Nation. And they will use the treaty to make the theft legal. They consider the Creek land spoils of war."

"What?"

"The Creek Nation will be forced to cede much of its lands to the United States. Even the tribes that kept the peace for the duration of the Red Stick uprising."

"That can't be right."

"No, it isn't right. It's dead wrong."

"You must be mistaken, Benjamin."

"Go and ask the general himself if you don't believe me."

"What are you going to do?"

Hawkins grimaced. "My first inclination is to warn

the chiefs not to sign. But I don't trust Jackson. He
might hang me from the nearest tree. Or, worse,
hang *them*."

"You're an agent of the United States government.
He wouldn't dare."

Hawkins snorted again. "I didn't think you were
quite so naïve, Timothy. I suppose you haven't been
around Jackson long enough. But let me tell you.
There is nothing he would not dare. He is a dangerous
man. Now I must go. Write a letter of protest to President Madison himself."

"You think that will do any good?"

"No," said Hawkins flatly. "But at least there will
be a record that someone protested this officially sanc-
tioned thievery."

Hawkins left Barlow standing there. The lieutenant
glanced at the recently constructed cabin that contained Andrew Jackson's office and private quarters.
He was of half a mind to take Hawkins's advice and
go ask the general if what the Indian agent had told
him was true. But that would be foolhardy. And, besides, he was pretty certain that Hawkins was telling
the truth. The man had no reason to lie. Barlow felt
slightly sick to his stomach. It was hard for him to
accept that the man he so admired—admired to the
extent that he had left the 39th Infantry, his home and
his brothers, to serve Jackson as aide, would be a
party to such blatant treachery.

As it happened, Jackson himself broached the subject that evening; after the dinner the general shared
with his aides and subordinates, among them Barlow
and Colonel Coffee, there were cigars and brandy all
around, and once everyone had been seen to and Jackson's servant had discreetly withdrawn, the general
puffed a moment on his cigar and fastened his steely

blue gaze on Barlow through a veil of pungent tobacco smoke.

"I'm pleased to announce that Mr. Hawkins has done us proud, gentlemen. He has convinced the leaders of the Creek villages to come here and put their mark on a new treaty with the United States. They will begin arriving in a few days, I expect, and they will be shown every courtesy. You will make sure your men cause no difficulties, and pick no quarrels with the Indians, for if any do occur, by God you will answer to me personally."

"Benjamin may be the one who causes you the most difficulty, sir," said Barlow.

"Oh?" Jackson was watching him like the proverbial hawk. "And why do you say that, Lieutenant?"

"Because, according to him, the treaty you intend to have the Creeks sign is treachery of the worst sort. A betrayal of all the Creeks who kept the peace, even in the face of threats and violence from the Red Sticks. He seems to think it's wrong to repay such loyalty with a document that forces them to cede nearly all their land to the United States."

Barlow had tried his best to keep all emotion out of his voice, tried not to betray the anger and disenchantment that had been festering within him since his talk with Benjamin Hawkins earlier in the day.

"And you agree with Mr. Hawkins, don't you, Lieutenant?"

There was no point in denying the truth. "Yes, sir, I do. By taking the land of the friendly Creeks, you prove them fools for having kept the peace with us. And you prove the Red Sticks were right to fight against us."

"Sounds like a comment someone from Philadelphia would make," drawled Coffee. "You've never had to live on the same ground with Indians, Lieutenant. Believe you me, they do not make good neighbors."

"I wonder why?" said Barlow dryly.

"I don't believe I like your tone, sir," said Coffee, bristling.

"Step back, John," snapped Jackson, and Coffee, fuming, clamped his lips tightly shut and contented himself with glowering at Barlow.

"The fact is, Lieutenant," said Jackson, addressing Barlow, "that I don't consider what I am doing a betrayal at all. Rather, I'm doing the Creeks a favor. This land is fast filling up with settlers, sir. Every year, hundreds more wagons cross over the mountains. There are, perhaps, twelve thousand Creeks in the entire confederation. They claim for themselves land that could support a hundred thousand farmers and their families. The settlers are going to come here. They are going to stake their claims, build their cabins, plow their fields. The Creeks simply cannot keep all this land. Right or wrong, they must give up some of it. If they do so by this treaty, then the United States government will be better able to guarantee to them the land that remains. The settlers will not be allowed upon it. And the settlers will have plenty of land elsewhere from which to choose. It is the only hope for the Indians, Lieutenant. And while I realize he is your friend, I must say that Benjamin Hawkins is doing his Indian acquaintances no favor by refusing to see that."

"Respectfully, sir, I don't agree. Mr. Hawkins just believes the United States should conduct its affairs in an honorable fashion, and he can find no honor in repaying the Creeks who kept the peace with us—some of whom were killed by the Red Sticks precisely because they did so—by taking their land away from them."

Jackson's gaze was like cold steel. "So you keep saying. Mr. Hawkins is an idealist. He is from the East, where a man can afford the luxury of being idealistic. Here on the frontier, one must look at matters in the cold light of reality. One must be, above all, a pragmatist. The red man and the white will never be able to live in peace and harmony, side by side. Attempts to turn the Indian to the white man's way of life are as cruel a policy as any we might otherwise pursue. It is contrary to his nature. It is an exercise in futility. It cannot be done—and unless it could be, the red man will be driven from his land. You cannot civilize this wilderness and leave the savage in place, no matter how noble you may think him to be, to run amok."

"I was born in the East, sir," said Barlow, his voice without inflection. "In the city. That must be why I can sympathize with Mr. Hawkins."

"No doubt. But you are also an army officer. From our previous conversations, I gather it is your intent to make your career in the army."

"That is my intent, sir."

"Then I can highly recommend that you become more pragmatic where the Indian is concerned. We will defeat the British, Lieutenant, have no doubt on that score. And we will drive out the Spanish dons as well. The treaty that ended our war of independence, for freedom from the tyranny of King George III, made the Mississippi River our republic's western boundary. But that arrangement could not last, for the destiny of Americans is to have the whole of this blessed and bountiful continent. President Jefferson understood this and so, with the Louisiana Purchase, he made it possible for us to realize that destiny. The land beyond the Mississippi is vast and largely uncharted. It must be tamed. It is full of Indian tribes, some of them quite powerful, by all accounts. The army will be called upon to lead the way in taming that wilderness, and the Indians will prove to be obstructions in the path of progress. I think you see where this is going, sir. More often than not, your orders will be to fight the Indian, not to make friends with him."

"I don't want to make friends with him, General."

"Good. Then it's settled." And with that Jackson steered the conversation onto another topic.

But it wasn't settled in Barlow's mind. He still believed that Benjamin Hawkins had a valid point, and it challenged his well-developed sense of fair play that Indians who had not made war against the United States were going to have their lands taken away from them. He wished that he'd thought to point out to Jackson that if the United States earned a reputation for treating its allies that poorly, in the future few tribes would put any stock in a treaty of peace made with the republic. But there was little to be gained by resurrecting the subject with the general. Jackson's mind was made up. And Andrew Jackson was not a man who could be readily made to change his mind about anything. Besides, Barlow could understand the point of view of frontiersmen like the general. They had seldom known anything except conflict with the red man. The same could be said for Barlow's ancestors but two or three generations past; his grandfather had fought the French and their Iriquois allies in the Seven Years War, as a private in a militia company that served side by side with British regulars. Thanks in part to the sacrifices made by Nathaniel Barlow and his fellow militiamen, Barlow had grown up in a part of the country that had forgotten what it was like to be subjected to Indian raids. Perhaps, then, Jackson was right, and idealistic notions like living in peace with the red man were out of place on the frontier.

Still, Barlow experienced a persistent unease as the chiefs of the friendly villages arrived at Fort Jackson over the course of the next fortnight. Benjamin Hawkins tried to prepare them for what was coming—and, in Barlow's opinion, took a serious risk in doing so. Barlow felt sure that General Jackson would not take kindly to the activities of the Indian agent. Yet the general made no effort to silence Hawkins. As it turned out, he didn't need to. The chiefs would not heed Hawkins's warnings. The Great Father in Washington had given them his solemn word that they would keep their homes if they spurned Tecumseh and the Red Sticks and kept the peace. So their friend Hawkins had to be mistaken.

On the first day of August—a blistering hot day, one of those southern summer days when drawing breath was like swallowing fire, and the slightest exertion drenched a person with sweat—Jackson summoned the chiefs to a meeting. He presented them with a document entitled *Articles of Agreement and Capitulation*, read it to them, and made it clear to them that it meant the United States was taking more than half of the Creek Nation as a cession. Watching the stunned faces of the chiefs, Barlow for the first time felt ashamed of the uniform he was wearing. It was not, apparently, that easy to stop being an idealist.

A chief named Big Warrior grew indignant, and challenged Jackson, saying that the Great Father would not be a party to such an injustice visited upon his loyal Creek children.

"You are not children," snapped Jackson, "and you are under my direct authority. You deal with me, not with the Great Father, here and now."

Barlow glanced at the general, an eyebrow raised. That seemed to be an odd comment from a man who had just been made a major general in the army of the United States—and who was, therefore, a subordinate of the president.

"I could take every last acre of Creek land if I so chose," continued Jackson. "The Creek Nation has been deceitful. They listened to that devil Tecumseh. They made him welcome in their villages. He is an avowed enemy of the United States, and the friends of our enemy will be treated as enemies, as well."

"We did not take to the warpath," protested Big Warrior. "We turned our backs on the Red Sticks when they asked us to join them."

"That you betrayed your own kind does nothing to improve my opinion of you," replied Jackson coldly.

"What were we supposed to have done with Tecumseh?"

"You should have seized him. Turned him over to us. Or, better yet, you should have cut his throat. Had you done any one of those things, there would have been no uprising, and we would not be here today."

The chiefs conferred for several days. Hawkins urged them to sign the treaty. There was nothing else they could do. If they did not sign, they might lose everything.

On the ninth day of August, Barlow was on hand to watch thirty-six chiefs make their marks on the Treaty of Fort Jackson, a treaty that resolved that since two thirds of the Creek Nation had made war on the United States, the entire nation would have to make recompense. Barlow felt sure that the claim that two thirds of the Creeks had joined the Red Stick uprising was a rather large exaggeration.

Following the treaty-signing, Barlow's presence was required in the general's cabin, along with the other members of Jackson's staff and his brigadiers, like Colonel Coffee. Brandy was poured and the general made a toast to a campaign well fought and a peace well made.

"The republic is much the richer for our efforts, gentlemen," he said. "We have acquired twenty-two million acres of prime land, the whole of the Alabama River valley, and the best portions of the valleys of the Coosa and Cohaba Rivers. We've cut the Creek Nation off completely from the wicked influence of the Spaniards in Florida. And we've crushed the Red Stick rebellion, making our frontier safer by far than it was a year ago."

"It's my understanding that only one of the thirty-six chiefs who signed the treaty today was actually a Red Stick," remarked Barlow.

"Those who haven't been killed have fled into the swamps of Florida and joined up with the Seminoles, I suspect," said Coffee. "Peter McQueen is down there, I know."

"Yes, well, I've written to the Spanish governor in Pensacola about that," said Jackson, a twinkle in his eye. "I've warned him that should he continue to harbor Creek bandits like McQueen, and if they are not immediately arrested, tried and punished for their crimes, then we will have no recourse but to deal with them ourselves—and all those who have given them aid and shelter will be considered our enemies. It is an eye for an eye, a tooth for a tooth, and a scalp for a scalp."

"That's nothing less than a declaration of war," said Barlow, astonished.

Jackson smiled coldly. "I can only hope that His Excellency, Don Matteo Gonzales Manrique, takes it as such!"

Chapter Eight

For several days Rook and his family, accompanied by Joshua and Toquay, traveled along the eastern bank of the Tallapoosa River. It was slow going, because during that time Toquay traveled on a travois which Rook and Joshua had made, and which was pulled by the army mule. Most of the time Amara and Rook's sons walked, but as they day grew long Rook would see how they tired and he'd insist that they take turns riding the mule. Rook always led the way, while Joshua remained in charge of the mule.

On the second day, Toquay regained consciousness, but his wounds were already becoming inflamed, and a fever rendered him incoherent much of the time. Amara made a poultice that included elm bark and applied it to the wound. Though cauterized, the wound oozed the poison that had collected within, and for several days thereafter Rook wondered whether his friend was going to survive. The constant jostling that Toquay endured while strapped to the travois didn't help matters, either. But there was no help for that. They had to keep moving. They would not be safe from Old Mad Jackson and his long hunters until they reached Spanish Florida. Other perils awaited them there, of this Rook was certain. But there would be time enough to worry about that if and when they reached their destination.

Rook suspected that Jackson would send out large detachments, composed of both Tennessee long hunt-

ers and Cherokee warriors, in the event that any other
Red Sticks had escaped Cholocco Litabixee, or any
other group of Red Sticks happened to be in the vicinity. This was confirmed when Rook saw the sign left
by these scouting parties. Early one morning, before
daybreak, he even heard one of them. He was awakened from a light sleep by his oldest son, Tookla, who
had spelled his father on watch a few hours earlier.
Amara, Korak and Joshua were still asleep, and Toquay was unconscious. Tookla had put a finger to his
lips, then touched it to his ear before pointing west,
across the murmuring river. Rook listened, and in a
moment he heard voices—the voices of white men—
and then the whicker of a horse. It was too dark to
see anything, and soon the sounds faded into nothing.
But Rook had little doubt as to the identity of the
men across the river.

When they reached the confluence of the Coosa and
Tallapoosa rivers, they struck out to the southwest,
leaving the river behind and making for the headwa-
ters of Burnt Corn Creek. There were some white
settlers who lived along this course—in fact, it had
been the site of the Red Stick raid against the Cornell
farm, an attack that had mobilized the militia of Georgia and the Mississippi Territory against the Creeks.
Rook had not participated in that raid—he had not
approved of striking at isolated farms, waging war
against innocent women and children, as it only provoked the whites, and accomplished nothing useful.
The farmers along Burnt Corn Creek had abandoned
their homesteads after the raid, and many had gone
to Fort Mims to seek safety, only to be massacred by
William Weatherford's warriors. That, too, Rook had
missed, and he was glad of it. He had not joined the
uprising until after the attack on Tallushatchee by the
Tennesseans. He had fought Old Mad and his back-

woodsmen at Talladega, too, and at Emuckfau Creek, and yet again at Enotochopco. That was enough for him. Rook was weary of fighting, of bloodshed. Surely there was a place in Spanish Florida, somewhere very remote, where he would live with his family and be left alone.

By the time they reached Burnt Corn Creek, Toquay's condition had greatly improved. The fever had broken, and the infection had been beaten back. Toquay became conscious of his surroundings for the first time, and Rook was finally able to tell him what had transpired since Horseshoe Bend. Toquay remembered nothing from the moment of his wounding at the breastwork. When Rook told him of the death and destruction wrought upon the Red Sticks at Cholocco Litabixee, Toquay's expression was bleak.

"I wish you had left me there, Rook," he muttered. "So that I could have died with my brothers on the field of battle."

"There is no honor in death."

"You spent too much time among the white men. Sometimes you say things a true Creek warrior would never say."

Rook was stung by Toquay's harsh words. But they were true words, this he could not deny.

"I could not leave you there to die," he said flatly. And as he said it, he wondered if a true friend would have left Toquay behind, knowing how he felt. Perhaps he was just being selfish, trying to keep the only friend he had alive.

Rook thought that, had he the strength, Toquay would have gotten off the travois and walked away. But he was still too weak. And so they continued on their way together. They lived off the land; Rook and his sons caught rabbits in cleverly laid snares, or used sharpened sticks to fish in shallow water when a stream or lake was near at hand. Quite apart from the fact that he was very low on powder and shot, Rook thought it would be unwise to fire a rifle in country that was probably swarming with enemies.

The farms they saw remained abandoned. For a week they followed the creek, which ran almost due south. Thanks largely to Amara, Toquay's recovery was steady during this time. She kept his wounds cleaned and talked him into eating so that he could more quickly regain his strength. Eventually he was able to get up and walk for a little while—a few minutes the first day, nearly an hour the next, and twice that long on the third day. He said nothing to Rook, and Rook left him alone, expecting his friend to leave them soon, as soon as he felt well enough to do so. Toquay would probably go back to the Red Sticks— assuming there were any still fighting. If not, he would no doubt return to his village. And if the whites tried to root out all those who had taken part in the uprising, Toquay would die. That seemed to be what he wanted, after all. Rook tried to reconcile himself to that. He had saved his friend's life, and apparently lost the friendship that meant so much to him in the process. He could not prevent Toquay from going his own way. He had done all that he could do.

Rook knew that Burnt Corn Creek emptied into a river that in turn fed into the Big Water, and that somewhere along the coast was the Spanish town of Pensacola and the fortress of Barrancas where the Red Sticks had gone to buy rifles and ammunition. Long before they reached the Big Water they would be in Spanish Florida—and safe, at least, from Old Mad's long hunters. But Rook had no way of knowing where the border was, so he could not stop worrying about his enemies until he reached the Big Water.

They reached the swamps first—swampland that

seemed to go on for days. Rook disposed of the travois; when he grew too weak to walk, Toquay rode the mule. Joshua worried incessantly about copperheads and alligators. Rook was more concerned about the Seminoles. This was their country, and he could not be sure of the reception they would give him and his party. From everything he'd heard about them, they were little more than cutthroats. But while they saw plenty of snakes and gators, there were no Seminoles—at least none that they could see. In fact, it seemed as though they were the only humans in the whole gloomy expanse of the swampland.

Finally they came to the Big Water. Rook smelled the sea long before he topped the last sand dune and gazed across a strip of white sand at the water that stretched as far as the eye could see. He and Toquay and Amara and the boys stood and stared for quite some time. This was a spectacle they had never witnessed before. Joshua was just relieved to be free of the swamp; he ran down to the surf and waded in until the waves knocked him down and washed over him. He came up laughing. Korak and Tookla glanced hopefully at their father. Rook smiled and nodded. His sons took off running, stumbling into the surf, falling into the cold saltwater. Like Joshua, they came up laughing. That sound was a salve applied to Rook's wounded and worried heart. He thought now that he might dare to believe his family would be safe.

They camped that night in the dunes, building a small fire to cook the meat of the sea turtle that Joshua had caught, and of the small quail that Tookla had flushed from the reeds that grew in the shelter of the dunes and then brought down with a slingshot. It was meager fare for six hungry people, but by now they were all accustomed to not having enough to eat. Despite this, Rook could sense that the spirits of the others were lifted. They were all glad to be out of the swamp, and in Spanish Florida. Even Toquay seemed to be in a much better frame of mind than had been the case.

"So what do we do now?" asked Joshua, putting into words the question that was foremost on everyone's mind, and directing the query at Rook.

"We will go to Pensacola. The Spanish governor has been a friend to the Creeks. Maybe he will tell us where we can find a place we can live in peace."

"There is no peace in this world," said Toquay.

"Maybe not," said Rook. "But even so, I want to find a place that is far away from war. I am done with fighting, Toquay."

"I will go with you to Pensacola," said Toquay. "There I will find others who, like me, will continue to fight against the long hunters."

Rook just shook his head. He glanced at Joshua. "What about you?"

"Me?" The runaway shrugged and flashed a grin. "Me, I'm a lover, not a fighter. I ain't interested in gettin' in the middle of no war. I hear tell there are a passel of runaway slaves just like me down here somewhere. Reckon the thing for me to do is join up with my own kind. So looks like we all aim to go to Pensacola. Only question is—which way do we go to get there?"

"I think it lies to the west of us."

"You think," said Joshua. "But you ain't sure, are you?"

Rook admitted that he wasn't certain in which direction Pensacola lay.

"Too bad there's nobody around here to ask," said Joshua. "Fact is, we ain't seen another living soul for more than a fortnight. I'm beginning to think we're the only folks left in the whole world."

Rook thought, *If only that was so.*

Amara took his hand and stood up. "Come. Tookla says the Big Water made him feel clean. I would like to feel clean again."

Rook turned to his oldest son. "Tookla, take the rifle and stand guard until I return."

"We may no longer be friends," said Toquay coolly, "but that doesn't mean I will not watch over your sons."

Rook nodded his thanks and walked with his wife down to the sea. Amara glanced back to make sure they were hidden from the view of anyone in the camp by the sand dunes before slipping out of her dress. Her smile was one of promise, and longing. Rook understood. She needed his touch, and he needed hers. There had been no time to even think of such things since their departure from Cholocco Litabixee. For weeks, their only thought had been of survival. But now they had reached their destination, and they were still alive.

She ran into the sea. Rook hastily shed his war shirt and leggings and moccasins and followed her. She waited for him in waist-deep water and there they embraced, her soft breasts pressed against his powerful chest—and then a wave knocked them over, and they allowed themselves to be tossed about in the surf for a while, laughing like children at play. Finally Amara rose and returned to the beach. Rook followed her, put his arms around her from behind and held her glistening body close. She laid her head back on his shoulder and gazed up at the stars.

"I wish we could just live here forever," she sighed. "And never see anyone else."

"Here?" Rook smiled. "On a strip of sand between the Big Water and a black swamp?"

"Why not?"

Rook answered her with a kiss, and she responded with hungry, almost desperate passion, turning in his arms to face him. A moment later they lay, arms and legs entwined, in the surf, the starlight captured by their gleaming bodies joined together as one, and for a little while they could find solace and pleasure in that joining, forgetting the dangers of the harrowing journey that had brought them to this place, and the uncertainty of what the future might hold in store for them.

Rook awoke to find the muzzle of a long rifle inches from his face. Even so, he instinctively reached for the rifle that lay by his side. Or used to. The rifle was gone. Only then did he realize that he was looking up the barrel of his own weapon.

Tookla, his oldest son, had taken the last watch, and Rook experienced a moment of gut-wrenching alarm, for Tookla had proven himself a reliable sentry and, if he had not been able to give warning of intruders then perhaps he was . . .

No, Tookla was alive—and in the grasp of a very large Indian, whose big hand was clamped tightly over Tookla's mouth, and whose burly arm was locked around the boy's neck. In the man's grasp, Tookla's feet were lifted completely off the ground; still he struggled, but to no avail. He seemed to be of no more bother to his captor than a mosquito would be. Tookla's eyes were locked on his father, so he saw Rook shake his head—and understood. He stopped struggling.

Rook looked up at the Indian who held the rifle on him. His dress was odd—a yellow deerskin hunting shirt, long to the knees, secured at the waist with a broad leather belt, and a bright red-and-yellow sash draped over the left shoulder and tucked under the belt on the right side. His buckskin leggings were adorned with beaded strips of cloth tied at the knees, and he wore gaiters that fit over the top of his moccasins. On his head was a turban adorned with large feathers. Only his hands and face were exposed to the elements. He was armed with a powerful bow of yewwood and a quiver of arrows, both carried on his back, as well as a short blowgun made from a bamboo stalk, along with a knife, under his belt.

There were five of them, and they were all dressed in similar fashion, and armed similarly as well—except for one, a black man who wore only leggings and a loincloth. This one was massive in the chest and shoulders, and his head was shaven. He was armed, Rook noticed, with only a knife. He sat on his heels atop a sand dune, gazing impassively down at the scene in the camp below, and occasionally surveying the beach in both directions.

Rook then looked around the camp at the rest of his party. Toquay, Joshua, Amara and Korak were all still sleeping. He saw that a thread of dawn light streaked the eastern sky. Daybreak was only minutes away.

The man with the rifle aimed at Rook's head asked him something in the Mikasuki dialect of the Lower Creeks. There were some similarities between this tongue and the Muskogee of the Upper Creeks, which Rook spoke. Rook surmised that he was being asked to identify himself.

"I am Rook, of the Oakchay," he said.

"He's a Red Stick, sure 'nuff," said the black man atop the dune, speaking in English.

"That's right," said Rook, also in English.

This exchange woke the others. Toquay leaped to his feet, and the man swung the rifle in his direction, even as one of the man's companions whipped an arrow from his quiver, fitted it to his bow and drew the bowstring back—all in one quick, sure motion that was almost too fast for the eye to follow.

"Don't, Toquay!" snapped Rook. "If they had wanted to kill us, we would be dead already."

Toquay made no move. The one with the bow and arrow gestured for him to sit. Toquay sat on his heels, as watchful as a panther prepared to spring upon his prey if an opportunity presented itself.

"I am Kinachi," said the man with the rifle, speaking to Rook in English. "I am Seminole, from the town of Tallahassee, also known as Tonaby's Town."

"Let my son go," said Rook. "He will do you no harm."

Kinachi nodded at the man who held Tookla, and Tookla was released. He came to kneel at Rook's side.

"I am sorry, Father," he murmured, ashamed. "I saw nothing. Heard nothing. One minute there was nothing, and then . . ." He shook his head morosely. "It is like they rose up out of the ground at my feet."

Rook put a hand on his son's shoulder. "Don't worry," he said.

The burly Seminole who had been the one restraining Tookla spoke to Kinachi in their native tongue.

"Chaito says a child should not be made to do a man's job," said Kinachi, translating into English.

Tookla bristled. Rook had taught both his sons to speak and understand the white man's language. "I am not a child," he said angrily.

"You have the courage of a man," said Kinachi approvingly. He turned his attention back to Rook. "What are you doing here, so far from home?"

"I have no home," replied Rook. "The Red Stick cause was lost at a place called Cholocco Litabixee one moon ago."

Kinachi nodded. "We have heard of the battle there. You are not the first Red Stick to come to our land seeking refuge. Some of them do not believe the cause is lost. There is one who is called Menawa who wants the Seminoles to join with him and go north to fight the long hunters."

"Menawa!" exclaimed Toquay.

"So the Great Warrior lives," said Rook ambivalently.

"Yes. He was wounded many times, yet he lives," said Kinachi.

At Toquay's behest, Rook asked where Menawa could be found.

"He is in Pensacola, in the care of the Spanish governor," replied Kinachi. "It will be many weeks before he is able to go to war again. But his will to do so remains strong. I myself have seen him. He was brought to Tallahassee by some of his followers. We took him to Pensacola."

"Then the cause is not lost," declared an excited Toquay, speaking to Rook in their own tongue. "Now I see that it was fate that brought me here to Florida. I will join with Menawa when his wounds have healed, and we will once again go on the warpath against the long hunters. Ask him if the Seminoles will join with the Great Warrior."

Rook sighed. "I am tired of fighting," he told Kinachi. "But my friend is not. He would have died with honor at Cholocco Litabixee, had it not been for me. Now he sees another chance to die the way a Creek warrior should."

Kinachi glanced at Toquay. His features betrayed nothing of what he was thinking. "I cannot speak for all the Seminole. No one man can do so. But most who live in Tallahassee do not want a war with the whites."

Rook told Toquay that Kinachi could not speak for all Seminoles, and left it at that.

"Then I must go at once to Pensacola," said Toquay.

Kinachi surmised Toquay's intent and said, in English, "You will all come with us to Tallahassee. Our chief, Hopaunee, will decide what is to be done with you."

"I have come here for one reason," said Rook. "To find a place where I can live with my family in peace."

Kinachi nodded. "I believe you. But it is not up to me to decide your fate. Who is that one?" He pointed at Joshua. "Is he your slave?"

"I ain't nobody's slave no more," said Joshua. "I'm a runaway. Come to find a life with my own kind."

The black man with the shaven head suddenly rose and came bounding down the slope of the dune, pulling up just as he came face-to-face with Joshua—and grinned like a wolf.

"So you be wantin' to join up with them other niggers at Barracoon," he said.

"Sounds good to me. Can you take me there?"

"My name is Tom, Tom Walker. I was given my master's last name. Then the Creeks stole me and sold me on the auction block at Pensacola to a Spaniard. Then the Spaniard give me to Kinachi here, in exchange for skins."

"So you're still a slave."

"I like livin' with the Seminoles. They don't ask much of me. I even got me a Seminole wife. But I don't come and go as I please. If that makes me a slave, so be it. I'd rather be a slave than be one of them runaways at Barracoon, that's for sure."

"How come you say that?" asked Joshua. "What's wrong with 'em?"

"They be outlaws, that's what. Thieves and killers,

most of 'em. Life is cheap in Barracoon. The law of the gun and the knife is the only law that place knows."

"We go now," said Kinachi.

"Mark my words," Tom told Joshua, still grinning. "You be better off stayin' with the Seminoles than goin' to that hell they call Barracoon."

In moments they were leaving the beach, plunging back into the blackwater swamp just as dawn broke. The sunlight barely penetrated the canopy of moss-draped cypress trees. Chaito took charge of Joshua's mule, and Kinachi kept Rook's rifle. That left Rook with a knife. But he wasn't about to try anything. To do so would be to put his family in even greater jeopardy. No, they would have to take their chances in Tallahassee. Their future lay in the hands of the Seminoles.

Part II

January–February, 1815

Chapter Nine

When Barlow came downstairs into the main hallway on his way to the boardinghouse dining room, hoping he wasn't too late for breakfast, he heard a commotion in the street outside. A glance out a convenient window revealed that people were rushing to and fro in the street, afoot and on horseback. His first thought was that the British were coming back. They had marched on Washington three months ago, five thousand of them, carried up the Chesapeake Bay by a massive flotilla of ships. Their arrival had been completely unexpected and threw the citizens of the city into panic and flight. Banks shut down and the contents of their vaults were spirited away to safer locations. Men bundled their families and what belongings they could carry into wagons and carriages and fled for the countryside. Government clerks rushed to pack important documents into crates and haul them off; one of them, in the State Department, thought to locate the Declaration of Independence and take it away to safety.

There had been no regular army troops near enough to put up a defense of the republic's capital city. That task fell to a few Maryland militia units, ill trained and ill equipped. They broke and ran after a brief skirmish with an advance detachment of Sir George Cockburn's veteran redcoats. President Madison and the rest of the government were forced to take to the hills as the enemy marched unopposed into Washington. The redcoats burned the Capitol building, some dockyards, and an arsenal, and set fire to the president's house. Then they headed north to seize the port of Baltimore. The date—August 24, 1814—was etched in blackest shame in the mind of every single patriot.

Barlow had still been with General Jackson when the news of the disaster reached him, and he was of the opinion that it had played a crucial role in the general's decision to send him to Washington.

Now, as he descended the boardinghouse stairs and entered the dining room, he wondered if he was about to see battle again. It was a wonder to many that Cockburn had not put the entire city to the torch. Even the attempt to burn the president's house had, for the most part, been a failure, leaving the executive mansion only partially gutted, its outer walls scorched black by the flames—blemishes hidden by a coat of white paint. Maybe Cockburn had come back now to finish the job he'd started last summer.

A pair of congressmen—two of Barlow's fellow boarders—sat at the dining room table, along with Sarah Langford, the daughter of Mrs. Emma Langford, the landlady of the house. Henry Clay of Kentucky sat with a copy of a special edition of the *Gazette* clutched in his hands, his attention riveted to a front page story. Standing behind Clay's chair, bent over his shoulder and also reading intently, was John C. Calhoun of South Carolina. Sarah stood behind Clay's other shoulder. She looked up as soon as Barlow entered the dining room and—as always happened when she saw him—her gaze lingered upon him with a shy affection that never failed to make him feel extremely self-conscious.

"Have you heard the news?" she asked him.

"What news?"

"I'll be damned if your man Jackson hasn't won a

great victory!" exclaimed Clay, his naturally high-pitched voice pitched even higher than usual. He was a man of slight build, fair of hair and complexion, with aquiline features. Clay was one of the War Hawks—the band of young congressmen who had been instrumental in pushing the United States into a war with Great Britain. This was in response to the seizure of American merchant ships by the Royal Navy and the impressment of American citizens into service on British vessels.

Until recently, Britain had been at war with Napoleonic France, and the United States had tried to remain neutral in that conflict, intent on trading with both sides. Both sides, though, had refused to recognize American neutrality. While Napoleon issued letters of marque to French privateers that preyed on American ships, the British went a step further; quite apart from their arrogant search-and-seizure policy—stopping American vessels at will and seizing all cargo if they deemed it to be bound for France—the British were also taking American sailors and forcing them to join the crews of their warships. Interference with free commerce was one thing. Abducting Americans was quite another—and too much to bear where many were concerned.

"He has defeated a British army at New Orleans," said Calhoun. He was a tall young man with a dark complexion, jet-black hair and somber eyes. A solemn, thoughtful representative of the state of South Carolina, Calhoun was rarely known to smile, and Barlow had not once heard him laugh in the weeks they had spent under the same roof. Even now Calhoun looked very grave, brows knit in a perpetual scowl. Like Clay, he was a War Hawk. In fact, it had been Calhoun's job—he had deemed it a high honor—to write the *Report on the Causes and Reasons for the War*, the official justification for the congressional declaration of war against Britain back in the summer of 1812.

"The British losses are reported to be between fifteen hundred and two thousand," continued Calhoun. "Killed, wounded, or missing in action. Pakenham, their general, is also dead. Jackson lost only thirteen men, or so he says."

"If he said it, then it's true," replied Barlow.

"Well, it's an unbelievable triumph," said Clay.

"Indeed. It changes everything," said Calhoun. As always, he was thinking ahead, considering cause and effect, pondering the possible consequences of Jackson's victory. "With the British invasion from Canada thrown back, we are safe in the north, for the time being. General Harrison's victory on the Thames River, and the death of Tecumseh in that battle, has made the western frontier far safer than it has ever been. And now this. Had the British captured New Orleans, they would have controlled the Mississippi River, cutting the republic in half."

"This does much to wash the stain of Washington's sacking by the British from the national fabric," mused Clay.

"The question remains," said Calhoun, "what effect will it have on the negotiations taking place now at Ghent?"

Barlow was aware that Calhoun referred to the peace talks currently being undertaken in Europe between representatives of the British and American governments.

"The British have won their war against Napoleon," said Clay. "Now they are free to turn their full attention—and the whole formidable might of their army and navy—against us. They are a proud people who may wish to avenge the thrashing we've given them."

"Perhaps," said Calhoun. "But my guess is that the

British people are growing weary of war. They've been locked in mortal combat with the French for the better part of fifteen years. And, above all, they are a pragmatic people. What do they have to gain by prosecuting this war further?"

"We have something yet to gain," said Clay. "Canada."

Calhoun shook his head. "You westerners always set your sights too high, I fear. We are not strong enough to take Canada, much less hold it. Our one attempt to invade was a shameful debacle. To try to seize Canada now would be to give the British crown a reason to continue fighting."

"And why not continue fighting?" asked the fiery Clay. "We have the upper hand now. By God, we have them on the run. The British must be driven from Canada or the frontier will never be truly safe. They will continue to send their agents among the Indians to encourage the tribes to fight us."

"You may be right," conceded Calhoun. "Yet I suspect the British will offer us a peace, and we will accept the offer."

"Then we should demand Canada as a spoil of war," insisted Clay. "If the British remain there, we will simply have to fight them again at some point in the future."

Throughout this exchange, during which Clay and Calhoun had apparently forgotten that Barlow even existed, Sarah Langford kept her eyes on the lieutenant. For his part, Barlow scarcely noticed her scrutiny. While he was glad for the republic that Andrew Jackson had won his victory, he couldn't help but feel slighted. He should have been there, to share in the danger—and the glory. Whether the war continued or not, he had a sense that the battle at New Orleans would prove to be the one feat of American arms that

would be remembered the longest. Instead he was
here, as Jackson's personal emissary. And had been
here for weeks, waiting for a second audience from
the new Secretary of War, James Monroe, and a response from the secretary to the letters Jackson had
entrusted to him for delivery.

Not that these weeks had been a complete waste.
He had made the acquaintance of Sarah Langford,
and he considered that to be a stroke of good fortune.
He glanced at her—and when he realized she was gaz-
ing at him again he felt his cheeks grow hot. *My God,
I'm blushing,* he thought, disgusted with himself.

She crossed the dining room to join him, a willowy
young woman of nineteen years, five years his junior.
She had long, lustrous auburn hair and big sea-green
eyes, and freckles across her pert nose. She was pretty,
but Barlow had seen his share of pretty girls. What
set Sarah apart was her nature. She was shy and con-
siderate and always ready with a kind or encouraging
word. Quite a contrast to her mother, mused Barlow.
Mrs. Emma Langford was a bitter, sharp-tongued
woman. Clay had told him in confidence that this was
due to the chronic philandering of her late husband.
Daniel Langford had been a notorious womanizer.
They had found him a few years ago on the banks of
the Potomac, his head stove in. Some said a jealous
husband had performed the deed. Others believed it
had been the handiwork of a vengeful wife—namely,
Emma Langford. The murder remained unsolved, and
the rumors still circulated about the landlady, and
about how a carriage boy had seen her walking home
that night carrying a hatchet that dripped with gore.
Barlow didn't particularly care if Emma Langford was
a murderess or not. What he did care about was how
protective she was of her daughter. She distrusted

men, and did her best to keep all of them away from Sarah.

Now Sarah glanced at Clay and Calhoun, who were bent over the newspaper. "You'll never read about it if you wait for those two to be done," she said. "So I have something for you. Follow me."

Barlow did just that—into the downstairs hall, where Sarah opened a sideboard and extracted another copy of the *Gazette* that had been concealed within.

"Thank you, Sarah."

She smiled shyly, and then her eyes widened in horror at the *thump-thump-thumping* of heavy footsteps on the stairs. She fled into the front parlor and put her back against one of the doors that stood open. Barlow watched Mrs. Langford come to the foot of the stairs. She was a gray woman, her iron-hued hair pulled back in a severe bun, her thin bloodless lips turned downward in a perpetual scowl. She brandished a cigar butt at him.

"I found this upstairs," she said. "I trust you are familiar with the rules of the house, Lieutenant."

"I don't indulge in tobacco, Mrs. Langford."

"Then it must be that devil, Mr. Clay." Her eyes narrowed. "When I'm done with him, he'll rue the day he crossed me. Have you seen my daughter?"

"I think you might find her in the kitchen, Mrs. Langford. And you'll find Mr. Clay in the dining room."

Mrs. Langford spun on her heel and headed to the back of the hallway. Barlow could only hope that Henry Clay would hear her coming and make a quick exit. By nightfall Emma Langford would have found so many other things to complain about that she would like as not forget about the cigar smoking.

Glancing at Sarah, whom he could see just inside the parlor, Barlow smiled and winked. Her answering smile was one of immense relief. Had her mother caught them alone together, there would have been hell to pay. As soon as Mrs. Langford had disappeared into the dining room, Barlow stepped into the parlor, took Sarah by the arm and hurried her across the hallway to the reading room. Across this room was another door leading to the pantry. From there an exterior door led to a covered walk connecting the kitchen to the main house.

"Thanks again for the paper, Miss Langford," he whispered.

She put her hand over his so that, Barlow supposed, he would have to keep it on her arm. "I guess you must be wishing that you'd been with General Jackson."

"I can't deny that."

"I'm glad you weren't," she said, averting her eyes. "You might have been . . . hurt."

"You had better hurry," he said.

"Yes, of course." She looked disappointed that he had no response to the admission that she cared for his safety. Realizing his error, Barlow could think of nothing to do, save take her hand and raise it to his lips.

Blushing furiously, Sarah Langford hurried across the room to the other door. She paused there to smile at him, a smile as warm and dazzling as sunlight. Then she disappeared into the pantry.

Barlow lingered, taking a deep breath and smelling the fragrance of her in the air. He was confused by his feelings where Sarah was concerned. He was more than fond of her. She was the nicest girl he had ever met. He felt sorry for her, too, because she was constantly under her mother's thumb. Because of her own bad experience, Mrs. Langford was willing to deny her own daughter the happiness that could come of falling in love. And it was beginning to look as though Sarah had done just that—had fallen in love with him. At first Barlow had put her attentions down to the infatuation of a sheltered girl with a young man in uniform. But it seemed to be more than infatuation. Barlow thought it would be easy to fall in love with Sarah Langford. But did he dare? He was scarcely in a position, financially or otherwise, to settle down. Part of him cringed at the thought of leaving Sarah, but another part longed to be back in the field with Andrew Jackson. He had missed a battle, but it wouldn't be the last one Jackson would fight. Not so long as the Spanish remained in Florida and the Seminoles continued to conduct their raids along the frontier. He couldn't stop thinking about his friend Moulton—and Moulton's widow, Anne. That was a fate Sarah Langford should be spared.

Stepping out onto the front porch, Barlow saw a man fly past on a galloping horse, holding a newspaper aloft and shouting: "The republic's been saved! Hurrah for Jackson!" Somewhere farther along the street, pistols were being discharged. The celebration was beginning. Barlow sighed.

He had been with Jackson until the end of last summer. It was then that the general had made up his mind to invade Florida. He had no authorization from Washington, but he didn't feel he needed one. And he was convinced that President Madison would sanction what he was about to do—albeit after the fact. Still, he felt compelled to justify his audacity in a long letter to the new Secretary of War, James Monroe. That letter, along with a second insisting that the government provide food and blankets for the Creeks that winter, Jackson had entrusted to Barlow.

"I need someone who can articulate all the reasons both things must be done," explained Jackson. Though Barlow had lodged no complaint, the general could sense that his aide was dismayed by the possibility of missing the campaign into Florida. "With the land cession we have cut the Creeks off from the Spaniards and the Seminoles in Florida. But Mr. Hawkins has informed me that the villages are poorly prepared for the winter. We must provide for them or risk another uprising. If their families are cold and hungry, Creek warriors may go on the warpath again. And the last thing I need is another uprising to disrupt my lines of supply and communication when I advance on Pensacola."

"Of course, sir," said Barlow. So the general's concern for the welfare of the Creeks was purely practical rather than humanitarian. Now the letter regarding the Creeks made more sense to him.

"As for Florida, you may read the letter to Monroe for yourself."

Barlow had done just that. The letter read:

> *As I act without the orders of the government, I deem it important to state to you my reasons for the measure I am about to adopt. First, I conceive the safety of this section of the union depends upon it. The hostility of the Governor of Pensacola is evident in his permitting the place to assume the character of a British Territory by resigning the command of the fortresses to them, and permitting them to fit out an expedition against the United States. At the same time he made to me a declaration that he had armed the Indians and sent them into our territory. Knowing at the same time that these very Indians had under the command of a British officer captured our*

citizens and destroyed their property within our own territory, I feel a confidence that I shall stand justified to my government for having undertaken the expedition. Should I not, I shall have the consolation of having done the only thing in my own opinion which would give security to the country by putting down a savage war. And that to me will be an ample reward for the loss of my commission.

"Your opinion, Lieutenant?" Jackson had asked him.

"I would not even suggest that what I was about to undertake might cost me my commission, sir. I would be firm in my conviction. It might give them ideas."

Jackson laughed. "They'll try to cut me down whether I succeed or fail in Florida, mark my words."

Along with the letters, Barlow carried copies of reports made by one of the 39th Infantry's captains, John Jones, whom Jackson had dispatched to Pensacola on an intelligence mission. Since Spain was officially neutral in the war between the United States and Great Britain, the Spanish governor had no alternative to welcoming Captain Jones into the town. Jones had seen enough to convince him that the British were being outfitted there for an expedition. More than one hundred Royal Marines were in Fort Barrancas. Furthermore, their commander, Major Edward Nicholls, was encouraging the Indians and runaway slaves to make war on the Americans. Jones believed the target of the expedition was Mobile, and Jackson had agreed.

Barlow knew from previous newspaper accounts that Jackson had marched the four hundred miles from the juncture of the Coosa and Tallapoosa rivers to Mobile in just eleven days. Working round the clock, his men repaired the fort that commanded the entrance to Mobile Bay. Meanwhile, spies in Pensacola informed Jackson of the British strategy. They would capture Mobile and then launch a major offensive to take New Orleans. Whoever controlled that city controlled the Mississippi River. The loss of New Orleans—and the river—would be a disastrous, perhaps even fatal, blow to the United States.

But, thanks to Jackson, the British failed to take Mobile. On September 12, Admiral Sir William Percy reached Mobile Bay with four warships, carrying Nicholls's Marines and one hundred and thirty Indian allies. Percy set Nicholls ashore and proceeded with a naval assault on the American-held fort, which he had outgunned by a ratio of four to one. Nonetheless, a cannonball cut the anchor cable of HMS *Hermes* and the ship drifted aground under the American guns. The British abandoned the stricken vessel, spiked her guns, and set her ablaze. Her magazine exploded several hours later—an explosion heard in Mobile thirty miles away. Percy's squadron sailed away and Nicholls took his command back to Pensacola overland, knowing he could not achieve his objective without naval support.

Arriving in Washington five and a half weeks after leaving Fort Jackson, Barlow discovered that Secretary of War Monroe had written a letter to Jackson in Mobile, informing the general that American negotiators, in Ghent, Belgium, working on a treaty to end the war, had learned that a British expedition had departed Ireland in September, bound for New Orleans. Monroe also ordered the governors of Tennessee, Georgia and Kentucky to send as many men to Jackson as they could spare. But instead of taking his army to New Orleans and waiting there for reinforcements, Jackson had moved on Pensacola instead.

If nothing else, Andrew Jackson was daring and unpredictable. But Barlow wasn't the only person in Washington who wasn't surprised by this news. Apparently, the government had feared just such an action by Jackson. In October, Secretary Monroe had dispatched another letter to Mobile, informing Jackson that the president had decided no action should be taken against the Spanish, regardless of whether the dons had been violating their professed neutrality by aiding the British. The question posed by the critics of the administration was whether this letter was meant only as a cover; if so, it was designed to give the president official deniability in the event that Jackson failed in Florida. If the critics were right, Madison was hoping Jackson would ignore the caveat and march on Florida anyway.

And that was precisely what Jackson had done. With four thousand men—including the 39th Infantry and several hundred Cherokee warriors—he laid siege to Pensacola, which was guarded by three fortresses, the most formidable of which was Barrancas. His warning to Governor Manrique, including a demand for the possession of Barrancas, never reached its destination. British troops fired on the flag of truce under which it was to be delivered, as the Royal Marines feared the Spanish governor might be enticed to surrender. Jackson immediately attacked. It didn't take long for Pensacola to fall—in fact, the attack was so swift and successful that the British warships anchored in the bay had no time to swing around and bring their guns to bear on Jackson's advancing columns. Governor Manrique surrendered, but the British, who had possession of Barrancas, did not. Jackson prepared for an attack on the fortress the very next day. But before that could take place, the British blew up parts of the fort and withdrew to the waiting ships, which sailed away at dawn.

Jackson wasn't through doing the unexpected. Deeming Pensacola indefensible, and believing the Spanish had been taught a valuable lesson, he gave Pensacola back to an astonished Manrique and headed for New Orleans.

When news of the Pensacola adventure reached Washington, Barlow was on hand for an after-dinner debate between Henry Clay and John C. Calhoun on the subject of Andrew Jackson's activities in the South.

"It makes absolutely no sense to me that Jackson would seize Pensacola and then promptly return it to the Spaniards," said Clay, exasperated.

"It is my understanding," said Calhoun, "that the destruction wrought by the Royal Marines on Barrancas rendered the fort useless. Besides, General Jackson already knew the British were sailing for New Orleans."

"Then he was damned reckless for embarking on his Florida campaign in the first place." Clay had thrown a quick look around to make sure Mrs. Langford wasn't present to hear him curse—another violation of the house rules.

"Let us avail ourselves of a military man's opinion," suggested Calhoun, looking across the table at Barlow. "And one who is a graduate of the academy at West Point, to boot."

"I doubt I could shed any light on the subject," said Barlow hastily, hoping to avoid being dragged into the discussion.

"You are too modest, Lieutenant," said Clay. "What's more, you've served with Jackson. You are his aide and personal envoy. He knows you well enough to have entrusted you with an important mission that, indeed, involves Florida. You must be in his confidence."

Barlow smiled ruefully. "Frankly, I'm not so sure. I

can't help but wonder if he sent me on this mission just to be rid of me."

"Why would he do that, Lieutenant?" asked the Kentuckian.

"Because I was outspoken in my criticism of the Treaty of Fort Jackson. In that matter I took the side of the Indian agent, Benjamin Hawkins, who strongly protested seizing the land of the Creek tribes that had kept the peace by rejecting the Red Stick cause."

"So you are a man of principle, sir," said Clay. "That doesn't surprise me. But still, you know this fellow Jackson far better than anyone else in the room. Can you make any sense of his actions with respect to Pensacola?"

"Well," said Barlow, "it does make sense from a strategic point of view. He has secured his flank by driving the British, at least temporarily, out of Barrancas, which leaves him free to commit his forces to the defense of New Orleans. More than that, he has revealed to the British, the Seminoles—and the Spaniards themselves—that Spain will have a difficult time holding on to Florida. Our intelligence showed that the Spaniards did not take kindly to the British in the first place; apparently the Royal Marines treated the small Spanish garrison in Pensacola's forts with utter disdain, and, to add insult to injury, even freed some of the Spaniards' slaves. The Spanish opinion of the British could not have been improved by what transpired when Jackson attacked the town."

"You mean insofar as the British did not put up much of a fight," said Calhoun.

"Exactly. From what I've read, the British warships didn't fire a shot in support of the Spanish trying to defend the town, while the Royal Marines only fired at the general's flag of truce before withdrawing behind the walls of Barrancas."

"All I can say," concluded Clay, "is that Jackson is either a brilliant field commander or a dangerous lunatic."

"Or perhaps both," murmured Calhoun.

Barlow had made no comment, and was relieved when the congressmen refrained from asking him his personal opinion of Jackson. He wasn't altogether sure of the answer to that.

Now, though, standing on the porch of the Langford house, opening the copy of the *Gazette* that Sarah had acquired for him, Barlow *was* sure of one thing. He had missed participating in the most important battle of the war—a great victory that would make Andrew Jackson a hero to all Americans. And he was sure that Jackson would return to Florida eventually. The Spaniards might not pose a threat to the United States, but the Seminoles most certainly did, and this the general could not long tolerate. Barlow swore to himself that, come what may, he would *not* miss the next battle.

Chapter Ten

Feeling a bit sorry for himself, Barlow sat on the front porch of Mrs. Emma Langford's boarding-house and read about the Battle of New Orleans in the special edition of the *Gazette*. In minutes, he was thoroughly engrossed in the details of Andrew Jackson's great triumph, and hardly even heard the tumult in the streets as all of Washington proceeded to celebrate.

New Orleans was located a hundred miles from the mouth of the Mississippi River, and yet it had long been the most important port on the southern coast, as the river was navigable by seagoing vessels all the way upstream to the city. Sixty miles downstream of New Orleans was Fort St. Philip and, twenty-five miles downstream, Fort St. Leon—two strongholds that governed the river approach. The forts and the swamps of the delta country protected the city from attack from the south, while the broad Mississippi made an assault from the west highly improbable. A glance at a map was all Jackson needed to realize that when the British came, it would be from the east. There were two possible avenues—overland by way of the Plains of Gentilly or by water from the Gulf of Mexico into Lake Pontchartrain via Lake Borgne.

Jackson arrived in New Orleans to much fanfare, greeted effusively by Governor W.C.C. Claiborne and a large crowd of civilians who cheered him when he vowed to protect the city and all its inhabitants or die

in the attempt. Establishing his headquarters at 106
Royal Street in the Vieux Carré, the general immediately fell to the task of preparing the city's defense.
He ordered all water routes into the city closed off—
a Herculean job considering the sheer number of ca-
nals and bayous in the area. He reinforced Fort St.
Philip and stationed a fleet of five gunboats—with a
total of twenty-three guns among them—on Lake
Borgne.

Next Jackson addressed the problem of Jean Lafitte
and the pirates of Barataria Bay. The Haitian-born
Lafitte was as brilliant a businessman as he was daring
a pirate. He made sure that the merchants of New
Orleans profited nicely from their association with
him—and his stolen merchandise. That way there was
never a strong commitment by the powers that be to
remove him from the scene. The British had tried to
recruit Lafitte and his men to their cause; Lafitte po-
litely heard them out and then offered his services to
Governor Claiborne. Instead of accepting the offer,
Claiborne launched an expedition against the pirates.
He destroyed their lair at Barataria, capturing eighty
men and nine vessels in the process. But in spite of
Claiborne's intransigence where the pirates were concerned, most of the citizens of New Orleans were willing for Jackson to accept Lafitte's help. The Louisiana
legislature formally urged him to do so. The pirates
were courageous and bold. They were excellent gunners and marksmen. They knew the swamps and bayous better than just about anyone. And, the Claiborne
raid notwithstanding, Lafitte could muster a thousand fighters.

Jean Lafitte was granted safe conduct to come into
New Orleans and discuss the situation with Jackson. The
general accepted the pirate chief's offer. To the consternation of many, he also recruited and armed two battal-

ions worth of free blacks. Meanwhile, General Billy Carroll was coming down the Mississippi with two thousand fresh militia from western Tennessee.

The British armada—sixty ships carrying fourteen thousand men—appeared off Cat Island on December 14 and sailed into Lake Borgne. The five American gunboats tried to escape, but were becalmed near Malheureux Island. They put up a spirited fight as forty-five British barges manned by a thousand sailors and marines closed in. But it was a hopeless fight; all of the gunboats were captured and sunk, their crews either killed or taken prisoner.

Admiral Cochrane had won the first skirmish, but he followed up his victory with a mistake. Believing the American prisoners when they swore Jackson had an army of ten thousand men in New Orleans—four times the actual number—Cochrane grew cautious. The admiral decided to ferry the army to the mainland on his barges. This operation took nearly a week. The weather didn't help; it rained every day, and froze every night. Rather than venture into Lake Pontchartrain, Cochrane advised Major General John Keane to make a quick march overland to the city.

As the British troops came ashore, Billy Carroll arrived with his recruits, as did Colonel John Coffee with his mounted rifles. A regiment of Mississippi dragoons showed up the next day. But, even while the streets of New Orleans were filled with soldiers, the citizenry was panicked at news of the British arrival. Jackson proclaimed martial law to keep order, and called upon the people to do their part to protect their homes with a proclamation that the *Gazette* published in part:

Natives of the United States! The British are the oppressors of your infant political existence, with

*whom you are to contend—they are the men your
fathers conquered whom you are to oppose. De-
scendants of Frenchmen! Natives of France! They
are the English, the hereditary, the eternal enemies
of your ancient country—the invaders of that you
have adopted, who are your foes. Spaniards—remember the conduct of your allies at St. Sebas-
tiens, and recently at Pensacola, and rejoice that
you have an opportunity of avenging the brutal
injuries inflicted by men who dishonor the
human race.*

Meanwhile, Admiral Cochrane had discovered the
Bayou Bienvenu, which reached from Lake Borgne to
within a dozen miles of New Orleans. On December
22, Colonel William Thornton and eighteen hundred
men moved up the bayou on barges. American pickets
were surprised and overpowered. The next day, the
redcoats marched out of a canebrake onto the plantation of Gabriel Villere. Villere was made a prisoner,
but executed a daring escape and reached New Orleans to warn the city that the British were coming.
Thornton wanted to take full advantage of the element of surprise and press on to New Orleans, only
nine miles away. But the cautious General Keane
overruled him. It was a costly mistake on Keane's
part.

When Jackson heard of the enemy's advance, he
swore with smoldering eyes that the British would not
"sleep on American soil." He quickly gathered up
Coffee's cavalry, the free black battalions, the Mississippi dragoons and the city militia and set out for the
Villere plantation. The schooner *Carolina* sailed
downriver and slipped close to the British encampment under cover of darkness, firing a broadside into
the enemy's tents. At the sound of the schooner's

guns, Jackson ordered his troops to attack. For two hours the fighting raged, often hand to hand. At nine-thirty, a heavy fog rolled in from the river. Jackson disengaged his forces and pulled back to the Rodriquez Canal, a ditch four feet deep and ten feet wide that stretched from the river's edge to a cypress swamp, a distance of nearly a mile. Ramparts consisting of logs, cotton bales and earth were thrown up. The ditch was widened and deepened. While the Americans worked feverishly on their defenses, Colonel Thornton's advance force was joined by the rest of the British army. The *Carolina*, joined by her sister ship, the *Louisiana*, bombarded the redcoat camp day and night.

Jackson's daring impressed Barlow. Some would construe his hasty attack as rash behavior. But it had served to make General Keane even more irresolute than before, and bought the Americans precious time.

On Christmas Day, the British got a new commander, Sir Edward Pakenham, the Duke of Wellington's brother-in-law. A veteran of the Napoleonic Wars, Pakenham, at age thirty, was considered one of the British army's finest commanders. He took one look at the situation and chastised Keane for placing the army is such a position. But there was nothing for it but to go forward. Pakenham placed a battery of nine fieldpieces on the levee to drive away the pesky American vessels, the *Carolina* and *Louisiana*. The British gunners proved to be deadly accurate with their fire; the *Carolina* was set ablaze, and the *Louisiana* barely escaped.

On December 28, Pakenham attacked the American defenses, sending one column along the levee and a second along the edge of the cypress swamp, striking both enemy flanks simultaneously. The advance was covered by a sustained firing of Congreve rockets and artillery. But when the redcoats were six hundred yards from the American line, Jackson's artillery and the *Louisiana* opened up on the first column with devastating results. Pakenham ordered a general retreat.

Back in New Orleans, the Louisiana legislature was said to be considering capitulation behind closed doors. Hearing this, Jackson ordered Governor Claiborne to deal firmly with the wavering solons. Claiborne closed down the legislature. When an irate commission of politicians approached Jackson and asked his intentions in the event the British broke through his defenses, the general bluntly told them he would burn New Orleans to the ground and make a stand somewhere upriver. The commissioners swore their allegiance to the cause of defeating the British.

On the night of December 31, the British army advanced quietly to within five hundred yards of the Rodriquez Canal and waited for morning, when Pakenham's five batteries of artillery were to open fire to cover their assault. But New Year's Day dawned thick with a fog so dense it reduced visibility to a few yards. The British waited for the fog to lift; at ten o'clock, their cannon began to roar. Congreve rockets screamed overhead. One of their primary targets was the Macarte House, which Jackson had turned into his field headquarters. The general and his staff were just sitting down to a late breakfast following an early morning inspection of the lines when a barrage of cannonballs and rockets shook the house to its foundation. Amazingly, though the house was struck at least one hundred times, no one was killed. Jackson rushed to the front line to encourage his troops to stand fast.

When he read of this, Barlow had to smile. Like so many others, he had some reservations about Andrew Jackson. But the man's courage—and luck—could not be questioned.

The American batteries responded, and the artillery duel continued until midafternoon, at which time the British withdrew out of range. Pakenham had decided to await reinforcements. The crack 7th Fusiliers and 34th Infantry were on their way across Lake Borgne. He planned to ferry Colonel Thornton and fifteen hundred troops across the river, with orders to capture the American artillery positioned on the west bank; Thornton would then advance upriver, flanking Jackson's position along the Rodriquez Canal, and turn the captured fieldpieces on the Americans. To accomplish this manuever, Pakenham delayed a week so that his engineers could widen a canal to accommodate the barges that would then be transferred from Lake Borgne to the Mississippi. The delay was for naught; a dam built by the engineers broke and the product of their labors was washed away. During that week, Jackson received reinforcements of his own—two thousand Kentucky militiamen. Unfortunately, more than half of the Kentuckians were without rifles. New Orleans was combed for weapons of every description with which to arm the newcomers.

On January 7, the commander of the American forces located on the west bank of the Mississippi, Brigadier General David Morgan, pleaded with Jackson for more men, claiming he had reliable intelligence to indicate that the main British attack would occur on his side of the river. All he had on hand to stop such an assault were five hundred Kentuckians, many of whom remained unarmed. Jackson refused to strengthen Morgan's position; he was convinced the primary British effort would take place against his lines.

In the early morning hours of January 8, Thornton's redcoats began crossing the Mississippi. The river's strong current swept the barges downstream, so that

Thornton landed a mile and a half farther downriver than planned. His orders had been to flank Jackson's line before the main attack began, but he was unable to carry out those orders in time. At four in the morning, Pakenham put two columns of troops into motion. Some of the redcoats carried bundles of sugar cane with which they were to fill the canal in front of the American lines, while others carried ladders to use in scaling the enemy ramparts on the other side of the ditch.

Barlow shook his head. Pakenham had been a fool to attempt a frontal assault before Thornton's command had achieved its objective. That was the crucial element in the British plan, after all, and the only one that could have made the outcome of the January 8 attack any different from the failed attempt on December 28.

Two Congreve rockets fired from either edge of the battlefield was the signal for the redcoat advance. When they saw the British troops emerge from the morning mist, the Americans cheered. The moment they had been waiting for had finally come. The band of the Orleans Battalion began playing "Yankee Doodle." And when the British, marching forward in a dazzling display of military precision, came within range, Jackson gave the order to fire. A sheet of flame appeared all along the ramparts as rifles and cannon firing grapeshot spoke at once. The British paused to return fire when they should have rushed the American defenses. They fell by the dozens as the Americans relentlessly poured their fire into them. Bravely the British rallied and pressed on. Some even reached the ditch. But then the disciplined lines, ripped apart by American shot and shell, disintegrated. The surviving redcoats retreated in disarray. General Pakenham rode forward to urge his men to turn and fight. A bullet shattered his arm, and another killed his horse. Pakenham calmly commandeered an aide's horse and continued his efforts.

Then the tartan-clad Highlander Regiment appeared on the field, their bagpipers playing the regimental charge. The fleeing redcoats stopped. They reformed their lines. Inspired by the Highlanders, they advanced on the American ramparts a second time. But the result was as it had been before. As brave as they were, the British soldiers could not withstand the withering fire. Pakenham's second horse was killed under him, and he was struck a second time, as well. A bullet lodged in his groin, he died within minutes. General Keane also fell. Before long, not a single senior British officer remained alive on the field. A hundred yards from the ramparts the Highlanders faltered. Over five hundred of them lay dead or wounded on the blood-soaked ground—more than half their number. Once again the redcoats withdrew.

Thomas Hind, who commanded the Mississippi dragoons, begged Andrew Jackson to allow him to pursue the retreating British. But Jackson said no. It was too risky. He wasn't sure if the British were finished. Pakenham's reserves had not been committed. And there was fighting across the river. Colonel Thornton's redcoats were driving the Kentuckians back. The American battery was captured. Thornton was about to turn those cannon on Jackson's lines when he received orders to retire and cross back over the river to rejoin the main body.

British casualties totaled over two thousand, with nearly three hundred killed, over twelve hundred wounded, and almost five hundred missing or captured. Jackson reported the loss of thirteen men killed, thirty-nine wounded, and nineteen missing, and acknowledged that the numbers were so lopsided that they defied belief. Under a flag of truce, the British buried their dead in mass graves and then withdrew to the fleet and sailed for home. It was rumored that Pakenham's remains were placed in a cask of rum to preserve the body during the long voyage home.

Barlow put the newspaper down and drew a deep breath. He reconsidered the deep disappointment he had felt when first he'd realized that he had missed the battle. Though he was happy and relieved that the British had been defeated, he was now glad that he had not taken part in the slaughter of so many brave men. The valor of the redcoats fairly leaped from the *Gazette*'s account of Jackson's triumph. Barlow resolved not to engage in any celebration of the victory, as so many others were already doing all across Washington. War was entirely too grim and bloody a business.

A horseman checked his mount in front of the Langford boardinghouse. He was a pale and thin young man, clad in somber and somewhat threadbare black broadcloth. The suit was a bit too small for him; the coat sleeves and trouser legs rode high on his limbs, exposing bony wrists and ankles.

"I beg your pardon, sir," said the rider. "Might this be the Langford home?"

"It is."

"Are you Lieutenant Timothy Barlow by any chance?"

"I am. And who are you?"

"Jonathan Adler, Lieutenant. I am a clerk at the Department of War."

"I see. What do you want with me, Mr. Adler?"

Adler stepped cautiously down out of the saddle. He was clearly a man altogether unfamiliar, and therefore uncomfortable, with horseback riding, and seemed much relieved when his feet found the street's cobblestones. He came up the porch steps on unsteady legs and brandished a letter from beneath his coat, which he presented to Barlow. Barlow noted that the letter was written on superior parchment and carried the wax seal of the War Department.

"Secretary Monroe requests your presence in his office at your earliest convenience, Lieutenant."

Barlow opened the letter. It merely confirmed what the clerk had just told him. What did it mean? Perhaps, finally, the Secretary of War was prepared to respond to Jackson's letters concerning his plans for Spanish Florida and the plight of the Creeks. Barlow could only hope this was the case, for it would mean he could soon be on his way back to Jackson and the army. So long as Florida remained in Spanish hands, Jackson would not rest easy, and Barlow was determined not to miss the next campaign.

"I will come straightaway," he said.

"I trust you will not take offense, Lieutenant, but I have been instructed to accompany you." Adler smiled, embarrassed. "In truth, I was told not to come back without you, under any circumstances."

"I see." Barlow did take offense. He didn't need an escort. He'd said he would respond to the secretary's summons, and his word ought to have been enough. But he reminded himself that Adler was merely a messenger. More than that, the clerk had been sensitive enough to comprehend the impropriety of his orders. "One moment, then," said Barlow, and went inside.

Bounding up the stairs to his room, he strapped on his dress sword and retrieved his shako. One had to be in full uniform to meet the Secretary of War. Thanks to Sarah, his uniform was clean, the brass shiny, his boots polished to a high gloss.

On his way back down the stairs, he met Mrs. Langford, with Sarah in tow.

"Who is the gentleman on my stoop, Lieutenant?" asked Mrs. Langford. "A friend of yours?"

"He was sent by Secretary Monroe to fetch me, ma'am."

"Ah, so at last you'll have your meeting. I take it, then, that you will probably be leaving us soon."

Barlow thought he detected a note of hopefulness in her query, and that made him wonder whether Mrs. Langford suspected that feelings had developed between him and her daughter. Or maybe he was just imagining it. Still, he studiously avoided looking at Sarah.

"That's quite likely, yes, ma'am," he replied.

"You've been a good tenant, Lieutenant. We shall miss you. Shan't we, Sarah?"

Eyes downcast, Sarah murmured, "Yes."

Now Barlow was sure that he'd been right; Mrs. Langford *did* suspect, and she *was* happy to learn of his imminent departure. Worst of all, she was gloating about it in front of her daughter, knowing that the news caused Sarah pain.

"If you will excuse me," said Barlow stiffly, trying to mask his anger, "I shouldn't keep the secretary waiting."

Outside, Adler looked at Barlow's frown and asked if something was wrong.

"Wrong?" Barlow had scarcely heard Adler's query. "No, nothing's wrong. Let's go."

"You are welcome to my horse, Lieutenant."

"I'll walk, thanks all the same."

"Then, if you don't object, I will walk with you."

Barlow didn't respond, and headed up the street with Adler, leading the horse, falling in step alongside. Suddenly Barlow found himself in no big hurry to meet James Monroe, or leave Washington. He was torn between his desire to get back to the army and his reluctance to leave Sarah Langford behind. It was a dilemma he knew, with dismay, that had no easy solution.

Chapter Eleven

The War Department was located in a large building within sight of the president's house, and about a half mile from the Langford home, through the middle of town. All of Washington, it seemed, had heard the news of Jackson's victory at New Orleans by now, and had taken to the streets to share in the revelry. They were on the rooftops, too, and on the balconies, and hanging out of windows. A number of men saw Barlow's uniform and came up to shake his hand, merely because he was in the army.

Adler left him in a long, bright waiting room and entered the secretary's adjacent office to inform Monroe of the lieutenant's arrival. There were chairs lining the walls of the room, and several were occupied by men in civilian dress. Barlow didn't sit down, but paced along a row of tall, narrow windows overlooking Pennsylvania Avenue. He did not have long to wait. Adler stuck his head out the door of the secretary's inner sanctum and bade him enter.

Monroe's office was a high-ceilinged room with windows along one side, a large and cluttered desk, some chairs, a globe on an ornately carved wooden stand, and a couple of tables laden with maps. Portraits of Monroe's predecessors decorated the walls. Monroe came around from behind the desk and extended a hand. He was a tall, pale, ascetic-looking man, with a frank and serious expression on a rather plain-featured face. He dressed in the old style, with pantaloons and stockings, a dark blue swallowtail coat and white stock.

"Lieutenant Barlow, I am pleased to see you again." Monroe's voice was soft, melodic, his elocution impeccable. His handclasp was firm, his gaze direct. "I trust you have heard the excellent news from down south."

"Yes, I have, sir."

"I am glad the loss of life was light on our side," said Monroe, turning to pluck a document out of the clutter on his desk, "as the battle, I am sorry to say, was for naught."

"What do you mean, sir?" Barlow was mystified.

"This just arrived from Ghent." Monroe handed him the document. "An end to the hostilities that have existed between the United States and Great Britain was agreed to weeks ago. The war was technically over when General Jackson won his victory." The secretary glanced at the row of windows. "That just arrived this very morning. I suppose we shall wait until the morrow to make the announcement, so as not to dampen the mood of the public."

Barlow read the document quickly. It was, indeed, a treaty of peace, signed by all the American and British delegates to the negotiations in Ghent. How ironic, he mused, that the republic's greatest triumph had occurred *after* the war. And what a waste that all those brave British soldiers had died for nothing! Shaking his head, he handed the treaty back to Monroe.

"I see the British will keep Canada," he remarked.

"Of course. Everything will be as it was before." Monroe remembered Adler, and nodded to the clerk, who quietly departed the room. Then the secretary circled around behind his desk and, with a gesture for Barlow to take a chair, waited until his guest was seated before sitting down himself. Barlow reviewed what he knew about this man. A Virginian, Monroe had been a graduate of the prestigious College of William and Mary, practiced law, and served with distinction in the Continental Army. After the War for Independence, he had been elected to the Congress. He had also served as minister to France, and with Robert Livingston had negotiated the Louisiana Purchase. A Jeffersonian and trusted associate of President Madison, Monroe was expected to succeed Madison when the latter's second term was concluded in 1816.

"Some things *have* changed, sir, in my opinion," said Barlow. "We will get a good deal more respect now from the courts of Europe because of what happened at New Orleans. We beat the best the British could pit against us. They should think twice before they venture to seize our ships and abduct our citizens again."

Monroe nodded approvingly. "I am impressed, Lieutenant. You don't always find that a military man knows how to look beyond the battle to its ramifications."

"War is only a means to an end, Mr. Secretary."

"Quite right. But this war is over, thank the Almighty. We do not have Canada, but personally I am rather relieved that we do not. Though I'm sure men like Henry Clay will raise a hue and cry about it remaining in British hands."

"I don't know if it's Canada that men like Congressman Clay want so much as it is wanting the British gone from continent. And the Spanish, as well."

Monroe smiled. "Ah, yes. The Spaniards. Well done, Lieutenant. You've brought us neatly to the reason I have summoned you here today."

Barlow shifted forward in his chair. "Forgive me if

I'm too bold, Mr. Secretary, but now is the perfect time to take Florida away from Spain."

"Is that you talking, Lieutenant? Or is it that you've spent too much time with Andrew Jackson?"

"Not recently I haven't," said Barlow wryly.

"And why, pray tell, would this be the perfect time?"

"Because I doubt the dons would put up much of a fight, sir. And even if they tried, they wouldn't have the British to help them."

"I see."

Barlow sensed that Monroe disapproved of his line of reasoning, but he threw caution to the wind—maybe Jackson *was* rubbing off on him—and continued.

"There is another reason, Mr. Secretary. General Jackson is down there with an army that just defeated the British. When he hears that the general is coming his way, Governor Manrique will probably have the white flag flying even before the army reaches Pensacola."

"And you do not believe that Spain would declare war on the United States if we presumed to invade Florida?"

"No, sir, I do not. But even if they did, we would handle them the same way we handled the British."

Monroe pursed his lips. "May the Lord see fit to save the republic from military men!"

Barlow thought that was an odd comment to come from the Secretary of War—and one who had served in the Continental Army, to boot.

"You talk as though our surviving the war with the British was never in doubt," continued Monroe. "But one victory does not a war win, Lieutenant. We were hard pressed on all sides for two years. And we're just fortunate that the British are weary of war, else they would probably dispatch Wellington and another army over here to take on your General Jackson."

"If that were to happen, sir, I'd put my money on General Jackson."

Monroe sighed. "And I suppose that once Florida is safely in the bag, your general will continue on to Texas, and then to California. Or perhaps even into Mexico."

"The argument for taking Florida, sir, is to end the Seminole threat to our southern frontier. No such threat emanates from Texas or California. Or Mexico."

Monroe rose, picked up a sealed letter, and brought it round the desk to Barlow.

"You will depart Washington at once, Lieutenant, and return as quickly as possible to your general. Present him with this. And with my compliments."

Barlow accepted the letter. "Yes, sir."

"In case something happens to those instructions en route, I will relay their essence to you verbally now, with the expectation that you would then relay what I say to Jackson."

"Of course, sir."

"According to letters from our envoys at Ghent— letters that accompanied the treaty—the British made it clear that their signing of the treaty should in no way be construed as recognition of our claim to any territory along the Gulf of Mexico. Great Britain has in the past, and continues to, dispute the legality of the Louisiana Purchase. France had no right, they say, to sell Louisiana to us, as by the terms of the Treaty of San Ildefonso, by which the Spanish surrendered that territory to Napoleon Bonaparte, the latter promised not to sell it to anyone else without at least first offering to return it to Spain. This Napoleon did not do prior to our purchase of it. I am not alone in the opinion that had the British won at New Orleans, they would have given the city back to the Spaniards, whom they consider its rightful owners. Naturally, the British do not recognize our title to West Florida, either; therefore, in their view, Mobile also belongs to Spain. Furthermore, the British do not consider that New Orleans or Mobile or any of the disputed territory I have mentioned are covered by the Treaty of Ghent. The treaty clearly establishes a *status quo antebellum.* That is, everything is to be as it was before the war. Though they question our right to New Orleans and Mobile, the British will not make demands regarding them, as they were in our possession, legally or not, when the war broke out. But they do request that all Indian tribes be restored to the lands they held prior to the start of the hostilities."

"What?" Barlow was certain he must have misunderstood that last part.

"Indian rights and property are to be restored to what they were in 1811, according to the agreement reached in Ghent."

"But that would mean the Fort Jackson treaty . . ."

"Is null and void."

Barlow stared at Monroe. "Surely we did not agree to that, sir!"

"Indeed, we did. The Red Stick uprising was part and parcel of the war, Lieutenant. It was instigated by Tecumseh, a known ally of the British. You might even say he was their agent."

Barlow could only shake his head in amazement. He knew with absolute certainty that Andrew Jackson would not stand for the nullification of the treaty he had forced upon the Creek Nation, nor the return of the land cession to the Indians. What would the general do? There was no way of knowing. This was a development Jackson had never envisioned. Barlow thought it possible that Old Mad would march his Tennessee long hunters all the way up to Washington to take on the federal government.

And I have to be the bearer of these bad tidings, mused Barlow, in disbelief.

"The negotiations required to abide by the letter of Ghent treaty will be conducted by representatives of this government who have not yet been selected," continued Monroe. "General Jackson, rest assured, will play no active part in them. But neither will he act in any way that might be construed as an effort to undermine them."

"He doesn't work that way, sir."

"Your loyalty to your commanding officer is commendable. But you will forgive me, I trust, when I voice the opinion that it is misplaced. I would have thought you would stand opposed to the terms of the Treaty of Fort Jackson."

"I didn't think it right to penalize the peaceful Creek villages by seizing their land," admitted Barlow. "But the deed—and the damage—is done. The Creeks won't trust the United States anymore, even if they get their land back. And by returning the ceded land, you will be reuniting the Creek Nation with the Seminoles in Florida, and make the defense of the frontier much more difficult."

"Perhaps," said Monroe. "However, defending the southern frontier is General Jackson's problem, as he is commander of that military district. We must abide by the terms of the Ghent agreement. Our reputation in the family of nations depends upon it."

"Yes, sir," said Barlow, without enthusiasm.

"I am relying on you to carry that letter—and my message—to your general. You are to make sure he understands that he is not to interfere with our negotiations with the Creeks—and he is to leave the Spanish in Florida alone!"

"I understand, Mr. Secretary."

Monroe nodded. "Excellent. You have a long journey ahead of you. You had better be on your way. I wish you Godspeed."

"Thank you, sir." Barlow rose, put the letter under his coatee and, snapping to attention, made a slight head bow, as befitted a civilian of high station, before turning on his heel to leave.

"One other thing, Lieutenant."

Barlow paused at the door and turned. "Yes, sir?"

"In your opinion, how will General Jackson respond to the instructions you carry?"

Barlow carefully considered the question, recognizing that it was fraught with peril for him—and for Andrew Jackson.

"He will respond like a patriot, sir."

Closing the door to Monroe's office behind him, Barlow stood there a moment, taking a deep breath and trying to come to terms with what the War Secretary had told him. Belatedly, he realized that the men in the waiting room were staring at him. Barlow cleared his throat, gave his coatee a tug, put on his shako and walked briskly out of the room.

Back at the Langford boardinghouse, Barlow slipped up to his room unseen and quickly packed his single valise. He was hoping to get in and out without being discovered. He had paid his board in full to the end of the week. And he fully realized that, at least where Sarah was concerned, there was nothing but pure cowardice in his skulking about like a thief. Facing a woman—a woman he thought he was falling in love with—was a far more terrifying prospect than going into battle. He would write her when he reached his destination, if not before; it would all depend on when he figured out what to put in the letter to her.

But he was unable to escape undetected. There was a firm and insistent knocking at the door. Barlow cast a quick look around. There was no other egress save the window, and he was not quite so desperate as to leap from the second floor of the house. Besides, he was certain that it wasn't Sarah at the door.

He was right. Opening the door, he found Henry Clay standing in the hallway.

"Ah, good. You're back," said Clay, with a smile that was both affable and sly. It never failed—Barlow was reminded of a fox every time he set eyes on the Kentuckian. "You are leaving us, I see." Clay nodded at the bulging valise on the bed.

"Yes, I am."

"On your way back to Jackson, then."

"That's right."

Clay peered at him. Clearly, he had hoped Barlow would be more forthcoming with information about his meeting with Secretary Monroe. But even if he wasn't going to be, Clay would not be easily deterred.

"Mrs. Langford said a clerk from the War Department came for you. Now you're packing to go. I trust it is safe for me to conclude that you have received the official response to the letters you brought to Washington."

"I have, yes."

Clay chuckled, and draped an arm around Barlow's shoulder. "Come now, Lieutenant. We've been messmates for many a week now. Surely there is something you can tell me!"

Barlow had no intention of sharing with anyone the instructions Secretary Monroe was passing on to General Jackson through him. Yet he knew Clay would not relent until he was told something.

"I can tell you this," he said, in a conspiratorial whisper, "the war is over."

"What?" Clay was stunned. "You jest!"

Barlow shook his head. "A treaty was signed in Ghent. It just today reached Washington."

"And the terms? The terms, man!"

"According to Mr. Monroe, *status quo antebellum.*"

"*Status quo . . .*" Clay's jaw dropped. "Everything as it was before? No! Then the British remain in possession of Canada!" The Kentuckian's cheeks darkened. "By God, that's damned intolerable!" he rasped, fists clenched. "I must go tell Calhoun at once. Good luck to you, Lieutenant." And with that Clay was gone.

Leaving the door open, Barlow turned back into the room to retrieve his valise and longcoat. But as he reached for the bag, his conscience got the better of him. He could not leave Sarah without saying goodbye, no matter how painful the parting might be. Stepping out of the room, he went along the upstairs hall to the top of the stairs—and she was there, coming up. The distraught look on her face told him that she already knew. She stopped, gripping the bannister so hard her knuckles were white, looking up at him with an unspoken plea in her eyes that pained Barlow to see.

"You're going away," she whispered.

"I-I have to," he said, wincing at the lameness of his response.

"Can't you stay just a day or two longer?"

"I have urgent and most important news for General Jackson."

"Sarah! Sarah, where are you?"

It was Mrs. Langford, calling from somewhere downstairs. Barlow reacted instantly. He reached out and took Sarah by the hand and pulled her up the steps. They hurried down the hall and into his room. She shut the door behind them. It was highly improper for a young lady to be in a man's private quarters with the door closed, and to be found there by her mother would cause her no end of trouble. But Sarah was past caring about that sort of thing. She had something far more important to deal with. Her heart was breaking.

"Take me with you," she whispered, clutching at his arm.

"Sarah, I . . ." Barlow was thrown off guard by her fervent plea.

"It doesn't matter to me where we go," she continued. "As long as we are together. Nothing else matters."

"But, Sarah, I will probably be involved in a campaign against the . . . Against the Indians. That life is not for you."

"*This* life is not for me," she said, with real urgency as they heard her mother calling out for her yet again. "Any place would be better than this one. I simply can't stand it here another day. Especially with you gone. These past weeks, only your presence here has kept hope alive inside me. Without you I shall . . . I shall lose my mind. I feel . . . I feel as though I am being suffocated. I would rather die than . . ."

Barlow put a finger to her lips. "Calm down, Sarah."

She nodded, took a calming breath—and jumped into his protective embrace when an angry tapping sounded on the door.

"Lieutenant?" It was Mrs. Langford. "Lieutenant Barlow! Are you in there?"

Barlow saw the door knob beginning to turn. He pushed Sarah against the wall so that when he threw the door open she was concealed behind it.

"Oh, there you are," said Mrs. Langford, startled by the sudden way he had flung open the door. She looked at him suspiciously, peering around him at the room beyond. "Would you happen to know the whereabouts of my daughter, Lieutenant?"

"Why no, Mrs. Langford. I assume she is downstairs."

"She is nowhere to be found. And she is not permitted to leave the house unless I know where she is going and when she is due back."

"I'm sure she's somewhere close by."

Mrs. Langford gave him another long look before turning on her heel and heading back to the stairwell.

Barlow shut the door and breathed a sigh of relief. Sarah melted into his arms, laying her head against his chest.

"You see, Timothy? It's simply unbearable. I can't live like this any longer."

"Soon you won't have to, Sarah."

She lifted her head and gazed at him, and he saw the tears on her cheek, and brushed them gently away with the tips of his fingers.

"What do you mean?" she asked, breathlessly.

"I mean . . . I mean that as soon as possible I will send for you."

"You'll send for me?"

"I will. And we'll get married and . . . And your mother won't be able to stop us."

"Oh, Timothy!" She threw her arms around his neck and kissed him passionately—so passionately that it made him blush. She blushed, too, and looked away, suddenly her shy self again.

Barlow had to smile. "So you see, you mustn't die

on me, Sarah. All you have to do is endure this for a little while longer. You can manage that, can't you?"

"How much longer?"

Barlow had no way of knowing. But he couldn't tell her *that*. She was clinging to his promise like a drowning woman.

"Just a few months, I'm sure," he said.

"A few months. Yes—yes, I can stand it for a few more months. Just as long as I *know* you will send for me at the end of that time. You must promise me, Timothy."

"I promise."

"But how will you send for me? If you try to get a letter to me, my mother will probably destroy it before I ever see it."

"I know—I'll send it to Clay or Calhoun, with another letter that will explain the circumstances."

"Send it to Mr. Clay. He would understand, and keep our confidence. He doesn't like my mother, and would enjoy being party to a conspiracy against her. Mr. Calhoun—well, there's no way to be sure what *he* might do."

"As you wish. Mr. Clay it is. Now, give me a smile."

She smiled for him, her eyes still wet with tears— only now he thought they were tears of happiness and relief.

"You *do* love me, don't you?" she asked.

"Yes, I do love you."

"I just . . . I wouldn't want you to marry me simply because you felt sorry for me, simply to rescue me from my plight."

"No. That isn't what I'm doing, Sarah." He cupped her chin in the palm of a hand and kissed her softly on the lips. The kiss lingered—and when he pulled away, she didn't move, her face tilted upward, her eyes shut, her lips slightly parted, and he thought she had never been prettier. Finally her eyes opened, and they were dreamy.

"You had better go," she said, her voice husky with emotion.

"You'll wait for me?"

"Yes. Oh, yes, I'll wait."

He nodded, gave her one last smile, then fetched his valise and longcoat. She helped him put on the latter, and her hands lingered on his chest.

"But please don't be too long, darling," she begged.

"I won't." He opened the door with caution, peering up and down the hall to make sure Mrs. Langford wasn't lurking in ambush. Then, with one last look at Sarah, he walked out.

The horse he had arrived in Washington on was boarded at a livery several blocks away. Barlow walked that distance completely wrapped up in his thoughts. What had he done? How was he to keep his promise to Sarah? When a man took a bride, he was obligated to provide for her. But he didn't even have a home to call his own.

One thing he was certain of—he did love Sarah Langford. And he derived a kind of inner warmth, a pervasive sense of well-being unlike any he had ever experienced, at the thought of being her husband. The scent of flowers from her hair and the sweet aftertaste of her lips lingered with him. She was going to be his wife, and that added a bounce to his step despite all the uncertainty that accompanied his proposal.

He was four miles away from Washington, on the road to Harper's Ferry, when he heard a galloping horse and turned in the saddle to see a man in civilian clothes coming quickly up the lane he had just traveled. Barlow checked his horse at the roadside, expecting the rider to pass on by. Instead, the man stopped his horse alongside him and peered at Barlow, and the uniform he was wearing.

"Are you Lieutenant Timothy Barlow, by any chance?"

"Yes, I'm Barlow."

"Aide to General Andrew Jackson?"

"That's right. And who might you be?"

The man stuck out a hand. "John Rhea, congressman from Tennessee."

Barlow shook the proffered hand. Rhea appeared to be a man in his forties, stoutly built, with his hair shaded with gray and his face square and craggy.

"It seems I only just missed you at the boardinghouse, Lieutenant. Mr. Clay told me you had departed. I had hoped you were taking this route."

"What can I do for you, Mr. Rhea?"

"I have a message for the general that I hope you will take the utmost care to pass on to him."

"I will do that, and gladly, sir."

"Good. Then tell Jackson that if he decides to take Florida, the Congress will stand behind him all the way."

Barlow just stared at the man. Rhea smiled.

"I know you had a visit this morning with the Secretary of War," said the congressman. "And I venture to guess that what I have just relayed to you directly contradicts Mr. Monroe's instructions to the general."

"I'm afraid I'm not in a position to . . ."

Rhea held up a hand. "You do not need to confirm or deny it, Lieutenant. I am aware that a treaty has arrived from Ghent. And I know at least the gist of the terms it contains."

"How could you know that?"

"Some things you're better off having no knowledge of. I can therefore safely assume that Secretary Monroe has instructed General Jackson to refrain from invading Florida. But we trust the general will do what is best for the republic. He has always done so in the past."

"Do you know the general personally, sir?"

"That I do, I'm proud to say. And he knows me. Well enough, I am confident, to know that I would not under any circumstances mislead him. The Congress will back him completely. Make certain he is clear on that score, Lieutenant."

"I'll tell him what you've told me, sir," said Barlow.

Rhea nodded. "Then may God speed you on your way."

With that the congressman wheeled his horse around and headed back for Washington.

Barlow watched him go. He didn't know what to make of Rhea's message. And he had no idea what Andrew Jackson would make of it, either. James Monroe was the general's superior, and his orders were clear, while, in Barlow's opinion, Rhea's suggestion smacked of conspiracy, or worse. Apparently the War Hawk–dominated Congress knew what Monroe expected of Jackson. Did they have eyes and ears in the War Department? And they were not as willing as the administration to see the war end without the acquisition of Florida. The Congress, then, was prepared to challenge the president's authority. Assuming that Rhea spoke for the Congress, as he implied.

Barlow shook his head and rode on, all too aware that the messages he was carrying to Andrew Jackson could fundamentally change the course of his country's future.

Chapter Twelve

"**Y**ou sure you'd have us leave you here on your own, Lieutenant?"

Robert Ambrister scanned the length of the beach he had just set foot on. They had brought him ashore in a sheltered cove. Behind him, beyond the reef, stood the frigate, HMS *Resolution*, that had carried him here. The bosun's mate and six oarsmen had muscled the dingy over the reef and into the calm, clear waters of the cove. Before him rose a wall of moss-draped cypress trees, marking the edge of the swamp that, by all accounts, covered most of the island.

"So this is Goose Island," he murmured. "The Scotsman's little fiefdom."

"Pardon?" asked the bosun's mate.

"Nothing. You've done your duty, and have delivered me to the right address."

"Thing is, nobody's actually seen this fellow Arbuthnot for a couple of years. He might not even be here anymore. He could be dead. And if he is still here, they say he has Seminole warriors with him who'd just as soon kill you as look at you, sir."

"Let's hope they don't do that until I've had a word with Arbuthnot," said Ambrister cheerfully. "My compliments to Captain Fowler."

The bosun's mate understood that he was being dismissed. He shrugged and nodded at two of the sailors, who deposited Ambrister's trunk on the beach. At the bosun's mate's command, the dingy's crew pushed their sturdy craft into deeper water before clambering aboard and putting their backs into the arduous task of returning to the waiting warship. Ambrister watched them go. A cold, blustery wind buffeted him. He was a tall, slender man, handsome by anyone's measure, and as dashing as always in his Royal Marine uniform. He could only hope that if the Seminoles *did* come, the uniform would cause them to think twice about killing him. He had no desire to die in this Godforsaken spot, even if he would be dying for King and country.

Ambrister was still on the beach when the frigate set sail. He imagined Captain Fowler or one of his subordinates watching him by means of an eyeglass—and no doubt making some final comment regarding his chances of surviving until sundown. A midshipman had informed him that a wager was being offered in the officers' mess regarding the likelihood of his coming out of Florida alive, and the unanimous verdict was that he would never be seen again. Though he would never have admitted it, Ambrister also thought it unlikely that he would survive. But Major Nicholls had asked him to accept the mission—and a dangerous mission wasn't something an officer and a gentleman who had the privilege of serving in the Royal Marines could decline.

As the *Resolution* slowly moved away under billowing sail, Ambrister sighed and sat down on his trunk. He wasn't about to go traipsing off into the swamp. If Arbuthnot was still on Goose Island, then the Scotsman would find him. Ambrister decided he would just wait here until nightfall. If his presence had not been discovered by that time, he would gather up some driftwood and build a roaring fire. There was a risk that a fire would attract the wrong kind of attention—there were pirates all along this coast—but

Ambrister was willing to take that chance. Goose Island wasn't all that large, but it was large enough to get lost on, and Ambrister didn't relish ending his career as a meal for the alligators that infested the blackwater swamps in these parts. No, he would either die in battle or in the bed of a woman of loose morals; he refused to settle for less.

There was only one problem with sitting on a beach all day. It was boring. Ambrister thought of himself as a man of action, first and foremost. He had to be doing something every waking moment. He wasn't one of those people who could find contentment sitting still for hours, communing with nature, or pondering the mysteries of life. He did not possess the patience to enjoy a sunset, or read a good book. Or wait on an empty stretch of sand to be found. He had to act.

Standing, he opened the trunk, removed a shot pouch and silver-capped powder horn. He drew a pistol from his sash and looked about for a likely target. There was a piece of driftwood about thirty paces along the beach. That would have to do. One hand behind his back, Ambrister took aim and fired, striking one end of the log. Reloading, he aimed and fired again. This time he hit the other end of the log. He reloaded and fired a third time. The bullet clipped off the stub of a limb protruding some three inches from the log.

"Splendid," said Ambrister, congratulating himself.

Reloading, he surveyed the beach again, hoping that the gunfire had attracted attention.

He was surprised to see an Indian standing at the edge of the cypress swamp about a hundred yards away. The man was just standing there, staring at him. He wore the garb of a Seminole and was armed with a long rifle in addition to tomahawk, and bow and arrow. Ambrister considered his next move—and decided to put the pistol away and sit down on the trunk again, as though he hadn't a care in the world.

The Seminole gazed at him a moment longer before cupping a hand around his mouth and making a sound that resembled very closely the call of the raven.

Two more Seminoles emerged from the swamp about fifty yards behind Ambrister, who glanced at them and then turned his attention back to the first Indian. The other two were staying put, the first one was coming toward him now. He stopped a mere ten paces away.

"Who are you?" asked the Seminole.

"Ah, you speak the King's English," said Ambrister, delighted. "Outstanding. My grasp of sign language is rudimentary at best. I am Leftenant Robert Ambrister, of the Royal Marines, at your service. I would rise, but I do not want your comrades to shoot me."

The Seminole's expression remained impassive. "Why are you here?"

"I've come to see Mr. Alexander Arbuthnot. Would you happen to know the gentleman?"

"Why do you want to see him?'

"I've come bearing an important message for the Seminoles. A message from the King of England, who also sends his warmest regards to his Indian children. I depend on Mr. Arbuthnot to serve as my intermediary with the leaders of the Seminoles. Do you know him?"

The Seminole gazed intently at Ambrister for a moment before nodding.

"I know him."

"Then would you be so kind as to take me to see him?" .

Ambrister felt it was safe now to stand, and did so,

moving slowly, and making sure his hands were nowhere near his pistol or saber.

The Seminole called to his two companions in the
Seminole tongue. They came closer and, at the direction of the first Indian, picked up Ambrister's trunk
and headed into the swamp.

"Come with me," said the first Seminole, and
turned to follow his companions.

Ambrister fell in behind him.

They led him deep into the swamp and Ambrister
kept reminding himself that had the Seminoles wanted
to kill him they could have done so with relative ease
on the beach. Furthermore, they were allowing him to
keep his weapons, which he took to be a good sign
that they weren't going to turn suddenly belligerent.
Still, he breathed a sigh of relief when he saw the
rooftops of houses in a clearing up ahead. As they
drew nearer, he realized the structures were, more
precisely, huts rather than houses, virtually identical
one to the other. Each was large, circular, erected on
stilts a few feet off the ground, with a thatched roof
and walls made of sticks loosely woven together. Entering the village, Ambrister counted eleven huts. Beyond them stretched cultivated fields, and beyond the
fields a row of cypress trees marked the commence-
ment of the swamp. There was nothing growing this
time of year, but Ambrister was able to identify the
stubs of brittle cornstalks protruding from the rich
black soil of the fields. It seemed that every inhabitant
of the small village was gathering to get a closer look
at their visitor. Some of the men, he noticed—and a
few of the women—were smoking pipes made of cane
for the stem and clay for the bowl. Ambrister studied
the features of the villagers, trying to gauge their
frame of mind. He saw no anger, no fear, and no

resentment at his intrusion. Only curiosity. He'd seen Seminoles before, in Pensacola. But this was the first time he had set foot in one of their villages. He was on their ground now. And it was said of the Seminoles that they preferred to be left alone, especially by whites.

He was led to a hut that stood in the center of the village, his escort having grown from three to sixty or more. A white man whom Ambrister assumed was Alexander Arbuthnot sat on the steps of the hut, a large book balanced on his knees. He was a thin man, almost frail, with a gaunt and craggy face turned walnut brown by many years of exposure to the elements, and set off by a thick mane of long, unkempt white hair, tied up in a queue. A neglected pipe dangled from his lips. He didn't look up until Ambrister stood at the foot of the steps, flanked by the warriors who had found him and brought him here, and with the villagers arrayed quietly behind him.

"Whatever your reason for being here, you're wasting your time," said Arbuthnot brusquely, his Scottish brogue still heavy in spite of nearly a lifetime gone from his homeland.

"You're Arbuthnot, I take it. Robert Ambrister, Leftenant, Royal Marines, at your service, sir."

Arbuthnot merely grunted—a sound meant to reflect deep skepticism. "At my service, eh? I want nothing you can provide me. But I'll wager you'll be wanting something from me."

"Not I personally."

"The army, then. Something to do with the war. Well, I'm not interested in helping you with your damned war, Lieutenant."

"His Majesty the King expects his subjects to respond when he calls them to serve their country."

"Uh-huh." Arbuthnot shut the book—Ambrister

saw that it was a collection of the works of Shakespeare, once an expensively bound volume but now
much worn. The Scotsman rose to descend the steps
and stand almost nose to nose with the lieutenant.
"I've spent nearly thirty years with these people. I
owe my allegiance to them. Many years ago I wrote
letters to the government, urging Britain to honor the
commitments it had made to the tribes. But when His
Majesty lost the colonies he also, apparently, lost all
interest in the Indians, and left them to face the
Americans alone." He gestured at the villagers. "Most
of these people are Creeks. They've been forced from
their ancestral lands, or their parents before them
were. They've made a new life for themselves here,
under the most difficult of circumstances. They are
exiles. So am I."

"So you no longer consider yourself a subject of
the Crown?"

Arbuthnot's eyes narrowed. "I am a subject of my
own conscience. Nothing and no one else. If that be
treason, so be it."

Ambrister reviewed in his mind what he knew of
Alexander Arbuthnot. The Scotsman, now seventy
years of age, had traded with the Spanish and the
Seminoles for many years, first from a base in the
Bahamas before moving to Florida. He exchanged
knives, guns, powder, lead, beads and blankets for
skins. It was said that the Seminoles trusted him ex-
plicitly because he had always treated them fairly, and
had repeatedly demonstrated that his chief concern
was their welfare. It was true that on several occasions
he had pleaded with the government to intercede on
behalf of the southern tribes, whom he felt had been
abandoned by the Crown. As a result, the Americans,
who believed Arbuthnot encouraged the Seminoles to
war against them and supplied the Indians with weap-

ons, had put a price on the Scotsman's head. In fact, Arbuthnot had urged the Seminoles to leave the Americans alone.

A man who believed deeply in duty to God and country, Ambrister disapproved of Arbuthnot's disregard for his responsibilities as a subject of the British Empire. But, much as he was inclined to condemn the old man as a traitor, the lieutenant refrained from doing so. He needed Arbuthnot's help if he was to complete his mission. It wasn't as though Major Nicholls hadn't warned him that Arbuthnot would be a difficult nut to crack.

"I'll accept that your loyalty lies now with the Seminoles," said Ambrister, betraying nothing behind a polite smile. "I have but a simple request to make, and I am hopeful that you will see fit to grant it."

"And what might that be?" asked Arbuthnot suspiciously.

"I would like to be presented, under your aegis, to the leaders of the Seminoles."

"Do you now? And for what reason?"

"To persuade them to wage a vigorous war against the Americans."

"No." Arbuthnot made a dismissive gesture. "You can go back where you came from, Lieutenant."

"That would be a long swim."

"Then I'll see you to the mainland and you can make your way back to Pensacola. There you should be able to secure passage to a British possession." The Scotsman spoke to the warriors who had escorted Ambrister to the village, making fluent use of their own language. Then he turned to go into his hut.

"Arbuthnot!" snapped Ambrister. "If you profess to care what happens to these people, you will at least hear me out."

Arbuthnot turned back to face him—and Ambrister

wasn't sure if that was a smile or a snarl on the Scotsman's weathered features.

"You are hardly in a position to dictate to me, Lieutenant. Or was that a veiled threat you just issued?"

"I am issuing no threat, but rather a warning."

Arbuthnot pursed his lips. "You've got plenty of brass, I'll give you that. So tell me why I should do as you ask. You fellows have managed to lose the war. At least that's my understanding. A bunch of backwoodsmen whipped you at New Orleans, didn't they?"

"Many good men died on that field, sir. I find your gloating to be highly offensive."

"Yes, many good men. And I think there have been enough good men sacrificed in the name of empire. I have never understood why Britain wishes to rule the entire world."

"The fact remains that the Seminoles have no choice but to fight. Do you honestly think they can live in peace with the Americans? They won't even be given that option. The United States covets Florida. The only way now to prevent them from taking it is to persuade them that the cost would be too high. Now is the perfect time, for they are tired of war. The Seminoles must teach them that lesson. If they don't, they have no chance."

"And I suppose you will promise them a helping hand in this endeavor."

"I am authorized to assure them of a constant and sufficient flow of supplies. Guns, shot, powder, even food—whatever they need."

"So history repeats itself. Years ago we promised the Creeks, along with the Choctaws and the Cherokee and the Shawnees, that we would support them against the Americans, who were just then beginning to cross the mountains. They have been abandoned by Britain, left to the mercy of the Americans. And if you are a red man, Lieutenant, that mercy is in short supply."

"You know the Americans will come. They've done it once before. The next time they march into Florida they won't leave."

Arbuthnot gazed bleakly at him—then looked past him at the Indians. Ambrister thought he saw a flicker of resignation in the old Scotsman's eyes. Arbuthnot *did* know it was true. If nothing was done to dissuade the Americans, Florida would not long remain in Spanish hands. And when that fateful day arrived— when the Americans took control—it would be the beginning of the end for the Seminoles.

"Of course," Nicholls had told him, *"we don't actually expect the Seminoles to win the war we'll encourage them to fight. But a war for Florida will keep the Americans occupied in the south—and they'll be rather less likely to think of trying to seize Canada."*

The key, Nicholls had said, was to convince the Seminoles—and Arbuthnot—that they *did* stand a chance of winning. After all, desperate people tended to cling to straws.

"Very well," said Arbuthnot. "I will take you to Tallahassee. The chief there is named Hopaunee. If you can convince him, the others will be inclined to listen to you."

"Excellent," said Ambrister. "When do we leave?"

"There's no time like the present. But you'll have to leave the trunk behind. It's rough going through days of blackwater swamp."

"I've brought some presents for the chiefs."

"Keep your trinkets. That's not what the Seminoles need now."

"What is it that they do need, Arbuthnot?"

The Scotsman grimaced. "A bloody miracle," he said.

Chapter Thirteen

W hen Tom Walker came to Rook's home it was
at Kinachi's request. The latter had promised to
inform Rook when the time had come for the big
council. Hopaunee had asked the chiefs of a half
dozen other Seminole towns to come to Tallahassee
and hear what the redcoat officer named Ambrister
had to say. Walker told Rook that Menawa had arrived just before daybreak, bringing with him a dozen
warriors, all former Red Sticks, including Toquay. Hopaunee had said the council would begin today when
the sun reached its zenith.

Rook was eager to see his friend Toquay again. It
had been several months since Toquay had gone to
join Menawa. The Great Warrior had established a
new town called Awanoee about two days travel west
of Tallahassee. Not surprisingly, Awanoee had become a hotbed of Seminole militancy. It was known
that on a regular basis Menawa dispatched war parties
to raid the American settlements across the border.
Many Red Sticks had rejoined their leader, as had
other Creeks who, while they had not participated in
the uprising which had ended in disaster at Cholocco
Litabixee, were incensed by the land cession mandated
by the Treaty of Fort Jackson. They said Menawa
could now put three or four hundred warriors into the
field. He was quickly becoming the leading voice of
the war faction. And he was urging all Seminoles to
take up arms and join him in a campaign to take back

the lands stolen from the Creek Nation at Fort Jackson. More and more young Seminole warriors considered him a great hero, an almost mythical figure considering his miraculous recovery from numerous wounds received at Cholocco Litabixee. Surely, said the young warriors, this was evidence that Menawa had been chosen by the Great Spirit to accomplish great things. Menawa even had a shaman named Alakusah to preach that the visions that had been visited upon him courtesy of the Great Spirit revealed that victory was assured if only those who followed Menawa had the courage to master their own destiny.

All of this worried Rook. It was as it had been before, when Menawa and Monahee and others had stirred the Creeks into an ill-fated uprising against the Americans. Rook could only hope that Hopaunee exerted enough influence to keep the Seminoles from making the mistake the Red Sticks had made. It was bad enough that now and then bands of glory-seeking Seminole braves raided isolated American farms or towns. Hopaunee was widely respected, even beyond the boundaries of Tallahassee. And he was as much a voice for peace as Menawa was a voice for war.

Rook asked Walker to thank Kinachi for sending word of the council. Kinachi—the man who had taken Rook's rifle away from him and pointed it at his head on the beach by the Big Water—had become a real friend. Rook was convinced that Kinachi had played some role in the invitation Hopaunee had extended to him and his family to stay in Tallahassee, though Kinachi denied having had anything to do with the chief's offer. But there could be no denying that because Kinachi and his family had so readily accepted Rook and Amara and their sons into the community, the other Tallahassee Seminoles had been quick to accept them as well.

Shortly after Walker's departure, Rook and his family set out for the town of Tallahassee, two miles away. Rook had chosen to live apart from the others. He and Kinachi and Joshua had built the thatch-roofed hut—this was just prior to Joshua's departure for the place called Barracoon, a community where runaway slaves congregated. Rook had spent the winter preparing a field for planting, labor that consisted largely of cutting down several trees, converting the timber into firewood, and burning out the stumps. He looked forward to planting corn and beans in the coming spring. Until then, he kept his family fed by hunting. Game was plentiful. Sometimes Kinachi's wife would bring vegetables to Amara. The two women had become fast friends. And Tookla, Rook's oldest boy, had become infatuated with Kinachi's eldest daughter.

Sometimes Rook wondered if he was dreaming. He had come to Florida in an act of desperation, seeking sanctuary, a place his family could live in peace. A new home, far from the bloodshed of which he had witnessed far too much. He had never imagined he would find what he was looking for so quickly, however. That Kinachi had been the one to discover them on the beach had proven to be a great stroke of luck. But from the beginning, Rook had felt an unease, as though he had a premonition that something would happen to reveal that it was all an illusion, too good to be true. And now he had a strong feeling that this British officer, Ambrister, was going to be the agent of his disillusionment.

As always, Amara could tell that her husband was troubled. He had shared none of his fears with her, trying instead to pretend, for her sake and for his sons', that he was fully confident of their future. But he couldn't fool his wife. He should have known better. She had not asked him any questions—at least not until this morning, as they walked to Tallahassee.

"Will you have to go away and fight?" she asked, having waited until Tookla and Korak—impatient as always to reach the village—had run up the trail out of earshot.

He shook his head. "No. I am done with fighting."

"But what if the long hunters come?"

He looked at her. "Then we will go somewhere else to live."

"Where else is there?"

Rook grimaced. He had no answer to that question. Florida was the only sanctuary that he knew of. And now he had to wonder if the sanctuary had become a trap. One from which there would be no escape.

Tallahassee was a beehive of activity. The village of several hundred had swelled to three or four times that number with the arrival of Seminoles from other communities. Rook was not the only one to sense that what would be decided at the council here today would determine their future.

As he entered the village with his family, Rook heard his name called out—and turned to see Toquay striding through the crowd of Seminoles toward him. Rook automatically smiled at sight of his friend. But the smile froze, half-born, when Rook saw that Menawa was with Toquay. He turned to Amara.

"Take the boys to Kinachi's house and wait for me there."

Amara cast a worried look at Toquay and Menawa. She nodded and herded Tookla and Korak away.

As Toquay drew near, Rook forced the smile back into place. The two friends embraced. But there was something perfunctory about Toquay's greeting. He was just going through the motions. His smile was insincere. For his part, Menawa did not even bother smiling. He peered intently at Rook.

"Yes," he said to Toquay. "I remember him now. Rook. You fought bravely at Emuckfau and Enotochopco. I should thank you for saving the life of Toquay at Cholocco Litabixee. He has proven himself time and again when we attack the long hunters' settlements across the border. He has become a leader in his own right. His hatred for the whites burns stronger with each passing day."

Rook nodded. Some things, he mused, never changed. Menawa was as long winded as ever.

"Soon we will stand shoulder to shoulder in battle again, Rook," said Toquay. "On this day all the Seminoles and the Creeks will join together to take the warpath against the long hunters."

Rook noticed that both Toquay and the Great Warrior were painted for war. And both had plenty of scalps dangling from their belts. He had heard that Menawa's Red Sticks had been busy along the frontier these past few months, and clearly that was the case.

"In a few weeks it will be time for planting," he said. "I do not have time for the warpath."

"I would rather kill the long hunters and their families than plant corn," said Toquay. "That is work better left to women."

Rook bristled at the insulting implication of Toquay's remark. "Hopaunee does not believe in war. But he cannot keep the men of Tallahassee from taking the warpath if that is what they wish to do. I, for one, will not go with you."

Menawa shook his head, contempt etched on his face. "Toquay, your friend no longer has the courage to be a Red Stick. Come."

He walked away. Toquay lingered for a moment, gazing at Rook with hooded eyes. No trace of friendship lingered there. He looked at Rook as one would look at a potential enemy. Then, without a word, he followed the Great Warrior.

Rook proceeded to Kinachi's house. He saw that Tookla and his friend's oldest daughter were standing apart from the others, in earnest and whispered conversation, their shoulders nearly touching. Ordinarily, he would have been pleased, knowing that his son was experiencing those same wonderful feelings he experienced in the presence of Amara. But Tookla and Kinachi's daughter were too young—and too blinded by love—to notice the dark clouds that had gathered over their future. Rook could see those clouds all too clearly, though, and it deeply saddened him to think that his son's happiness might be fleeting.

Amara sat talking with Kinachi's wife at the cook fire in front of the house, while Kinachi was sitting on his heels discussing something with Korak, who strained to budge the taut bowstring on the Seminole warrior's yew-wood bow. When he saw Rook, Kinachi stood and mussed Korak's hair.

"The time has come," Kinachi told Rook. "Do you intend to speak at the council meeting?"

"I have come only to listen."

Kinachi nodded, then looked around to make sure no one was paying attention to them before leaning closer. "I think you *should* speak—against those who preach war with the Americans. You alone among the Red Sticks here today have the courage to tell the truth about the price the Creek Nation had to pay because of that uprising."

"The Red Sticks make war against all their enemies, Kinachi. Even Creek enemies. I would be putting the lives of my wife and sons in danger if I spoke out against Menawa."

"If they attacked you, they would have to take on

this entire village. Not even Menawa would dare do that."

"Don't be so sure."

The Seminole shook his head. "I do not understand the thinking of Menawa and his followers. They could not defeat the long hunters the first time. Now they have even fewer advantages. They must know in their hearts that they cannot win."

"They have lost hope," said Rook grimly. "They believe that whether they fight or not, the long hunters will kill them and their loved ones, eventually. So, since defeat and death are inevitable, they choose to die like warriors, fighting the enemy to their last breath."

"Is that the way you were thinking when you fought with them?"

"Yes. After the whites attacked a friendly village and killed women and children, I saw that the Creek Nation had no future."

"But you are no longer a Red Stick. Something must have changed your mind."

Rook glanced at Amara. At that exact moment she looked up from her conversation with Kinachi's wife and smiled at him—a pensive, troubled smile.

"Nothing happened," he replied bluntly. "I am just trying to keep my family safe for as long as possible."

"You do not believe there is any hope of living in peace with the Americans?"

"Not really, no. There are too many of them, Kinachi. They need more and more space. The land that today they say they do not want is the land that tomorrow they will covet. And whatever they want, they take."

"Look around you," said Kinachi. "Most of the land we call our own is swamp. Of what use is the swamp to the Americans?"

"When they find a use for it, they will take it. For now it is enough that they do not want the Spanish to have it. They do not want the Spanish to hold any land."

Kinachi carefully considered Rook's words, then smiled ruefully. "Maybe I was wrong. Maybe you should not speak at the council meeting, after all. Your words would only lead others to wonder whether we should fight the long hunters."

"It's a question of time," said Rook. "If Menawa gets his way, the long hunters will come this year, seeking vengeance for what the Red Sticks have done. If we keep the peace, it might be that several years will pass before they come."

"Well," said Kinachi, looking at his own family, "we had better go hear what Menawa and the English officer have to say."

The council was being held in the center of Talla-hassee, in an open space in front of Hopaunee's lodge. A large fire had been built in the middle, and hundreds had gathered round it. There were no women and children present. War was a topic fit only for men. Hopaunee and several other Seminole leaders sat crosslegged on a wooden platform raised a few feet off the ground. At either end of the platform stood tall poles decorated with Seminole totems. These were supposed to draw the attention of the Great Spirit who, it was hoped, would grant those who sat between the poles the wisdom to make the right decisions. With the Seminole chiefs was Menawa, the English officer named Ambrister and the Scots trader, Arbuthnot.

"I thought the Scotsman was supposed to be a friend of the Seminoles," Rook said to Kinachi.

"He has always been."

"And yet he brings the redcoat here to talk war."

"Maybe he did not have any choice."

Hopaunee spoke first, as the council host, giving an explanation where none was needed as to why the meeting had been called. Their good friend Arbuthnot had asked that they listen to the words of the English officer, and the officer was to speak of matters that concerned all Seminoles, which was why Hopaunee had decided to invite the chiefs from other towns to attend. With that, Hopaunee nodded to Ambrister.

The English lieutenant spoke through Arbuthnot, who translated his words into the Mikasuki dialect spoken by the majority of Seminoles. In the short time that he had lived at Tallahassee, Rook had picked up enough Mikasuki to grasp the gist of what the redcoat was saying. Ambrister began by assuring the Seminoles that their White Father, the King of England, had the welfare of his Indian children always in his heart. And while the war between Great Britain and the United States was over, the King was still committed to defending the Indians against American aggression. In the treaty that had ended the war, the King had insisted the Americans pledge to restore to the Creeks all the land that had been taken away from them. The Americans had promised to do this. But they had failed to keep their promises many times before, and the expectation was that they would fail this time, too. Therefore, it was up to the Seminoles and Creeks to drive the long hunters away. They were within their rights to do so. And it was in the best interests of the Seminoles because the Creek Nation, once it was fully restored, would serve as a buffer between the Seminoles and the Americans. To that end, the King would pledge all the supplies the Indians might need to prosecute the war. In two weeks time, a British warship would drop anchor in the harbor at Pensacola. The vessel would be laden with rifles, powder, shot, food, blankets and other items set aside solely for the Indians who chose for fight for what was rightfully theirs.

After Ambrister spoke it was Menawa's turn. The Great Warrior rose and addressed the crowd. He had fought the long hunters, he said, and knew that they could be beaten. He had defeated them at Emuckfau and Enotochopco, and would have won a great victory at Cholocco Litabixee, as the Great Spirit had promised, but for the fact that many of his warriors had lost faith in their cause, and had doubted the Great Spirit's ability to protect them from the bullets of their enemies. He himself had been struck by five bullets, receiving wounds any one of which should have taken his life. And yet he lived. By taking the bullets he had repaid the Great Spirit with his own blood for the lack of faith exhibited by those who followed him.

Rook had to shake his head in amazement. Menawa was taking on the role of Jesus Christ, the savior who suffered for the sins of his people in the Christian religion, to which Rook had been exposed during his years among the whites.

Menawa went on to say that he and the Red Sticks would never bury the hatchet and return to peaceful pursuits until all the whites had been driven from Creek land. He warned the Seminoles that they would meet the same fate as the Creeks unless they rose up now and drove the whites away. There was no time to lose. Every day more long hunters came. Soon there would be too many to kill.

Two chiefs from other towns were the next speakers. The gist of their words was that they were uncertain what to do, and looked to Hopaunee for guidance in that respect. Rook was relieved to hear this. Had the other chiefs rallied to Menawa and accepted the English offer, Hopaunee would have been the lone voice for restraint. But now Rook thought it possible that Hopaunee's wise council would prevent most of the other Seminole towns from going on the warpath, so that when Ambrister and Menawa departed, they would leave with relatively few new converts.

Hopaunee glanced at Arbuthnot, and the old Scotsman nodded. Rising slowly, Arbuthnot said he wanted to apologize for his race, and how shoddily they had treated the Indian. He was ashamed. The actions of the whites were the result of ignorance on their part. They could not see that the Indian way of life was a superior one. And he was grateful that the Seminole had welcomed him into their towns. He could not advise them what to do in this instance; he did not feel as though he had the right. But whatever the Seminoles decided, he would remain a steadfast friend to the end of his days.

When Arbuthnot was finished, Rook had a somewhat better opinion of the old trader than had previously been the case. The Scotsman's words rang true; his love for the Seminoles was evident. Rook still thought Arbuthnot had made a mistake by bringing Ambrister here. But at least he'd made it plain that he did not necessarily advocate accepting Ambrister's offer.

When he saw that no one else on the platform wished to speak, Hopaunee gravely got to his feet. He surveyed the gathering for a moment. The crowd was profoundly quiet. All eyes were on the Tallahassee chief. His words would sway many of those present.

"I have never sought a war with the white man," said Hopaunee. "The long hunters are many, the Seminoles few. My father came to Florida when I was only a child. He was the first to settle here. He came to get away from the Americans. He knew they would one day covet all the Creek lands. This has come to pass, and it saddens my heart.

"I do not blame the Red Sticks for fighting the long hunters. They fought for their homes and their families. But they should not have made war against their own people. This I do not approve of. What remains of the Red Sticks have come here. Already they have made raids on American farms and settlements across the border. They will continue to do so, and while I wish they did not, I know they will not stop if I ask them to, and I will not wage war against them to make them stop. The Creeks and the Seminoles are brothers. The same blood flows in all our veins.

"The Red Sticks will continue on the warpath, as I have said. This will bring the long hunters down upon us. They want to protect their farms and settlements, just as we would do if anyone took the warpath against us. They want Florida. They want the Spaniards to go away. And they want their slaves back. There can be no doubt that someday they will come here.

"For that reason I have decided to accept the English offer of supplies, and to join Menawa's Red Sticks. It makes my heart heavy to think of all the blood that will flow. But by taking the war to the Americans we may yet postpone the day when the long hunters take Florida away from the Spaniards, and drive us into the Big Water. It seems to me that the blood will flow no matter what we do. This is as certain as the rising and the setting of the sun. We must therefore keep the long hunters away as long as possible. I say we must fight to do this. And that is all I have to say."

A great hue and cry rose from hundreds of throats as the crowd exploded into a frenzy of excitement. Warriors raised bows and tomahawks and rifles and fists high over their heads and shouted their support for Hopaunee's decision until they were hoarse.

Kinachi glanced at Rook, who stood quite still in the midst of this melée. Recovering from his shock at Hopaunee's announcement, Rook felt sick to his stomach. Becoming aware of Kinachi's scrutiny, he could only shake his head before turning to walk away.

Kinachi caught up with him as he broke free of the crowd, and together they headed back to the house where their families were waiting.

"What will you do now?" asked Kinachi.

"I have seen all of this before," said Rook bitterly. "I will not go on the warpath again."

"You cannot be made to go. Every man in Tallahassee is free to heed his own heart. Hopaunee will not expect all the warriors here to follow him. He speaks only for himself, and any who follow him will do so of their own free will."

"And what will *you* do?"

Kinachi was grim. "I will follow Hopaunee. He has great wisdom, and if he says we have no choice but to join the Red Sticks, then I will agree that this must be so. All my life I have listened to him, and followed his counsel, and I will not stop listening to him now."

Rook nodded. Aware of Kinachi's intense loyalty to Hopaunee—a loyalty exhibited by all the other Seminole warriors of Tallahassee—he was not surprised by his new friend's decision.

As they drew near Kinachi's house, Rook grabbed his companion by the arm and brought him to a stop. "Look there," he said, pointing at his youngest son playing with Kinachi's two youngest children. All three of the children were laughing. "The Red Sticks do a lot of talking about courage and honor. And yet they cross the border and murder the children of the long hunters. At the same time they complain about how the long hunters are without honor because they sometimes kill Creek children. His hatred blinds Menawa and others like him to the truth. They say I am without honor because I will not fight. But I would be without honor if I made war on children." He shook his head. "I would fight the long hunters to protect my family, but for no other reason."

"One day you may have to, my friend," said Kinachi.

Rook nodded. He knew in his heart that this was so.

Chapter Fourteen

It took Timothy Barlow a day less than four weeks to arrive in New Orleans, two weeks less time than had been required to make the journey from Fort Jackson to Washington. The reason was that he did not have to travel overland the entire way. Instead, he took to the rivers as soon as he was across the Appalachian Mountains. He secured passage aboard a flatboat that took him down the Ohio all the way to that river's confluence with the Mississippi, where he had to wait but a single day to find himself aboard a keelboat heading down the Father of Waters. He switched boats once more at Natchez. His hosts were glad to have a soldier along, as river pirates were particularly troublesome, and every extra gun was appreciated. Yet the journey was uneventful. Barlow kept busy by taking up pole or rudder and helping with the navigation. There was ice on the rivers; a blizzard as severe as he had ever experienced had blown through during the first week of his river travel. The temperatures had plummeted dramatically, and a heavy coat of snow lay upon the land. So much ice, he was told, was exceedingly rare on the lower Mississippi, and sometimes they had to be wary of huge floes swirling downstream in the main current. On a couple of occasions a narrow channel past an island or sandbar was blocked by ice, which they had to cut through with axes—a perilous pastime, as falling into the river meant certain death. Barlow derived a new respect for the rough and rowdy river men who made their living by the commerce of the Mississippi.

Barlow was of special interest to his companions because he brought with him the news that the war was over. For the most part this news was most welcome, though some of the westerners he came into contact with grumbled a bit about the fact that the English remained in possession of Canada.

When at last he reached New Orleans, Barlow discovered that the news of the treaty had preceeded him, carried by sailing ship from the east coast. He found the city streets filled with soldiers, and it didn't take him long to locate the 39th Infantry's encampment, midway between the city and Lake Pontchartrain. He reported at once to Colonel Williams, whom he found in the field, inspecting a series of lookout posts placed along the shore of the lake.

"Well, well," said Williams, pleased. "It's good to see you alive and well, Mr. Barlow. How was Washington?"

Thinking of Monroe, Clay, Calhoun and Rhea, Barlow smiled ruefully. "Entirely too many politicians there, sir."

Williams chuckled. "Indeed. A den of snakes, eh?" Aware of Barlow's curiosity regarding the lookout posts, he added, "General Jackson has us keeping an eye out for the British, in case they return."

"Is that likely, sir? The war is over."

"Yes. We've only just received the word. But the general isn't taking any chances. There may be another fleet out there, carrying another redcoat army, and if that's the case, they might have set sail before the news of the treaty reached England. The general is simply being prudent. Too prudent, if you ask many of the inhabitants of the city, as he refuses to lift martial law. He says he will wait until he receives official confirmation. Do you carry such confirmation, Lieutenant?"

"In a manner of speaking, yes, I do, sir."

"Good. The Louisiana militia has been stirring up some trouble. The governor asked the general to discharge them. But he wouldn't do that, either. And just yesterday he had a member of the legislature arrested for inciting mutiny."

"What?" Barlow shook his head. Andrew Jackson certainly seemed to have a well-developed skill when it came to creating controversy.

"You see," said Williams dryly, "the Louisiana militia registered themselves as French citizens with the French consul here. A fellow by the name of Toussard proceeded to demand that the general discharge them on account of their newly acquired foreign status. The general promptly ordered all Frenchmen, including Toussard, to leave the city at once and keep a distance of a hundred miles.

"Then, a few days ago, an article appeared in the local French–language newspaper. It accused Jackson of acting like a tyrant, and denying citizens their rights. The editor of the newspaper was threatened with his liberty, and revealed that the author of the piece was a legislator named Louailler. Naturally, the general had Louailler arrested." Williams sighed. "I must say, Lieutenant, I'm beginning to think we may have the whole city up in arms against us before very much longer."

"Colonel, the correspondence I carry is from the Secretary of War, addressed to the general, and I deem it vitally important that he reads it as soon as possible."

"Of course, of course. You can find him, I suppose, at his headquarters in the Vieux Carré, near the levee. I'll have Ensign Houston escort you here." Williams turned and gestured for the ensign, who sat his horse among others of the colonel's entourage, to come over. Barlow shook Houston's hand enthusiastically. "You two know each other, I believe," said Williams.

"Yes, sir," said Barlow. "When I arrived at Horseshoe Bend, you had Mr. Houston show me the enemy breastwork."

"And we met again after the battle, in the hospital tent," said Houston.

"It's good to see you've made a complete recovery, Ensign," said Barlow. He and Houston had reached a first-name basis during their mutual convalescence, but he thought it best to keep things formal in the colonel's presence.

"Thank you, sir. And may I say you seem none the worse for wear."

"Ensign," said Williams, "be so good as to deliver Lieutenant Barlow to General Jackson's headquarters."

"Yes, sir."

"And then return promptly, without making any detours."

"Yes, sir!"

Borrowing the horse of another of the colonel's staff, Barlow rode alongside Houston toward New Orleans. When they were well beyond the colonel's earshot, Barlow fired a puzzled glance at the ensign. "Detours? What did the colonel mean, Sam?"

Houston cleared his throat self-consciously. "Let's just say that the colonel feels I have exhibited entirely too keen an interest in the local taverns and bordellos."

Barlow laughed. "Of course! I should have guessed."

"How was Washington?"

Barlow was pensive as he thought of Sarah Langford. "It wasn't all bad."

"Oh? I can tell by your tone of voice—and hangdog expression—that there's a woman involved."

"You can do no such thing."

Houston smirked. "I most certainly can. I'm a pretty astute student of human nature, if I do say so myself. And I know you well, Timothy Barlow. So come on, out with it. What's her name? Is she pretty?"

"Her name is Sarah. And yes, she's very pretty."

"So did you propose to her?"

Barlow was startled. "Well, not that it's any business of yours, but yes, in fact I did."

"Shame on you!" said Houston, and laughed. "Spending all your time in Washington chasing petticoats, you missed the big battle."

"Don't remind me."

"If it makes you feel any better, so did I. I was furloughed and sent home. My damned wounds refused to heal. The surgeon didn't hold out much hope for me, and they thought that if I was going to die, I should do it in my own bed."

"That was generous of them. You look well enough now."

Houston nodded. "I only just returned a week ago. I was determined that the Red Sticks would not be the death of me. But I confess I nearly passed away when I heard of General Jackson's great victory. I took solace in the knowledge that, while the war may be over, the general isn't done. He fully intends to take Florida. I'm sure of it."

"We'll see," said Barlow, carefully noncommittal. He was glad he could not speak of the letter from Secretary Monroe that he carried, as he didn't care to be the one to inform his friend that, if in fact he did march into Florida with Andrew Jackson, they would both be considered renegades by their government.

As they entered New Orleans, Barlow took a closer

look at the armed men that filled the streets. They were long hunters from Tennessee and Kentucky, as well as the dragoons from Mississippi, and apparently even Jean Lafitte's pirates, enjoying their new amnesty, courtesy of Jackson, and distinguishable from the other men by their outlandish attire, as well as their boisterous swagger.

Houston took him to Royal Street in the Vieux Carré, within sight of the levee that held back the mighty Mississippi. This was the oldest part of town, with narrow, cobblestone streets and old two-story and three-story houses of brick or clapboard. A score of fighting men stood outside the gate at 106 Royal. The gate gave access to a brick carriageway that led to an inner courtyard surrounded by the two-story house. There were several more soldiers on the balcony overhanging the street. The Stars and Stripes flew from a flagstaff secured to the roof. Barlow and Houston dismounted, tied their horses to an iron hitching post, and were met at the gate by Major John Reid, one of the inner circle of Tennesseans Jackson most trusted, and a man who served as the general's chief of staff.

"My God," said Reid, a grin spreading across his face as he recognized Barlow. "It's you!"

"Yes, sir. I have a letter for the general from the Secretary of War."

"Then come in! Come in!" Reid shepherded them down the carriageway. They entered the courtyard in time to see Jackson burst through French doors from a second-story room onto the inner balcony, a piece of paper crumpled in a fist, his face scarlet in hue.

"By the Eternal!" roared Jackson. "That damned scoundrel! I'll have him hanged." His gaze settled on Barlow, Houston and Reid. "You three! Get up here! And be quick about it!" With that, he whirled and stormed back inside.

"We've been having some difficulties with the locals," said Reid dryly. "I suspect that's what this is all about."

"You would think that by now they'd know better than to tangle with him," remarked Houston.

"They loved him like no other a couple of months ago," said Reid as they ascended a steep wooden staircase to the balcony. "But now they can't wait to see him go."

Shakos under arms, Barlow and Houston flanked Major Reid as they stood at attention on the threshold of a large, cluttered room warmed by a blazing fire in a brick hearth. The furnishings included a large desk, several chairs, a narrow iron bed. Maps covered the walls and there were even some scattered on the floor. The general was pacing like a caged lion. A man Barlow did not know was sprawled insouciantly in a chair near the desk; he was clad in a perfectly tailored clawhammer coat of the deepest crimson. His doeskin trousers were tucked into high black boots. His face was long and narrow, his complexion dark, his hair jet black. He sported a rakish mustache and sideburns that reached his jawline. His eyes looked black. Barlow surmised that he was either a Creole or a Spaniard.

Jackson stopped in his tracks, hands clasped tightly behind his back, and glanced at Barlow. "Welcome back, Lieutenant. It appears you are just in time. We're about to have another fight on our hands." He turned his piercing gaze on Reid. "Do you know a fellow by the name of Dominick Hall, Major?"

"Yes, sir—the federal district judge."

Jackson thrust the crumpled paper at Reid. "This is a writ of habeas corpus, issued this very day by Judge Hall, ordering me to produce Louis Louailler in his court at eleven o'clock tomorrow morning."

Reid took the writ, straightened it out, and looked it over.

"Judicial interference with my control of this city will not be allowed to serve as a screen behind which treason may stalk unmolested," said Jackson. "Judge Hall has challenged my authority, and he will rue that decision."

"Just say the word, *mon general*," said the man in the chair.

Jackson smiled coldly. "Lafitte here has suggested that one of his pirates will gladly deliver my answer— in the form of a knife between the judge's ribs."

Barlow looked again at the man in the chair. Jean Lafitte! The notorious pirate chieftain whose men had fought so valiantly for the American cause behind the ramparts on January 8.

Reid looked worried. "Surely, sir, you are not actually considering . . ."

Jackson grimaced. "If and when I want Hall dead, I'll do the job myself. But by the Eternal, that man has been a thorn in my side ever since I arrived here! And ever since the battle, he has been outspoken in his criticism of our continued presence in the city. I smell a rat, Major. Were I gone, Hall and his cronies would gladly turn New Orleans over to the British, if the redcoats happened to return. But they'll not have the chance. This city is too vital to the interests of the republic. Without it, we lose control of the Mississippi. If an enemy holds New Orleans, he has the republic by the throat! And that is something I will not allow."

He strode to the desk and angrily scrawled something on a piece of paper, which he presented to Reid.

"Execute this order at once, Major."

Reid read the order aloud for the benefit of Barlow and Houston. "Having received information that

Dominick Hall has been engaged in aiding, abetting and exciting mutiny within my camp, I forthwith authorize Major John Reid to arrest and confine him and make report of same to headquarters."

"Take these two gentlemen with you," said Jackson, with a gesture that indicated he meant Barlow and Houston.

"Sir, this is a federal judge we're talking about," cautioned Reid. "A man appointed by the president himself."

"And I have been appointed commander of the Seventh Military District, Major. When I impose martial law, everyone—including a federal judge—must bow to my authority."

"At least give the lieutenant and the ensign the option of foregoing the pleasure of accompanying me, General."

Jackson scowled. "What's come over you, John? Why should I do such a thing?"

"Unlike myself, they have chosen to make a career in the United States Army. This order could have serious repercussions that might adversely affect their futures."

Jackson glanced at Barlow. "Well, Lieutenant? Are you with me or not?"

Barlow was taken aback. He had not been prepared for this development. His mind raced. Major Reid had made a valid point. Jackson was charting a perilous course. His anger was blinding him to the possible consequences of Hall's arrest. If events turned against the general, they would most assuredly do likewise for anyone involved in the incarceration of so august a person as a federal district judge. But he had questioned the general's actions once before, with regard to the treatment of friendly Creeks at the signing of the Fort Jackson treaty. If he did so again he would likely find himself no longer a member of Jackson's staff—and perhaps not even a part of Jackson's army. Or he might be accused of mutiny. He glanced at Houston. The ensign was inscrutable. You never could tell what Houston was really thinking.

"I'm with you, General," said Barlow.

"Good. Good!"

"Before we go, sir, I should give you this," said Barlow, producing Secretary Monroe's letter from beneath his travel-stained coatee.

"Fine." Jackson took the letter from him and did not open it. His thoughts were entirely consumed by the crisis at hand, and he seemed totally disinterested in the letter's contents. "See me when you're done with the judge."

Barlow accompanied Reid and Houston out of the room. They filed down the stairs and paused in the courtyard to collect themselves.

"The two of you really should let me handle this," said Reid grimly.

"Thanks, Major," said Houston, "but we are under orders. That will protect us from any backlash that might occur."

"Maybe." Reid didn't sound too convinced. "Well, come on then. Let's get it over with."

They walked with Reid the four blocks to Dominick Hall's residence, and were admitted immediately into the presence of the judge. Hall was relaxing in a downstairs parlor with a glass of brandy. He was a stern, gray man, tall and thin—not unlike Andrew Jackson in appearance and presence.

"Good afternoon, gentlemen," said Hall with icy cordiality. "To what do I owe this pleasure?"

"General Jackson has sent us, sir," said Reid flatly.

Hall nodded, and looked them over. "To arrest me? Or perhaps assassinate me?"

Barlow bristled. "We are not assassins, sir."

"No, of course not. My apologies for having offended you, Lieutenant. Just because your general is a barbarian, I should not automatically assume that his subordinates are, too. On what charge am I being arrested?"

"Aiding, abetting and exciting a mutiny," said Reid.

"Really," murmured Hall. He sipped his brandy. "The man is mad. I fear for my city and its inhabitants. They are in the grip of a lunatic and a tyrant. There is no way to predict what he might do."

"If you cross Andrew Jackson, your fate is actually quite predictable," remarked Houston.

Hall finished his brandy, put the glass down and rose. "I hold no animus toward the three of you. You are only obeying orders, like good soldiers. From what I know of Jackson, to do otherwise would be to invite the attentions of a firing squad." He walked with stiff dignity right past them to the door. "But mark my words, gentlemen. Jackson will lose this battle—and it will be a defeat that will haunt him for the rest of his days."

After seeing Judge Hall safely locked away in the same barracks as the legislator, Louailler, Barlow bid Sam Houston farewell. The ensign returned to the 39th Infantry's encampment. Major Reid headed for Royal Street to report to Jackson. Barlow wanted a bath and a meal and ten hours sleep. He was exhausted after the long and difficult journey from the nation's capital. But he assumed that by now the general had read Secretary Monroe's letter, and if that were so, Jackson would probably have questions for him. And besides, he had not yet been afforded an opportunity to deliver Congressman Rhea's message to Jackson, a message he considered highly confidential in nature.

They found the general in the same room. The fire in the hearth had died down considerably, and been neglected. The French doors were open, letting in the cold air. The general didn't seem to notice. He sat behind the desk, head lowered so that his stubborn chin was resting on his chest. Barlow noticed that the letter he had carried with him all the way from Washington lay open on the desk in front of Jackson.

"Judge Hall has been placed in custody, sir," said Reid. He headed for the hearth, intent on putting another log on the fire.

"Leave it, Major," rumbled Jackson. "You may go. Lieutenant, stay for a moment, if you please."

Reid departed. Jackson gestured for Barlow to take a chair.

"I have not actually met James Monroe," said Jackson. "What do you make of him, Barlow?"

"He is . . . an extremely intelligent man, sir. I believe he prefers diplomacy to war. He is a true patriot, more concerned with the republic's welfare than his own aggrandizement."

Jackson peered at Barlow from beneath dark, bushy brows. "He is also a fool," snapped the general.

"I really couldn't speak to that, general."

Jackson nodded. "We will have to seize Florida. It is inevitable. The Seminoles will continue to raid our frontier settlements, probably with the aid and encouragement of the British."

"As I was leaving Washington, a congressman named Rhea caught up with me, sir. He said you knew him."

Jackson sat up and leaned forward. "I do. What did he say to you?"

"He indicated that the Congress would stand behind you, should you decide to take Florida."

"Ha!" Jackson leapt to his feet. He began to pace feverishly, deep in thought. Barlow watched him, expecting him to say more. But minutes passed, and Barlow shifted uncomfortably in his chair. It was as though Jackson had completely forgotten he was there. For weeks now Barlow had been wondering what the hero of New Orleans would do after reading Monroe's letter and hearing Rhea's message. Would he bow to the authority of the War Secretary who, presumably, spoke for the president? Or would he disobey orders and march on Florida? And if he did the latter, would the Congress support him, and stand in defiant contradiction of the executive branch? Barlow's curiosity got the better of his caution after five minutes of silence.

"So what will you do, sir?" he asked. "Are we going to Florida?"

Jackson stopped and turned, a taut smile on his lips. "We will go to Florida, yes. But not right away. I have in mind to visit my home. I have been away from my affairs—and my beloved Rachel—for more than a year now. I miss her terribly." He drew a long breath and nodded to himself. "Yes, I will go to Tennessee and let time prove Mr. Monroe to be the fool that he is. There are some in Washington who would like nothing better than to see me defy the administration. I would be blamed for starting a war, or precipitating a national crisis. They would paint me a reckless brigand, or worse."

"Are you referring to Congressman Rhea, sir?"

"No, not him. But rather the men who represent the ruling class. The easterners, the ones who have always held the reins of power. They know that those reins are slipping from their grasp. With each passing day the western states grow more populous—and therefore more powerful. Soon all the western states will lack is a leader, someone who will represent the common man against the monied interests. The Constitution says our government is by the people and for the people. Noble words, but so far that's all they are, just words. But one day the government *will* belong to the people."

Barlow understood then. He had always known that Andrew Jackson was an ambitious man. But he hadn't realized, until now, just how ambitious. The general had his sights set on the presidency. He hadn't actually come out and said so, but Barlow was sure of it. And Jackson understood that if he made a single mistake where Florida was concerned, his hopes of attaining that office would be dashed. He would not be denied his dream of taking Florida, but he would allow events to dictate the necessity of that action. He would bide his time. He could play the game of political intrigue with the best of them. Barlow wasn't sure if the general was right in saying that there were those in Washington who, because they feared his growing popularity, conspired against him. But if in fact they *weren't* worried about Andrew Jackson, then, indeed, there *were* fools in the halls of government.

"You will come with me to Tennessee, Lieutenant," said Jackson. He was upbeat now, an entirely changed man from the one slumped, disconsolate, behind his desk only moments earlier. "But don't worry. You'll see action before long. I promise you that!"

Chapter Fifteen

Like the rest of Andrew Jackson's staff, Barlow was quartered in the house at 106 Royal, and these turned out to be the nicest accommodations he could remember having. The town residence of a planter who had given it to Jackson for the duration of his stay in New Orleans, the house came complete with a platoon of house servants who made sure the occupants had every possible convenience and comfort available to them. Barlow didn't mind that the departure for Tennessee was put off until the little matter involving Louailler, Hall and the Louisiana militia was concluded. He found the city exotic and fascinating. The same could be said for its inhabitants. Its mixture of race and creed and culture made it a lively, cosmopolitan place. The northern cities of Philadelphia and New York, with which he was acquainted, seemed quite tame and dull by comparison. He spent all of his free time roaming the streets, gathering in the sights and sounds and smells.

Jackson decided to bring Louailler before a military tribunal. The legislature cried foul, assuming it would be a kangaroo court that would simply do the general's bidding, and justice be hanged. Everyone was surprised, therefore, when the tribunal agreed with Louailler's contention that since he was not in the military he could not be court-martialed. He was promptly acquitted. But Jackson refused to acknowledge the verdict and ordered Louailler kept in custody. As for Judge Hall, the general opted to send him packing. At dawn one morning, an escort of soldiers marched Hall out of the city and relayed to him Jackson's order that he not return to the general's jurisdiction. Hall was indignant—but he was also smart enough not to test Jackson's resolve, feeling if he did so that the next time the soldiers came for him at dawn it would be for the purpose of marching him in front of a firing squad. The best he could do, then, was to sit and wait for Jackson to loosen his iron grip on the city. Sit, wait—and plot revenge.

Hall did not have long to wait. A week later, Jackson finally relented. More information arrived that clearly indicated that the war with Britain was well and truly over. There would be no second British fleet to appear in Lake Pontchartrain, no second British army to march on New Orleans. Martial law was revoked. Louailler and others held in confinement were released. Judge Hall was allowed to return to his home. Jackson called on all the volunteers in his army to muster in the square near the river. Barlow was present with the general when the latter gave his farewell address to the troops.

"It is time for all of you to return to your homes," he said. "Go, my brave companions, full of honor, and crowned with laurels that will never fade. Farewell, fellow soldiers. The expression of your general's thanks is feeble, but the gratitude of a country of freemen is yours. Yours, too, is the applause of an admiring world."

The cheering seemed to go on forever. Hats were hurled into the air. Cannon lined up on the adjacent levee fired a salute. Barlow could tell Jackson was deeply moved by the obvious affection for him that the troops displayed. The general stood stern and ramrod straight, but tears welled up in his eyes.

They arrived back at 106 Royal Street to find an order from Judge Hall awaiting them. It demanded that Andrew Jackson appear in Hall's court on the following day to show cause why he should not be held in contempt for not obeying the writ of habeas corpus the judge had issued for Louis Louailler.

Barlow expected Jackson to explode in anger. Instead, the general smiled wryly after reading the order.

"The man is a worthy opponent, I'll give him that. He has nerve."

"He has too much nerve if you ask me," said Major Reid. "You should just ignore that order, sir. Return to Tennessee and let Hall stew in his own bitter juices."

"Nonsense. I've never run from a front, and I'm too old to learn a new trick."

The case of *United States* v. *Major General Andrew Jackson* drew a great deal of interest from the public—in fact, it seemed to Barlow that the entire city of New Orleans had turned out to fill the streets around the courthouse. Arriving in an open carriage with Major Reid, Barlow and his legal counsel, Edward Livingston, Jackson wore civilian clothes. Having never seen the man in anything but a military uniform, Barlow thought the general looked odd. Somehow older, more frail, diminished. But the people didn't seem to think so. They cheered him as though he were Caesar returning to Rome after the conquest of Gaul. Jackson was prompted to remark to his entourage that at least the citizens of New Orleans had forgiven him his transgressions. Major Reid replied that Judge Hall should forgive him, too, lest he become the target of mob action. Jackson listened gravely and said nothing.

The courtroom was as packed as the streets—and when Jackson entered the room, a roar went up from the crowd, one so lusty that it rattled the glass panes in the windows. Despite the apparent adoration of the people, Barlow stuck close by the general's side, as did Reid; they had agreed between them that the crowd might contain an assassin. Jackson had made some enemies during his sojourn here. And there might be a crackpot, someone who had no grievance against the general, but who sought to make a name for himself by slaying the hero of the hour. They had not told Jackson of their concerns. He would have scoffed. But they kept a close eye on all those who came near.

When Judge Hall entered the courtroom, he was greeted with a volley of boos, hisses and some invective. Scowling, he hammered on his desk with a gavel until the noise had subsided.

"If there are any further displays I will have this room cleared," declared Hall, furious.

Jackson rose. "There is no danger here, Your Honor," he said. "The same arm that protected this city from outrage shall shield and protect this court, or perish in the attempt."

Such noble sentiment triggered another spontaneous explosion of cheers from the people, and Hall had to use the gavel again to restore order. He smiled coldly at Jackson.

"The court appreciates the general's concern," he said dryly. "But as he may soon learn, it is perfectly capable of protecting itself."

Edward Livingston rose to address the judge. "Your Honor, we respectfully suggest that these proceedings are improper. By becoming the arbiter of your own grievances, sir, you have placed yourself in a situation where reason could have but little agency except to attach to any decision you might make nothing but suspicion and censure."

"No one has ever received anything less than a completely fair and impartial hearing in my court," snapped Hall.

"My client," continued Livingston, "demands his constitutional right to a trial by jury, which would, considering the circumstances, be a better instrument of justice."

"Your request is denied. Though I am heartened to know that the general is at least acquainted with the fact that citizens of this republic have constitutional rights. His actions of late had given me cause to wonder. Now, let us proceed."

Livingston sat down.

"I have a number of interrogatories which I will expect the general to answer," said Hall. "Did you, General Jackson, understand that the writ of habeas corpus I had delivered to you on fifteenth March last was a binding order of a duly authorized court, which you as a citizen were required to obey?"

For a second time Jackson got to his feet. "I will not answer any questions. I appear before Your Honor to receive the sentence of the court, and have nothing to add. I mean no disrespect to the court, but as no opportunity has been furnished to me to explain the motives which influenced my conduct, so it is expected that censure will form no part of that punishment which Your Honor may imagine it is your duty to perform."

Hall was silent for a moment, staring at Jackson with an expression that mixed disbelief with grudging admiration. The general was avoiding a confrontation without actually admitting guilt, and there was nothing for the judge to do but decide on a sentence.

"In light of the service you have rendered your country, General," said Hall, "I find this to be an unpleasant but necessary duty. Necessary because the answer must be made clear to a fundamental question:

Whether the Law should bend to the General or the General to the Law. I therefore impose upon you a fine of one thousand dollars."

Edward Livingston arose once more to address the court. "Your Honor, a number of us, in the spirit of the deepest gratitude for the general's heroic defense of our city, would like to pay the fine."

Hall peered at Jackson, smiling faintly. "Is that an acceptable arrangement in your mind, sir?"

"Absolutely not," said Jackson.

"Ah," said Hall. "I rather thought it would not be."

"I will pay the fine," continued Jackson, with stiff dignity. "I would, though, like to suggest that the money be divided among the families of the valiant soldiers who died in defense of New Orleans."

"Who could argue with that?" asked Hall. "It is so ordered." He banged the gavel once. "This court is adjourned."

As Hall left the courtroom, a man stood up in back and shouted: "Three cheers for Andy Jackson! Three cheers for Old Hickory!"

The audience erupted with huzzahs. Jackson departed the courthouse, with Barlow and Reid elbowing the press of well-wishers aside. Emerging onto the front steps, the general was greeted by another cheering throng. He raised a hand to silence them.

"I have, during the invasion, exerted every one of my faculties for the defense and preservation of the Constitution and the laws of this republic. On this day I have been called to submit to their operation under circumstances which many persons might have thought sufficient to justify resistance. However, obedience to the laws, even when we think them unjustly applied, is the first duty of every citizen. I did not hesitate to comply with the sentence you have heard, and entreat you to remember the example I have given you of respectful submission to the administration of justice. I now bid you all, and this great city, a fond farewell."

They cheered him more as Barlow and Reid escorted him to the waiting carriage. The last one in, Barlow shouted over the din to the driver, ordering him to drive on. Then he settled onto his seat with a sigh of relief.

"I must say, sir," he remarked wryly, "that you appear in their good graces once more."

"But I am surprised you didn't put up a fight in Hall's court, General," confessed Reid. "The point that seems to have been overlooked in all this talk about laws is that when martial law is in place, *you*, sir, are the sole arbiter of justice."

Jackson merely grunted. "We have many battles ahead of us, Major. One must learn to pick and choose the fight he will exert himself to win. The judge knows I was within my rights, and I daresay I got the better of him today. But he has saved face, and I have made the best of the situation. Besides, I must give the politicians in Washington no ammunition they might someday be able to use against me."

"Where to now, sir?" asked Barlow.

"Home," said Jackson, his voice husky. "Home to Nashville."

They traveled as far as Natchez by river, and from there struck out overland on the Natchez Trace, which would see them well into Tennessee. The first stop north of Natchez was the plantation called Springfield, the property of one Thomas Marston Green, an old friend of Jackson's. Barlow discovered that it was here that Jackson had married Rachel back in 1791. The place held many memories for the general. Barlow assumed they were all fond memories. But he was wrong.

"My dear Rachel," murmured Jackson, when they were all sitting on the front gallery with its tall white columns—one of which had been cracked by the great New Madrid earthquake of 1811—drinking brandy or whiskey depending on preference, and watching the night deepen, laying a star-spangled cloak across the sky. "Her first husband, Captain Robards, was an insanely jealous man who shamed her in public, so that she decided to flee to Natchez. I accompanied her. We traveled with the Stark family, by flatboat. Rachel was welcomed here, and I returned to Nashville. I had a thriving law practice and I wanted to be in a position to defend her good name if need be."

"I assume no one spoke ill of her in your presence, Andy," said Green wryly, "as I don't believe you had to kill anyone during that time."

"That's true. Word arrived that Robards, who had traveled to Virginia, had acquired a divorce there. This was necessary, as Kentucky, where he and Rachel had been wed, was at the time a district of Virginia, and he had to present his request to the Virginia legislature. I hastened back here with the news. It was the summer of '91. Rachel and I were married, right here in this grand home."

"In 1791, this was Spanish territory, wasn't it?" asked Barlow. "I take it, sir, that you could not obtain the services of a Catholic priest. Even were you Catholics, no priest would have presided over a union involving a divorcee if her previous husband was still living."

"He's a bright young man, isn't he, Andy?" asked Green.

"Yes," concurred Jackson. "Sometimes I think he might be *too* bright." He laughed softly, a dry and rasping sound. "But you're quite right, Lieutenant. This was Spanish territory then, and Catholic to boot.

There were some Protestants here, however. The Spaniards had encouraged Americans to settle in these parts, as they could find few of their own kind willing to do so. They allowed Protestants to practice their religion, and there were several ministers in the vicinity at that time. I admit that, in hindsight, I perhaps should have taken more care in arranging the event."

"You and Rachel were madly in love," said Green. "And being in love is a condition that is not conducive to clear thinking."

"True words," said Jackson, nodding ruefully. "For you see, Barlow, as it turned out Robards hadn't gotten that divorce, after all. All he had acquired from the Virginia legislature was an enabling act which permitted him to bring suit against Rachel. This he had not done. It wasn't until two years later that we learned the truth. Rachel was distraught, to put it mildly. Technically, we had been living in adultery all that time. She found little comfort in the knowledge that we had done so innocently. You must understand—that scoundrel Robards had falsely accused her of being an adultress all during the time they were together. And suddenly, a cruel twist of fate had made her one in the eyes of the law."

"So what did you do, sir?" asked Barlow.

"I was persuaded to marry her a second time. At first I was reluctant to do so, as it seemed tantamount to a confession of adultery. But legally there was nothing else we could do." He sighed, gazing at the north star, which was clearly visible from where they sat. Thinking, Barlow was sure, that Nashville lay in that direction. "I do not believe my dear wife has altogether recovered from the shame and embarrassment of that situation."

"What of you two gentlemen?" asked Green, glancing at Barlow and Reid. "Either one of you married?"

"Not I!" said Reid, with feeling.

Green chuckled. "I detect the tone of a committed bachelor."

"I'm not married," said Barlow. "Yet."

"Yet?" Green's eyes twinkled mischief in the light of the storm lanterns that illuminated the gallery. "So you've been captured, I take it. When is the fateful day?"

"I'm not entirely sure," admitted Barlow, wishing fervently that the subject had not come up. "I met her in Washington. Told her I would send for her as soon as I could, and that we would be wed."

"Splendid!" exclaimed Jackson. "Then you *must* send for her as soon as we reach the Hermitage."

"Yes, sir."

Jackson smiled. "That's not actually an order, Barlow. Merely a suggestion. If you love a woman, as I love my Rachel, you should waste no time and spare no effort to make her yours. I made mistakes in my haste to marry Rachel, I grant you. But I treasure every moment I have spent with my wife. I am sure you feel the same way where your beloved is concerned."

"Yes, of course," said Barlow, as though that went without saying.

As the conversation turned to other matters, Barlow became lost in thought. The way Jackson had described his feelings for Rachel made him wonder if his feelings for Sarah were really strong enough to warrant marriage. Was he truly in love with her? Enough to warrant the commitment he had said he would make? These were doubts he would never admit to anyone, but neither could he deny them to himself. Yet there was no escaping the fact that he had made a promise to Sarah Langford, and a gentleman always kept his promise.

* * *

During the journey up the Natchez Trace, Andrew Jackson was greeted at nearly every turn by citizens who hailed him as their hero, the man who almost single-handedly had won the war against the British— and had saved the republic in the process. In Barlow's opinion, a humble Jackson was at his best, acquitting himself well in this flood of adoration that might have inflated the ego of a lesser man. Jackson was consistently quick to point out that the men who had served under him were the ones who deserved all the credit. They were the true heroes, not he.

There was an undercurrent to the remarks made by those who came from far and wide to make Jackson's return home a kind of triumphal procession. The men who spoke to the general at the inns and taverns and river crossings sounded very confident about the future of the republic. It was something that Barlow realized had always been missing from the American discourse. Always before there had been profound anxiety regarding the future. The United States had struggled through one crisis after another in the thirty-odd years of its existence. In the family of nations she was still just an infant, still learning to walk, and virtually defenseless. But now freedom was secured. The republic had won respect abroad. More importantly, her people had faith in her permanence. And it was all due to Jackson's victory at New Orleans. Barlow could tell that he had been right when, upon first hearing of the battle, he had predicted it would go down as the single most important feat of arms in the nation's history. It was only natural, then, that he continued to feel deep regret at having missed it. He sensed that Jackson knew of his disappointment, even though Barlow had been careful not to speak of it to anyone save Ensign Sam Houston. That was why, surmised

Barlow, the general had on more than one occasion assured him that another fight was in the offing.

As they traveled north, they encountered snow. The winter had been a long and severe one, but finally the days were growing steadily warmer. The snow was melting. This resulted in rivers running high, and they had to exercise caution at the numerous crossings. But at last they arrived at the Hermitage, not much the worse for wear. Jackson's home, located a few miles from the bustling frontier community of Nashville, consisted of a group of log buildings, the largest being a two-story blockhouse built with resisting Indian attacks in mind. Here Jackson and his wife resided. Guests stayed in the three smaller cabins. There was a spring just to the west of the cabins, and beyond the spring was a garden and a field where, when the last of the snow was gone, corn would be planted. All of this crowned a low hill covered with elm, oak and sycamore trees, overlooking the valley of the Tennessee River.

Rachel Jackson was not what Barlow had expected. The general had spoken of her often, describing the high-spirited, vivacious girl he had met years ago, a sprightly dancer and superb horsewoman. But the Rachel Barlow met was a plump, pale woman, subdued in manner, and with a trace of perpetual sadness in her kind smile.

"I feel as though we've already met, ma'am," said Barlow, "as much as your husband talks about you."

Rachel laughed softly and shook his hand. "Andy, where did you find this young fellow? He has impeccable manners."

"Well, he's a city boy," replied Jackson, "so what do you expect?"

"I expect that all the belles in Nashville will swoon when they lay eyes on him."

"They'd be wasting their time," said Jackson. "He has his cap set for a young lady he met back in Washington."

In the days to follow, Jackson had precious little time to spend alone with Rachel. A constant flow of visitors came to the Hermitage to greet the hero of New Orleans, including nearly all the men of wealth and influence in and around Nashville. The general was a gracious and patient host in every case. Some of them brought newspapers that heaped praise on Jackson for the service he had rendered his country. "Glory be to God that the barbarians have been defeated," proclaimed the *Niles Weekly Register*. "Glory to Jackson! Glory to the militia! Sons of freedom, benefactors of your country—all hail!" "We demonstrated to mankind a capacity to acquire a skill in arms to conquer 'the unconquerable,' as Wellington's invincible were modestly styled," read an account in another newspaper. "Who would not be an American? Long live the republic! Last asylum of oppressed humanity! Long live Andrew Jackson! Since Washington our greatest warrior!"

Many were the callers who attempted to coax from the general some indication of his future plans, and more than one openly encouraged him to pursue political office—governor of Tennessee, or senator, or even president in 1816. But Jackson kept his ambitions to himself. He portrayed himself as a modern-day Cincinnatus, a humble farmer who had become a reluctant warrior to fight for his nation, desirous only of returning to hearth and plow now that the great struggle was over.

A few weeks later, Jackson was the guest of honor at a grand banquet given in his honor in Nashville, attended by Tennessee's most distinguished citizens, including Governor Blount. Barlow and Reid accompanied the general. Speeches were made honoring Jackson. An ornamental sword voted by the legislature of Mississippi was presented to him. And a Congressional resolution was read aloud:

Resolved, By the Senate and House of Representatives of the United States of America in Congress assembled. That the thanks of Congress be, and they are hereby, given to Major General Jackson, and through him, to the officers and soldiers of the regular army, of the volunteers, and of the militia under his command, for their uniform gallantry and good conduct conspicuously displayed against the enemy, from the time of his landing before New Orleans until his final expulsion therefrom, and particularly for their valor, skill and good conduct on the 8th of January last, in repulsing, with great slaughter, a numerous British army of chosen veteran troops, and thereby obtaining a most signal victory over the enemy with a disparity of loss, on his part, unexampled in military annals.

Resolved, That the President of the United States be requested to cause to be struck a gold medal, with devices emblematical of this splendid achievement, and presented to Major General Jackson as a testimony of the high sense entertained by Congress of his judicious and distinguished conduct on that memorable occasion.

Jackson humbly accepted all the homage paid him, not only in the hall where the banquet was held, but also in the streets, thronged by people who, despite the lateness of the hour, wanted to see the hero with their own eyes. A chorus of girls dressed in virgin white sang a song composed to honor him.

Come all ye sons of freedom
Come all ye brave who lead 'em
Come all who say God speed 'em
And sing a song of joy!
To Jackson ever brave
Who nobly did behave
Unto Immortal Jackson
The British turned their backs on
He's ready still for action
O Jackson is the boy.
Our country is our mother
Then let each son and brother
Stand firm by one another
And sing a song of joy!
Let party spirit cease
Here's "Victory and Peace"
And here's Immortal Jackson
The British turned their backs on
He's ready still for action
O Jackson is the boy.

During the carriage ride home, Major Reid congratulated the general. "You're another Washington, sir. Without doubt the most respected man in the country at this moment in time."

"Ah, but fame is fleeting, Major, and not to be too relied upon." He looked across at Barlow. "By the way, Lieutenant, I've been meaning to ask if you've sent for your bride-to-be."

"Well, um, no, sir. Not as yet."

"I wrote to Congressman Rhea over a week ago, asking that he provide whatever assistance might be required in her journey here. I am confident he will make every effort to meet my request. So, when we get home you should write to her straight away as

Rhea will be expecting her soon. That is, if you haven't changed your mind."

"No, sir, of course not."

"Good. Good! The two of you will be welcome at the Hermitage. We have the several cabins, and you may claim the one you favor. Rachel has told me that she hopes you will see fit to let us host your wedding."

"That's too kind, General."

"We would be both pleased and honored. Now, I do have a good bit of property in Nashville. Frontier lawyers must become accustomed to receiving land, houses and livestock in lieu of cash payments for services rendered, you know. There are several good, solid houses available, if you and your bride would prefer to reside in town."

"I'm not sure that in my present condition I could pay you what a house would be worth, sir. Especially a good solid one."

Jackson dismissed that detail with a wave of his hand. "I'm sure we could make some arrangement satisfactory to both of us. Personally, I would be content to gift a house to you. But were I in your shoes, I would insist on paying my own way, so I will not insult you by declining payment altogether."

"Thank you, sir."

"In addition, if you wish to take leave to travel to Philadelphia and see your family, either before or after you are wed, just say the word."

"I suppose afterwards would be the better choice."

"Yes. That way you will be able to introduce them to your new bride. Then it's all settled."

"I don't know what to say, General."

Jackson shook his head. "No need to say anything. I take care of those who take care of me. It is not a matter of trying to purchase your loyalty, of course. I know that's not for sale. No, mark it down to profound gratitude on my part. In a small way I can repay you for services rendered."

"It's I who am grateful, sir."

Barlow glanced at Reid, aware that the major was watching him closely. Had he betrayed a lack of enthusiasm for the wedding arrangements? He had tried his best not to. Thankfully, Reid made no comment—until after they had arrived at the Hermitage. It was late, and Jackson wanted to go straight to bed: Reid and Barlow repaired to the log cabin that they shared.

"Not getting a case of cold feet about this marriage business, are you, Barlow?" asked Reid, smiling, as he built up the fire in the hearth.

"No, of course not. It's just that . . ." He looked at Reid, wanting someone to confide in, and yet restrained by an innate reluctance to speak of personal matters with anyone else. "It's just that the general and his wife are so devoted to one another that it gives me cause to wonder whether my feelings for Sarah run . . . Well, run deep enough."

"That devotion that the general and his wife display is the product of more than twenty years together, remember," said Reid.

"I never thought I'd hear you sing the praises of married life, Major!"

Reid laughed softly. "No. I guess I've just had rotten luck when it comes to affairs of the heart. But enough about me. This is about you. Marriage is a big step. So I suggest you refrain from taking that step unless you're absolutely certain that's the direction in which you wish to go."

Barlow shrugged. "I'm not sure. I probably never would be sure. But I made a promise."

"Oh, I see. Then you are in a quandary!"

"So it would seem."

"Well," sighed Reid, sitting in a rocking chair near

the hearth and extending his long legs in order to warm his feet by the fire. "The way I see it, it would be better to break a promise than to break a young lady's heart."

"I don't understand your reasoning. Breaking my promise would do just that. Break her heart, I mean."

"Not nearly as much as it would bring her heartbreak to discover that she was married to a man who did not truly love her with all his heart and soul. She would be doomed to a life of emptiness."

"I see."

Reid yawned, rose, and clapped Barlow on the shoulder. "It's been a long day. I think I'll turn in."

Barlow occupied the rocking chair Reid had vacated and sat there for a long while, staring into the crackling fire, trying to decide what to do. Finally he drew a long breath and went to a table standing beneath a window, and upon which was a box containing paper, ink and pen. He sat down, dipped his pen in ink, and wrote: *Dear Sarah.* Then he hesitated, her words ringing in his ears. *I wouldn't want you to marry me simply because you felt sorry for me, simply to rescue me from my plight.*

Barlow grimly put pen to paper and began to write the most important letter of his life.

Part III

January–April 1818

Chapter Sixteen

When Barlow walked into John Henry Eaton's office, the lawyer was bent over a huge tome, one of many on his desk, scattered among a clutter of papers. By the pale winter light shining in through the snow-rimmed windows, Barlow saw a square-built man about his own age who had a shock of sandy hair and good, strong features. When Eaton looked up to identify his visitor, Barlow noted that his eyes were a very pale blue, and his gaze was both honest and direct.

Since he was not here on official business, Barlow wore civilian clothes—his one good suit of plain brown wool.

"What can I do for you, sir?" asked Eaton.

"Are you John Eaton?"

Eaton leaned back in his chair. "I am. And you are?"

"Lieutenant Timothy Barlow, United States Army, at your service."

"Oh yes. I've heard of you. The general's aide."

"One of them anyway." A postwar military rendering had divided the country into two military districts, northern and southern, and Andrew Jackson had been given command of the latter. There were other generals in the area, but in Tennessee when one referred to the "general," it was understood that Jackson was the subject matter. The expansion of authority and responsibility inherent in the redistricting had caused

Jackson to increase his staff. Some of the men chosen were trusted friends of long duration—Andrew Jackson Donelson, Robert Butler, John Overton and Richard Keith Call. Barlow had suggested the addition of Sam Houston, a suggestion which Jackson had heartily embraced. Almost all of these men lived on or near the Hermitage.

"How may I help you, Lieutenant?" asked Eaton.

"I am here on behalf of General Jackson. It is a personal rather than a military matter."

"Does the general need a lawyer? I thought he was one himself."

"He doesn't need a lawyer. He needs a writer."

"A writer?"

"A project was undertaken by Major John Reid to write a biography of the general entitled *The Life of Andrew Jackson*. The idea was enthusiastically endorsed by many of the general's friends. Unfortunately, Major Reid has died an untimely death, succumbing to pneumonia, and the manuscript has not been completed. While at first the general did not approve of the project, he now wishes to see it through, more than anything to honor the memory of the major, who was not only a trusted subordinate but also a close personal acquaintance."

"Of yours as well, I think," said Eaton astutely.

Barlow nodded. "Yes, he was my friend, too."

"So why come to me?"

"You have a reputation as a writer as well as a lawyer, Mr. Eaton."

"Well, I have written a few editorials for the newspaper, and a story or two. It's an intriguing proposal you've presented, Lieutenant. Considering the general's tremendous popularity throughout the nation, such a book would fare extremely well, I should think."

"If well-written, it would. And the general insists on someone outside his circle of friends and aides. Someone who will write an unbiased account of his life."

"An *unbiased* contemporary biography," mused Eaton. "Now that would be a nice change of pace."

Barlow smiled. "Then you'll do it?"

"Not so fast. I don't know, frankly." Eaton gestured wearily at the books and papers piled high on his desk. "As you can see, I am extremely busy with my practice."

"Then at least consider it."

Eaton nodded. "That I can promise to do. Though I must say, I have not kept abreast of the general's career to the extent that many others have."

"I can help you there," said Barlow. "In fact, why don't you come to dinner tonight? We can discuss the matter further. And I can tell you more of what General Jackson has been involved in lately."

"Are you married, Lieutenant?"

The unexpected nature of the question caught Barlow off guard. "Why, yes, I am married."

"Then I accept your invitation!" Eaton chuckled at the expression on Barlow's face. "I am a bachelor, you see, and a bachelor would be a fool to pass up a good home-cooked meal."

"Ah. Then I will expect you tonight. Say around six?" He gave Eaton directions to his house, and left with the lawyer's assurance that he would be right on time.

When dinner was done, Eaton was effusive in the praise he heaped on Sarah Barlow. He declared the meal to be the best he'd had since coming to Tenessee. And after he and Barlow had retired to the sitting room of the small but comfortable frame house which

the Barlows had called home for nearly two years, the
lawyer congratulated his host.

"You are a very lucky man, Lieutenant, to have
such a lovely wife."

Barlow couldn't have agreed more, and—as he had
done daily since becoming a married man—thanked
the Almighty that he had decided to keep his promise
to Sarah Langford. He had certainly never had cause
to regret doing so. Sarah was the perfect wife. She
was deeply in love with her husband, and it showed
in everything that she did. She was completely committed to his happiness. In public she was discreet and
proper. In private she was full of passion for him.
Everyone who had made her acquaintance was happy
to have done so. Rachel Jackson thought she was an
angel from heaven. Even Barlow's parents were enam-
ored with her. The trip to Philadelphia which Barlow
had undertaken with his new bride shortly after the
marriage ceremony—which had been held under the
trees at the Hermitage one fine summer day the summer before last—had gone far better than he had anticipated. His fears that his mother would find fault
with Sarah (as she would find fault with any woman
whom her son chose as a life's mate) had proven un-
founded. He had also been afraid that his father's
gruffness would put Sarah off. But Sarah had won
them both over completely. "You could not have done
better for yourself, son," his father had told him. And
Barlow was inclined to agree. He was especially
pleased to see how his younger brother and sisters
took to Sarah like fish to water. Barlow no longer
entertained any doubts about his love for his bride. If
anything, his feelings for her had grown stronger with
each passing day. Sarah made it easy to love her.

Only one cloud overshadowed their married bliss.
A year had passed since Sarah's miscarriage. The phy-

sician said she would bear no more children, news that had mortified her. Barlow had been able to accept that diagnosis with equanimity; Sarah had barely survived the miscarriage, and by that time he had reached the point where he did not think he could bear to lose her. The choice between keeping her and having offspring was not a difficult one for him to make. Sarah, though, had never fully recovered, at least emotionally. She could not shed the feeling that she had let her husband down. She had been slow to come out of a deep melancholy. Even now Barlow thought he saw the sorrow behind her eyes whenever she saw a small child. A most caring and giving person, she would have made a splendid mother, and Barlow's main regret in the whole tragic business was that she would never have that opportunity.

Barlow offered his guest a brandy and, when Eaton accepted, poured two glasses from a decanter atop a sideboard. The lawyer, examining the parlor's modest but comfortable furnishings, nodded his head. "Yes, a very lucky man. Your home is a good one, Barlow."

"It's not actually mine. It belongs to General Jackson. He has been kind enough to let us live here."

Accepting the brandy, Eaton took a sip before saying, "I've given your proposal a good deal of thought—and have decided to accept."

"Excellent. The general will be pleased." Barlow opened the sideboard and took out a thick leather portfolio, which he passed to Eaton. "Those are the chapters completed by John . . . I mean, Major Reid. I have read them. In fact, I believe I am one of the few privileged to have done so. They cover the general's early years, up to his arrival in Tennessee to pursue a career in the law."

"Will I be able to interview the general?"

"He has told me to assure you that he will be at

your disposal. I'm sure his many friends in these parts will also make themselves available to you, as well."

"And you? What do you think of the man?"

"He's a great American. A born leader of men."

"You are extremely loyal to him," surmised Eaton.

"He inspires such loyalty in all who get to know him."

"There is a saying that a man's greatness is best measured by the stature of his enemies. And from what I hear, Jackson has made some powerful enemies over the situation with the southern tribes."

"That's a complicated story."

"Made more so, I should think, by the contradictory nature of some of the general's statements on the subject."

"How do you mean?"

"Well, he calls them savages in one breath, and his friends and brothers in the next."

Barlow smiled. "I see you've been paying attention."

"It's a matter of the greatest import on the frontier. You're close to the general. You of all people must know how he really thinks."

"Sometimes I'm not so sure," admitted Barlow.

"Then tell me what Jackson thinks of the former Secretary of War, William Crawford? I understand they have fundamentally different views on how to handle the Indians. Crawford supporters insist he will be president someday. I hear the same from Jackson men. With the possible exception of the up-and-coming John Calhoun of South Carolina, Crawford is the best hope of the Southern states to maintain their grip on the executive mansion. At the same time, the general is the West's favorite son."

"The general has been openly critical of Crawford,

but not from any political consideration. It was Crawford who accepted the argument of the Cherokees that
four million acres of the land cession acquired from
the Creeks in the Treaty of Fort Jackson actually belonged to them."

"And, according to newspaper accounts, General
Jackson has fired off some angry letters to Washington, saying that Tennessee will never stand for returning all that land to 'savages.' Yet those savages
were his trusted allies in the fight against the Creeks,
were they not?"

"I feel as though I'm being cross-examined," said
Barlow.

Eaton laughed. "I apologize. I have a tendency to
ask questions until I get to the bottom of something.
And Andrew Jackson is, you must admit, a fascinating
subject. An enigma. A man of contradictions. He is
entirely predictable in some respects, yet prone to
doing the unexpected. Sometimes he acts rashly, and
at others he exercises the patience of Job. He is a man
who would appear to be extremely ambitious, and yet
he often refuses to wield his power and prestige for
self-aggrandizement. I confess, the more I considered
the offer to write his biography, the more intrigued I
became. I'll say this, though. I will not be satisfied
with doing anything less than a completely honest appraisal of the man. I have no interest in painting the
portrait of a saint. Saints are much less interesting
than sinners, don't you think?"

"Absolutely. And I'm sure General Jackson would
expect nothing less than an honest appraisal from your
pen. But as to Crawford, he backed down, you know.
He appointed three commissioners to examine the
Cherokee claim and to conclude treaties with them,
as well as the Choctaws and Chickasaws."

"And the general got them to agree to more land cessions. So just what *does* he think of Indians, Lieutenant?"

Barlow pondered that question a moment before answering.

"I know this much. He is convinced that Congress has the right to occupy any Indian lands deemed necessary for the defense of the republic. He wrote to President Monroe last year to express his opinion that Indians had no rights other than to hunt and fish. They were not a sovereign nation. They were more like subjects, so Congress also had the power to regulate all of their concerns. He believes they occupy far more land than they need, considering their numbers. And I know that, prior to the treaty talks last fall, the general told Colonel Coffee that Indians were by nature treacherous. If they said they would do something you could not always rely on them to carry through on the promise."

"So the Indians, in his view, are much like British tenants. They can use the land, but it's owned by the squire, and the squire makes all the decisions regarding the use of the land."

"Yes, I suppose it's something along those lines."

"You were present at those negotiations last year?"

"Yes. At the Chickasaw Council House, last September."

"Haven't the Chickasaws always been friendly towards us?"

"Yes, always. But that didn't matter as far as the general was concerned."

"In fact, I'm told George Washington himself presented the Chickasaws with a charter that guaranteed their title to the lands."

"Right again. That was back in 1794."

"But that doesn't matter to Jackson either, does it?"

"Not at all. The general persuaded the Cherokees to cede millions of acres south and west of a line running south of the Tennessee River to the Tombigbee, then east to the Coosa. This for an annuity of six thousand dollars for a period of ten years. He told them it was the price they had to pay for the continued good will of their beloved father, the president."

"Then he convinced the Chickasaws and the Chocktaws to make land cessions, as well."

"He did, though it required bribing most of the chiefs, a practice he finds distasteful. Nonetheless, in the end, he got exactly what he wanted."

"Clear title to the land necessary for a good military road stretching from Tennessee to the Gulf of Mexico," said Eaton. "Nearly five hundred miles of road. Construction was begun a couple of months ago, wasn't it? People say it's just part of Jackson's scheme to one day take Florida away from the Spaniards."

"Is that what they say?"

"With settlers pouring into the Indian cessions, the incidence of Seminole raids has increased substantially."

"That is apparently the case."

Eaton leaned forward. "So when will he do it, Barlow? When will General Jackson march on Spanish Florida?"

Barlow watched the brandy as he swirled the amber liquid around in his glass. "The situation has been further complicated now by the general's relations with the War Department."

"I think I do recall hearing something about that. Something to do with one of the general's aides being posted to New York without his knowledge."

"Well, that never actually happened. I never had to report to New York."

"So it was you!"

Barlow nodded ruefully. "To join a company detached from my regiment, the 39th Infantry. I was to replace an officer who died of tuberculosis. The general, however, insisted that I stay. And he issued an order of his own, one that forbade any of his officers from obeying War Department instructions unless he personally approved them."

"That must have gone over real well at the War Department."

Barlow nodded. "It got worse. The general was informed that Brigadier Winfield Scott had written a newspaper article describing his actions as mutinous. They traded insulting letters. General Scott insisted he had not written any such article, but he stressed that this didn't necessarily mean he was in disagreement with its sentiments. And General Jackson called him a pompous, hectoring bully—and went on to label all of those who worked in the War Department as pimps and spies."

Eaton thought it over. "I would have to say that Andrew Jackson is a dangerous man—if you cross him. How does he get along with the new Secretary of War, Mr. Calhoun?"

"Calhoun was not the man he wanted to see in that office. But so far there have been no problems. Secretary Calhoun announced that all orders emanating from the department would pass through commanding officers. Both he and President Monroe, I think, realize that no one other than General Jackson can command the unquestioning loyalty and obedience of western militia."

Eaton finished off his brandy and Barlow immediately rose to fetch the decanter from the sideboard and refill his guest's glass.

"Thank you," said Eaton. "Now, let's get back to Florida, shall we? It seems to be the chief topic of conversation west of the Blue Ridge these days. Everyone is speculating as to *when* Jackson will march against the Spanish dons. It's no longer a question of *whether* he will do it."

"It never has been, really."

"And when the time comes," said Eaton, "you will go off to war."

"That's right."

"How does Mrs. Barlow feel about that?"

"You can ask her yourself. Here she is now."

Both men got to their feet as Sarah entered the room. She insisted that they resume their seats, and went to stand behind her husband's chair. Her hands, with their long, delicate fingers, rested lightly on Barlow's broad shoulders.

"I will miss Timothy awfully," she told Eaton, with a smile. "But I knew when I married him that he was a soldier. It is all he has ever wanted to be. His father himself told me as much. He told me how Timothy, when he was a young boy, would find a stick and, pretending the stick was a rifle, would march vigorously back and forth in front of their house, like a sentry on guard duty. Sometimes he would march for hours on end."

"I also killed more imaginary redcoats than the Continental Army managed to kill real ones," added Barlow.

Eaton laughed. "All I know is," he said, looking again at the warm and well-appointed room, "that I would be extremely reluctant to give up all this, and the company of such a pretty and intelligent woman, one who obviously loved me with all the power of her being, for the dangers of the Florida swamps."

"I do not look forward to the day," confessed Barlow, placing a hand over one of Sarah's. "But it is my duty."

"Besides," said Sarah, "he missed the battle at New Orleans, and has made it abundantly clear to the general that he will not miss the next one. Though I must tell you, Mr. Eaton, I for one am glad he wasn't at New Orleans. Because then he would not have been in Washington that winter, and I would not have been afforded the opportunity to fall so madly in love with him as I did. Much to my mother's dismay, I might add."

"Oh? She didn't approve of your marrying a military man?"

"She didn't approve of me marrying *any* man!" said Sarah, with a soft laugh. "It was like a military mission just getting me away from her. Timothy had to write me under the cover of a letter to Henry Clay, who was a boarder at my mother's house. And Congressman Rhea provided me with a carriage and a driver to spirit me out of the city in the dead of night. Then two men took me across the mountains, where Timothy was waiting. He brought me the rest of the way here."

"Have you heard from your mother since?"

"Yes. I left her a letter, telling her that I loved her and always would, but that I had to be with Timothy, as he was the source of my greatest happiness. Some months later I received a letter from her in return. She wished me well, and expressed the hope that we would one day come to Washington and visit her."

Eaton shook his head. "I have for years harbored a deep skepticism regarding the institution of marriage. But now, seeing the two of you, I'm beginning to have second thoughts. The problem is finding a suitable wife. There are entirely too few women of your character, Mrs. Barlow, especially out here on the edge of civilization."

Sarah blushed. "Why, thank you, Mr. Eaton. You're too kind. I'm nothing special."

"I beg to differ," said Barlow.

"You will find the right woman," Sarah assured their guest. "And it will probably happen when you least expect it."

"Well then, it's promising that I don't expect to at all, I suppose!"

They all laughed. Not wishing to overstay his welcome, Eaton finished his brandy, rose, and made his excuses. Barlow showed him to the door.

"So when do I get to meet the general?" asked Eaton.

"I will relay to him the good news that you have accepted the proposal. He will be pleased, and will want to discuss it with you at your earliest convenience, I'm sure."

"We had better make it soon," said Eaton. "I have a hunch that he—and you—will be on your way to Florida to battle the Seminoles before very much longer."

Barlow nodded. They shook hands and bade each other good night. Closing the door on the winter night, Barlow shuddered as a sudden chill coursed through his body. He turned to find Sarah standing there, watching him, smiling at him, pretty as a picture in the soft lamplight.

"Was everything all right?" she asked.

"Everything was wonderful, as always. It was a perfect evening, thanks to you."

She came forward to take his hands in hers. "The evening isn't over yet, is it?"

He pulled her even closer. "No. Not by a long shot."

"I think Mr. Eaton is right. Quite soon you'll be

going away to war, possibly for a long time. I want another promise from you, Timothy. I hate to be so demanding, but I want you to promise that you will love me every night until that day comes. That way I will have fresh memories of your arms around me to keep me warm during your absence."

Barlow grinned. "Now *that's* a promise I'll make sure I keep!"

She laughed softly—a laugh he interrupted with a kiss.

Chapter Seventeen

Several days later, Barlow was on his way to the Hermitage when he met Sam Houston. The ensign was mounted on a hard-run horse, and the usual scowl he wore to mask his feelings had been betrayed by an enthusiasm too great to conceal. Seeing his friend coming down the road at a gallop, Barlow checked his horse. He pulled the collar of his longcoat up. It was a blustery winter's day, the sun veiled by a thin sheet of ruffled clouds, and a brisk wind blowing in from the northwest over the sun-draped ground. Houston stopped his steam-snorting horse alongside.

"The day we've been waiting for all these years has come at last, Timothy!" exclaimed Houston. "The general has issued the order. We leave the day after tomorrow. The militia is to organize immediately. We're going to Florida!"

Barlow was surprised by his own reaction to the news. Where was his own anticipation at the prospect of a campaign against the Seminoles? This was, after all, what he had been hoping would happen ever since he'd heard about the battle at New Orleans. Yet all he could think of at this moment was Sarah. He had left her, asleep in their warm bed, and the image was vivid in his mind's eye—her long, lustrous auburn hair fanned out in disarray across the pillow upon which she rested her head. He had awakened not an hour ago to find her nestled against him, an arm and a leg thrown in intimate abandon over him, and he had reluctantly slipped slowly out from under them, trying not to wake her. Florida seemed suddenly a very long way from that warm bed, that auburn hair, that soft skin.

"Really," he said, noncommittal. "That's good news. I should go home and tell Sarah."

"That will have to wait for later. The general wants to see his entire staff this morning. I was coming in to town to bring you out."

"What has happened to bring all this about?" asked Barlow.

"The Seminoles have committed a terrible atrocity. It seems they have a village called Fowltown that happens to be located north of the Florida border, in the territory ceded by the Creeks. The chief of Fowltown refused an order to vacate the town, so General Gaines attacked and drove them out. The Seminoles had a terrible revenge. They ambushed a flatboat on the Apalachicola River that was carrying some soldiers as well as women and children to Fort Scott. All but one woman, who was captured, were slain. The Indians murdered the children by taking them by their heels and smashing their heads open against the sides of the boat."

"Good God," breathed Barlow.

"There's more. An expedition led by one Gregor MacGregor has seized Amelia Island off the Florida coast and proclaimed the entire territory independent of Spanish rule."

"MacGregor? Who is he?"

"A Britisher, and a troublemaker, by all accounts. It isn't clear what his motives are. Rumor has it that he plans to use Amelia Island as a staging ground for an invasion of Cuba. But it's apparent to our government that he does not have our best interests at heart. The general has been ordered to deal with MacGregor's filibusters as well as the Seminoles. We are going to Fort Scott."

"What are the orders with respect to the Spaniards?"

Houston shook his head. "That I couldn't tell you. But President Monroe has to know that if he sends the general, the dons will be driven out of Florida. The general won't take half measures."

Barlow nodded, and urged his horse into motion up the road to the Hermitage.

They arrived to a scene of tumult. Various aides were going in and out of the blockhouse, some of them leaping aboard horses to ride away at a gallop. Barlow assumed they were carrying orders from Jackson to his militia commanders. He noticed that Rachel was sitting, all bundled up, on a split-log bench alongside the east wall of the blockhouse. She was smoking a pipe and watching the comings and goings. When Barlow looked in her direction, she motioned to him. He walked over. Houston went inside the blockhouse.

"Good morning, Mrs. Jackson. How are you?"

She smiled wanly. "I am well, thank you, Lieutenant. I trust you and Sarah are also well?"

"Yes, ma'am."

"It would seem that you and my husband are going off to war again," she said pensively. "You must tell Sarah that she is welcome to come and stay with me while our men are away. I would appreciate the company."

"I will tell her, thank you."

"You had better get inside. You know how Andy gets when he is kept waiting."

"Yes, ma'am." Barlow started to turn away.

"Come back safe," she said.

Entering the blockhouse, Barlow had a real sense of how difficult it had to be for wives like Rachel

Jackson—and his own Sarah—during the absence of their husbands gone off to war, and not knowing if they would see their men alive again. He was grateful for Rachel's offer, and resolved to persuade his wife to accept it; he did not care to think of Sarah being alone all those months, without even a child to occupy her thoughts and her time.

Andrew Jackson's long, lanky frame was bent over a table in the common room that took up the entire ground floor of the blockhouse, studying a map. He was flanked by Houston and John Overton. When Barlow entered, Jackson glanced up.

"Ah, there you are at last, Lieutenant. I am pleased to be able to tell you that we are bound for Florida. You will finally get that fight you've been hankering after."

"Yes, sir."

"We will march immediately to Fort Scott. You and Ensign Houston will oversee the acquisition of sufficient supplies for one thousand men for a fortnight. But I want no more than twenty wagons to accompany the column, so keep it to the barest essentials."

"Provisions for a fortnight only, sir?"

"That's right. We will live off the land when they are gone."

"Yes, sir. How do we pay for the supplies, General?"

"Give the merchants scrip. The government will settle all accounts. And if for any reason there are difficulties in that regard, I shall make good on the debts myself. Tell them that. And make sure they understand that I will take any hesitancy on their part as a personal affront."

"Very well, sir."

"I have a letter here for Governor Blount. See that

he gets it today. It requests authorization to acquire powder and shot from the state arsenal. You will also be in charge of that. We shall need plenty of it—a hundred rounds per man, I should think."

Barlow did some rough calculations in his mind. One hundred thousand rounds and the powder to go with it would take up a good deal of the space in twenty wagons. At best Jackson's army would have to endure half rations during the march to Fort Scott. That, coupled with the winter weather that would make the journey that much more difficult, promised an arduous beginning to the campaign. And after the supplies ran out? This time of year game would be hard to come by. Living off the land would prove easier said than done. But Jackson wanted to move quickly. And he was a man who could endure the most severe hardships—and expected every man who served under him to do the same.

"I want to be on the march day after tomorrow," continued Jackson, "so there is no time to waste. No dickering with the merchants. Pay them what they ask. On the other hand, brook no resistance. If it's something the army needs, and there is no other convenient source, take whatever measures are necessary. Confiscate it at the point of your saber, if it comes to that. We will set things right at a later date."

"I understand, sir." Barlow took the letter for Blount. "Is there anything else, General?"

"Yes," said Jackson brusquely. "Make sure all your affairs are in order, Lieutenant. This will not be another New Orleans. The Seminoles will not be so obliging as to come at us in nice neat rows across open ground. We will have to go into the swamps after them and root them out. I expect our casualties will be high. But regardless of the cost, we will not

fail. We will make the frontier safe once and for all.
The task will not be completed until the Seminoles
are crushed—and the dons are driven out of Florida."

"Yes, sir," said Barlow.

The trek Barlow had made with the 39th Infantry
during the winter of 1813–1814 in order to join Andrew Jackson and fight the Red Sticks at Horseshoe
Bend had been a long and difficult one. Many, including Barlow, had grown ill due to the privations in-
curred on that march. The memory of it was still
strong in Barlow's mind. But it was nothing compared
to the ordeal that was the march to Fort Scott.

They started down the military road, but as it had
only been started a couple of months earlier, it wasn't
long before the army of one thousand Tennessee volunteers had to resort to roads and trails that were bad
to begin with—and made infinitely worse by heavy
rains that pounded the column almost on a daily basis.
The heavily laden wagons were a constant headache;
it seemed that every hour at least one would become
bogged down in the mire. The situation would have
been even worse had Barlow not acquired oxen to
pull the wagons; these big, lumbering beasts managed
to keep the wagons rolling through all but the worst
conditions. Prying wagons out of the muck was a back-
breaking business. Barlow was usually in the middle
of it. The general had given him the responsibility of
taking charge of the supply train. The wagon drivers,
civilians all, proved more intractable than even the
oxen. They were not at all inclined to take orders
from a young lieutenant, especially a city boy from
Philadelphia. They greatly taxed Barlow's patience.
But he consoled himself with the knowledge that at
least this time he hadn't been sent off to Washington.
This time he would be in the thick of things. This time

he would surely see action. It was just a shame, he mused, that he had so little enthusiasm for the adventure. Usually, all he could think about was Sarah. He missed her terribly. He confided in no one about this, however. Not even his friend Houston. The ensign would just tell him that married life had made him soft. And Barlow wasn't sure that this wasn't in fact the case.

Three weeks into the march they had made less than two thousand miles; their destination lay that far again, and more, ahead of them. It seemed that even the hardy backwoodsmen of the Tennessee militia were being dragged down by the hardships of the winter march. A good many of them got sick. Jackson had to leave nearly two hundred men by the wayside, as they became too sick to travel.

He summoned Barlow and Houston to his tent one night to discuss a solution to the matter.

"We will need more men to defeat the Seminoles, gentlemen. The president has written to the governors of Georgia and Mississippi, requesting that they provide me with as many volunteers as can be called up on short notice. And General Gaines is south of here, somewhere along the border, with your old regiment and a few militia. But time is of the essence. I will not sit and wait for weeks on end at Fort Scott in hopes of receiving reinforcements. So I want the two of you to carry a message to the Cherokees. I have need of their warriors. They served me well against the Red Sticks. They may do so once more against the Seminoles."

Barlow stared at the general in disbelief, and before he could think better of it, the words escaped him. "You can't be serious, sir."

Jackson fastened a piercing gaze on him. "I assure you, Lieutenant, that I am in deadly earnest."

"But, General, at the Chickasaw Council House you forced the Cherokees, who had never warred against us—indeed, who had often fought alongside us against some common enemy—to cede a third of their land to the United States. With that act you turned a people we could once rely on as allies into possible adversaries."

"I am aware," said Jackson stiffly, "that I once told you to feel free in speaking your mind, Lieutenant. At the moment, however, I am in no mood to debate our policy toward the Indians. You have your orders. Now I expect you to carry them out."

"What do we buy their services with, sir?" asked Barlow.

"I don't care what you promise them, as long as it does not include the return of the lands they have surrendered to the United States."

When he and Houston left the general's tent, Barlow was shaking his head. "Well, Sam, looks like we may well miss the next battle, too."

"Why do you say that?"

"Because we can expect the Cherokees to kill us."

They traveled by horseback in the direction of the Cherokee village of Tahlequah, which Barlow estimated was two days travel to the southeast. They saw no one on the first day as they traversed verdant valleys, negotiated steep, pine-cloaked ridges, and skirted the occasional thicket or bog. That night they camped on a wooded southern slope above a gurgling stream. The early moon's light shimmered on the water, making it look like a ribbon of quicksilver. They built a crackling fire for warmth and to brew some coffee, in which they could soften the hard biscuits that constituted their supper.

"You haven't said much today," observed Houston.

"If it helps any, I don't fancy this assignment any more than you do. But we have our instructions, and we're bound as soldiers to carry them out, whether we like them or not."

"I have no intentions of doing anything less."

"The Cherokees would have to be fools to fight for General Jackson again."

"Well, they are not fools. But they *are* desperate. So desperate, in fact, that they might be compelled to cut a deal with devil."

"Thinking that by ending the Seminole threat they might be able to hold on to their land a while longer. If there is peace on the frontier, that might result in less immediate pressure on the government to remove all the Indians from this part of the country."

Barlow nodded. "Something like that. In other words, they may try to prolong the inevitable. But sooner or later all their land will be taken from them, and they'll be moved, every last man, woman and child, somewhere west of the Mississippi. Somewhere out of the way. I know for a fact that this is the ultimate solution General Jackson prefers. It's just a matter of time until we find some pretext or other to embark upon that course."

"Well," said Houston, "let's just hope the Cherokees are in the mood to at least listen to our proposal. Because if they aren't, we're dead men, as you've said. And we probably won't even see it coming."

Houston's words proved to be prophetic. They had been on the move but an hour the next morning, proceeding along a narrow trace, single file, through thick timber, with Barlow in the lead, when the Cherokees sprang their ambush. Barlow heard Houston's shout of alarm and turned in the saddle in time to see the ensign carried off his horse by the impact of a buckskin-clad brave who had dropped from the branches that overhung the trail. An instant later a war cry that froze the blood in Barlow's veins made him swing round to look the other way, a hand flying instinctively to the butt of the pistol in his belt. Two warriors were leaping out of the brush alongside the trail. Barlow's startled horse shied away—a movement not anticipated by the first warrior as he launched himself at the lieutenant. He missed his mark and went sprawling. The second Cherokee, however, did not. He hurled himself at Barlow, as agile as a panther, and tried to drag him from the saddle. Barlow drew the pistol and was on the verge at firing it point-blank at the warrior when he thought better of it— and instead used the pistol like a club, slamming the barrel against his assailant's skull while at the same time spurring his horse forward. Stunned by the blow, the Cherokee lost his grip and fell as Barlow's mount surged up the trail.

He was free—but Barlow didn't even consider escaping. He would not leave Houston behind. Instead, he turned the horse sharply, prepared to shoot if the ensign's life was in imminent danger. As he did so, a fourth Cherokee emerged from the timber. Barlow recognized this one. Years had passed, but Mondegah was little changed. He barked a curt order to the warrior who had borne Houston to the ground, and the warrior responded by rising and letting the ensign regain his feet. The two braves who had tried to waylay Barlow also stood, brushing themselves off and glancing sheepishly in Mondegah's direction. But Mondegah wasn't paying them any attention. He studied Barlow.

"I know you," he said, in English.

"We met on the road to Horseshoe Bend several years ago."

Mondegah nodded. "You rode with Sharp Knife."

"I still do."

"We have heard stories that Sharp Knife and his long hunters have returned. There is much debate around the council fire as to why. Some say he has come to take away the rest of our land."

Barlow shook his head. "No, that's not why. He has come to fight the Seminoles."

"Then why are you here?"

Barlow glanced at Houston. The ensign was fuming at having been caught off guard, and with angry sweeps of a hand was brushing mud and snow and wet leaves off his uniform.

"He wants the Cherokees to help him," said Houston curtly. "What do you think?"

Barlow watched Mondegah's face, trying to gauge the warrior's reaction. He could not, however, tell what the Indian was thinking.

"Why did you not fire your pistol?" Mondegah asked him.

"It occurred to me that had you wanted the two of us dead it could have been accomplished at once. And I have not come all this way to kill the Cherokees whom I once fought alongside."

"Yesterday's friends can become tomorrow's enemies."

"True. But not this time."

Mondegah spoke to his fellow braves. They went into the brush, retrieved their bows and rifles, while Mondegah made the call of the crow, which brought a fifth Cherokee out of the timber. This one led five ponies. Once mounted, the warriors proceeded up the trail. Mondegah was the last one to ride past Barlow.

"That remains to be seen," he said to Barlow, in passing.

Barlow turned to Houston. "Are you hurt?"

"Only my pride."

"At least we're still alive."

"You sound surprised."

"I am," confessed Barlow. "Wait here. I'll get your horse."

Barlow wasn't sure what to expect when they reached Tahlequah, but then he wasn't too surprised, either, when some of the Cherokees greeted the arrival of two white men—and soldiers, at that—with considerably less equanimity than Mondegah had displayed. They walked into the Cherokee town, leading their horses; to have entered on horseback would have been an affront. But afoot they were easy targets for some angry young bucks. They were spit at, and insults were hurled at them. Barlow ignored this, but he could not ignore the brave who rushed in with a knife in hand and made as though to cut him open. It was a feint, an attempt to make Barlow flinch—or perhaps to make him react violently, which might have provoked a brawl, one in which he and Houston would almost surely perish. But Barlow had the presence of mind to just keep walking, maintaining eye contact with the young warrior while betraying nothing by his expression. Mondegah shoved the brave aside with a stern rebuke. Then he glanced Barlow's way and nodded approval.

"My God, Timothy," breathed Houston, falling in step alongside Barlow. "How did you know that buck wasn't going to gut you with that knife?"

"I didn't know for certain," admitted Barlow. "But had he done so he would have shamed Mondegah—indeed, he would have shamed the entire town. I was betting he wouldn't go that far, no matter how much he might have wanted to."

"He's not the only one who wants to have our

hides. Did you see the hate in his eyes? The purest hate I've seen in a long while."

"Do you blame them for hating us?"

Mondegah escorted them to a lodge, where they waited for what seemed like an eternity until, finally, they were visited by several elderly Cherokees, none of whom Barlow recognized.

"Mondegah says Sharp Knife has sent you," said the oldest of the lot, in English. "Once the Cherokee called Sharp Knife true friend. We were proud to fight with him against our common enemy, the Creeks. But now our hearts they are broken because Sharp Knife took our land away. Why did he do this? We do not understand. We have always kept our peace with the Americans. Many of our young men are angry. But you will not be harmed while you are here with us. Tell us, why has Sharp Knife sent you?"

"There are Red Sticks in Florida," said Barlow. "They have joined with the Seminoles, and they still make war, attacking our farms and settlements, killing innocent women and children. General Jackson has come to defeat them once and for all. He asks that the Cherokees join him in this fight."

"Give us a reason why we should help Sharp Knife," said another of the elders, his tone one of bitterness. "Why should we help the man who has taken so much of our land. We trusted Sharp Knife and he has betrayed that trust."

Barlow nodded. "I agree with you. He did betray the Cherokees. Your people have been wronged by my people, and I am ashamed. But I cannot change what has happened, and neither can you. All we can do now is to try to shape the future to our best interests. If you fight, you should not do so for Sharp Knife, but rather for yourselves."

"If we fight for the Americans," said the first elder, "will the Americans then promise not to take away any more Cherokee land?"

Barlow shook his head. "I won't lie to you. I don't think you could elicit such a promise. And even if you did, I don't think that promise would be kept."

"It would be easy for you to lie to us to get what you have come for."

"I do not lie. I think, however, that if the Cherokees help bring peace to the frontier it would be in their best interests."

The first elder nodded. "We will talk between us of this matter, and come to a decision. Until then you will be our guests. No harm will come to you."

With that, he rose and, joined by the others, left the lodge.

"You put entirely too much sugar on that entreaty, my friend," said Houston wryly.

"I thought it was time we started being honest with these people," replied Barlow.

They were free to come and go as they pleased, and Barlow took full advantage of this to move about the town and try to learn what he could of the Cherokee way of life. He sensed some animosity, but the elders had made it clear that the two American soldiers were their guests, and should be afforded the respect that guests deserved. No one raised a hand against him.

Several days passed without further discussions with the elders. Barlow thought Houston would grow impatient, that the ensign would be eager to leave Tahlequah and rejoin the army. But Houston seemed to have forgotten that there was a war going on. The reason for this was a Cherokee maiden called Walks in the Sun, who had been assigned the task of bringing the two white men their food. Walks in the Sun spoke a little English—Barlow was surprised to find that a good many of the Cherokees had mastered at least the basics of his native language. Houston fell head over heels in love with her, and before long they were spending almost every waking hour together, talking for hours on end, taking long walks, or just sitting quietly together on moonlit evenings in front of the lodge, enjoying one another's company. Walks in the Sun was clearly as stricken with Houston as he was with her. For his part, Barlow was happy for his friend. Walks was a beautiful young woman—the prettiest he had seen in Tahlequah—and she had many fine attributes. She was kind and gentle and full of life. But Barlow's happiness was tainted with a foreboding as he wondered if Houston had fully considered the ramifications of falling in love with a Cherokee girl at this point in time. Despite the fact that Jackson was at present trying to recruit the Cherokees for his campaign against the Seminoles, that didn't change the fact that the outlook was bleak for Cherokee–American relations. What would Houston do if ever the two peoples went to war? But then, love was blind to such considerations, and Barlow didn't try to educate his friend on the risks involved. It would have been pointless.

Their sojourn in Tahlequah stretched into a week, then ten days. Barlow was aware of the fact that there was no one person in the town who could alone make a decision on Jackson's proposal. That wasn't how things worked in an Indian community, especially not in a matter that had the potential for determining the future of the entire tribe. The Tahlequah elders consulted not only among themselves, but also with their counterparts from several nearby towns. And though he figured that by this time Jackson was drawing near Fort Scott, and while he believed the general when he'd vowed not to tarry at the fort to await the arrival of reinforcements, Barlow found himself in no more hurry to rejoin the army than Sam Houston appeared to be.

All good things, however, eventually come to an end, and on the twelfth day the three elders returned to the lodge where Barlow and Houston were staying. This time Mondegah accompanied them.

"We have made up our minds," said the eldest. "We will ask our warriors to join you in your fight against the Seminoles."

"I will relay this welcome news to Sharp Knife," said Barlow. "He will be grateful for the help of the Cherokees in his efforts to bring peace to the frontier."

"You do not understand," said the old one. "Our warriors will not fight for Sharp Knife."

Barlow was puzzled. "You're right, I don't understand, sir. I thought you just said . . ."

"We have decided to fight for you," said Mondegah. "Not Sharp Knife. Even so, I do not think all of our warriors will choose to go."

"We ask only one thing in return," said the elder. "That you will speak on our behalf to the White Father."

"President Monroe," said Barlow. "I could do what you ask, yes. But I'm not sure any good would come of it. I'm just a lieutenant in the United States Army. I'm a person that others, particularly presidents, do not feel compelled to listen to."

"But you do not lie to us," said Mondegah. "You are an honest man. Surely that must count for something among your people."

"Well, I'd like to think so."

"You go to fight the Seminoles," said the elder.

"Our warriors will stand beside you, and when the fighting is over, you will speak for us."

Barlow reflected on all that he had seen during his stay in Tahlequah. The long hunters were prone to call the Cherokees—along with all the other tribes—a bunch of "savages." But Barlow knew better.

"I will do as you ask," he said. "But I make no promises as to the result."

The elder seemed eminently satisfied with that response, and nodded his approval. "It is just as well. We no longer put our trust in empty promises."

The next morning, Barlow and Houston emerged from the lodge to find Mondegah and what appeared at first glance to be about two hundred Cherokee warriors waiting for them. A great crowd of loved ones and well-wishers had gathered to see the warriors off. Houston said his farewells to a tearful Walks in the Sun. Then he and Barlow mounted up and led the Cherokee fighters out of Tahlequah.

"I'm coming back here," murmured Houston, turning in his saddle to look back, hoping to catch a last glimpse of the Cherokee maiden who had captured his heart. "As soon as this damned war is over, I'm coming back, and I will never leave her again."

Chapter Eighteen

Barlow and the Cherokees arrived at Fort Scott in three days, and discovered that Jackson had reached the stronghold only the day before. Fearing that the sudden appearance of so many Indians painted for war might elicit a violent reaction from the long hunters, Barlow bade the warriors make camp several miles away. Leaving Mondegah in charge—and leaving Houston behind, too, just in case the camp was discovered by scouts from the fort—Barlow rode in alone. He was taken at once to Jackson, who had set up his headquarters in a cramped room barely large enough to contain a narrow bed and a table. No sooner was Barlow across the threshold than the general was firing questions at him.

"How did you fare at Tahlequah, Lieutenant? Where is Ensign Houston? Where are the Cherokees?"

"I've brought two hundred warriors. Most from Tahlequah, some from surrounding towns."

"Outstanding. Good work! They will be placed under Colonel Coffee's command, as was the case at Horseshoe Bend. He knows how to handle them."

"I'm afraid that won't be possible, sir."

"What?" Jackson stared at him, perplexed. "What do you mean it won't be possible?"

"They won't be *handled* by Colonel Coffee, this time, or anyone else but me."

"What are you talking about, Barlow?"

"The Cherokees are here only because they've agreed to fight with me. They'll obey your orders, as long as they pass through me, sir."

"And just how did you manage that?"

"Actually, I had very little to do with it, sir. They just don't trust you anymore. But apparently they do trust me."

Jackson's eyes narrowed suspiciously. "Just what did you promise them? What did you use to buy their loyalty?"

"The truth, General. I promised them nothing. If I had, they would not have believed me and they wouldn't be here today. I did agree to plead their case to the president after this campaign is over."

Jackson stared at him for another moment, and at the risk of seeming defiant, Barlow met and held the general's gaze.

"I warned you long ago, Lieutenant, that one day you would have to make a choice where the Indians are concerned," said Jackson coldly. "It would appear as though you have made that choice. Regrettably, it was the wrong one for a soldier who entertains any hope of making a career out of the army."

"I care less about that than I do about seeing that tribes who have never intended us harm receive fair treatment at our hands."

"Fair treatment! They're damned lucky we've let them keep what they have."

"I don't see it that way, sir."

"You profess to be a student of history. You know that a stronger people or nation conquers the weaker. It is the natural order of things."

"Might makes right, in other words."

"Exactly. Just ask your Cherokee friends if you

don't believe me. Long ago they took much of the land they now call their own away from some other tribe."

"I'd like to think my country will behave differently."

"Then what about Florida? I suppose you would rather it remained in Spanish hands?"

"No, sir. The Spaniards have conspired against us. They will continue to make trouble for us until they are driven out. The same cannot be said for the Cherokees, sir, and you know it."

"I'll thank you not to presume to tell me what I know," snapped Jackson. Fuming, he moved around the confines of the small room, hands clasped tightly behind his back. Finally he came to a stop and slammed a fist on the table. "Very well, damn it. I don't like this. But you have me over a barrel, Lieutenant. I need those warriors. We will proceed on their terms. I regret that you intend to throw away a promising career on a hopeless cause. But I cannot be concerned with that now. I have matters of far greater import to address. Come." He gestured for Barlow to draw closer to the table, and then stabbed a finger at a map that was spread out on top of it.

"Here is the bay at the mouth of the Apalachicola River. I have just received word that two ships laden with supplies left New Orleans a fortnight ago. By now they must lay at anchor in this bay. We are in desperate need of the supplies they carry. Today we will kill most of the oxen for meat. The men will carry all the ammunition that they can, and we will leave the wagons here in order to make a forced march to the bay. Along the way we will strike at a place along the Apalachicola that some call Barracoon. You've heard of it?"

"Supposedly a town of runaway slaves."

"Correct. And those runaways have been as much trouble along the border as the Red Sticks and the Seminoles. They have been fighting alongside the hostiles, and sometimes they conduct raids of their own. They loot, burn, rape and murder. We will destroy Barracoon. Those of its inhabitants who surrender will be taken to Mobile in chains and returned to slavery. Those who resist will be cut down without mercy."

"Yes, sir."

"You and the Cherokees will leave an hour before dawn, make for the Apalachicola by the most direct route, and then proceed downriver. I will follow with the militia, and will be no more than half a day behind you. I have sent word to General Gaines to rendezvous with us at the bay. From there we will attack St. Marks, which is located here, and then a Seminole town on the Suwanee River where, I am told, many of the braves who have attacked our frontier have congregated."

"Very well, sir."

"If you encounter the enemy, send runners to inform me and hold your ground until I arrive with the army."

"Understood, General."

"And if I encounter the enemy first, I shall send word to you. I trust," added Jackson dryly, "that your Cherokees will see fit to come to my rescue, if that turns out to be the case."

"You've always been able to count on them, sir. That has never been the problem."

"You are dismissed, Lieutenant."

When Barlow arrived back at the Cherokee encampment, Houston asked him how things had gone with Jackson.

"Fine," said Barlow ruefully. "Though I expect I'll have to find another place to live when I get back to Nashville."

*   *   *

Five days later, Barlow was surveying the exterior of the stronghold called Barracoon through Ensign Houston's field glasses. Houston and Mondegah were with him, along with two other Cherokee braves. The rest of the Cherokees were hidden in the thick timber a half mile to the north. Barracoon was a collection of huts and shanties surrounded by a palisade. On its west side was the Apalachicola River. On the other three sides the forest had been cleared to a distance of about one hundred yards. This open "killing ground" was studded with tree stumps.

It was minutes until sunrise, and in the gray and uncertain morning light, Barlow could see a few men—sentries—on the walls. Behind the palisade, smoke rose from cook fires. He spotted only one gate, in the north wall, but he thought it likely there would be another, most likely on the west side, closest to the river—the side he could not see from his vantage point. It was his understanding that the Spaniards had built this outpost more than sixty years ago. It had stood abandoned for a long time, until a band of runaway slaves had moved in. Since then it had become a community almost exclusively populated by runaways.

"The walls are in some disrepair," he muttered to Houston. "There are several lookouts."

"By now everyone in Florida must know we're coming," remarked Houston. "I wonder how many people there are inside?"

Barlow shook his head. No one knew for sure how many people called Barracoon home. But it was important to find out, and the sooner the better. General Jackson would arrive by this afternoon, and Barlow felt sure he would launch an immediate assault. He would not spend the time necessary to conduct a siege that would eventually starve the runaways into surrender. He had to take St. Marks and get to the supply ships as soon as possible.

"Look," said Houston, "maybe we could send a few men in there. Indians probably come and go all the time. We know some of the men in that fort have joined the Seminoles in raids. Even if they've heard that General Jackson is on the way, they might not be aware that we've come with the Cherokees."

"I don't think so," said Barlow. Although they had seen no one during the past five days, he wasn't convinced that no one had seen them. And if the runaways knew that the men Houston wanted to send into Barracoon were with Jackson's army, they would probably be killed on the spot. It was a risk Barlow wasn't willing to take. "I have a better idea. We'll sit tight and wait until someone comes out. With any luck we'll be able to capture him without alerting the fort."

And so they waited. About an hour later the gates opened and two men emerged. They were armed with rifles. Barlow surmised that they were hunters. He watched them cross the open ground; they walked at a carefree, unhurried pace, and were engaged in animated conversation.

"We'll take those two," Barlow told Houston. Turning to Mondegah, he said, "I want at least one of them taken alive. And they must not be given a chance to fire their rifles, or the entire town will be alerted."

Mondegah nodded and, with a gesture at the other two warriors, headed deeper into the woods. Barlow lingered long enough to survey Barracoon once more with the field glasses before returning them to their owner. "Everything seems quiet. Let's go," he said curtly, and set out in the footsteps of the Cherokees, followed by Houston.

He left the ambuscade up to the warriors, being quite willing to concede that they were both more talented and more experienced than he in the art of pulling one off. While he and Houston hung back, Mondegah and his brothers melted into the brush, along a deer trail that the two runaways were taking as they entered the forest. Barlow was confident that once they were twenty yards deep into the trees they would be lost from the sight of anyone at the fort. A hundred yards deeper into the timber, they walked into the trap. The Cherokees appeared out of thin air—or so it seemed to the two hunters, who were caught completely unawares. They did not have time to cry out in alarm, much less bring their rifles to bear. One died on his feet, a Cherokee tomahawk cleaving his ribcage and exploding his heart in a great shower of dark blood. The other was borne to the ground by one warrior, while Mondegah ripped an old flintlock rifle from his grasp. The black man started to struggle, opening his mouth—perhaps to shout for help, or maybe to beg for mercy. But the pressure of a knife blade against his Adam's apple kept him silent, and he lay still as Barlow and Houston moved in.

"By God," breathed Barlow, looking down at the man. "I know you. Captain Hatcher's slave. You vanished at Horseshoe Bend."

Joshua stared, wide-eyed, at Barlow, and said nothing.

"What's your name?" asked Barlow. "I'm afraid it escapes me at the moment. Come on, man, speak up!"

"My name is Joshua, suh. Thank the Lord you done found me!"

"Really," said Barlow, his tone pregnant with skepticism. "You wanted to be found?"

"Yessuh, I sure did. I was in the camp jis' like I was s'pose to be, when I seen this mule go by. A regimental mule what it was, Lieutenant. So's I went after it. And that's when them red heathens jumped me. Come out of nowhere. Just-just like these ones."

Barlow glanced at Houston. "Do you think he is telling the truth?"

"You must be joking. He ran away. If ever there *was* a mule, it was one he probably stole."

Barlow nodded. "I'm inclined to agree. Not that it matters at this point." He sat on his haunches beside Joshua, who remained pinned to the ground by the Cherokee warrior who straddled his chest and held a knife to his throat. "See your friend over there?" asked Barlow, with a nod in the direction of the dead man.

Very slowly, very carefully, Joshua turned his head. "Yessuh, I sees him."

"That he's dead and you're alive is the result of an arbitrary decision by these Indians," said Barlow coldly. "That could just as easily have been you. And if you don't tell me what I want to know, you'll end up in the same condition. Do you understand me?"

"I understand. Yessuh, I sure do understand."

"How many people are behind those walls?"

"Around a hunnerd and fifty, I'd say. Men, women and children."

"How many armed men?"

" 'Bout fifty or sixty, I reckon."

"Is there another way in besides the main gate?"

"There's a small gate on the other side. It's used by them that go to fetch water from the river."

"Is that side guarded?"

"No, suh, not usually. River runs deep and strong along here. Too deep and strong, they say, for anyone to swim across."

"Is the gate kept locked?"

"Most of the time it is, yessuh."

"What are you thinking?" Houston asked Barlow.

Barlow stood up. "We can take this place," he said. "And if we don't, a lot of men will lose their lives once the general gets here and orders an attack."

"How do we take it?"

"You and I and a few others will float down the river until we're abreast of the fort. Then we go ashore, get through the gate, and, once inside, fight our way to the main gate. If we can get it open, Mondegah brings the others through."

Houston thought it over—and nodded. "That might work. I'm for it. When do we go?"

"There's no time like the present."

"Good idea." Houston flashed a rare smile. "The more time I have to think about your plan the less I may like it. And what about him?" The ensign nodded at Joshua.

"We can spare a man to keep an eye on him." Barlow turned to Mondegah. "But if he makes trouble, or tries to escape, he's to be killed."

"I won't be makin' no trouble for you, nosuh," said Joshua fervently.

Barlow just turned away.

When Barlow emerged from the river, he crouched among the thick reeds that grew along the bank and scanned the wall that loomed above him. He saw the gate Joshua had mentioned, at the top of a trail that ended at the water's edge nearby. He saw no lookout on the wall or guard at the gate. Apparently, Joshua had been telling the truth. From within Barracoon came the typical sounds of a community—a dog barking, the clang of a blacksmith's hammer on iron, the laughter of a woman. Nothing, though, to indicate that the inhabitants of the fort had any idea that an enemy lurked just outside the walls. That, mused Barlow, was about to change in a very dramatic fashion.

Behind him, Sam Houston and three Cherokee warriors emerged from the Apalachicola. Though the water was quite cold, the Indians had stripped down to loinclothes, while Barlow and Houston wore only trousers and boots—this, to facilitate swimming. Each of the Cherokees carried a knife, a bow and a quiver of arrows, while Barlow and Houston had brought along only their sabers.

Once his companions were kneeling, like him, in the reeds, Barlow nodded to them and made his move, hurrying up the trail to the gate while the others watched from their hiding places. The gate was hardly larger than an ordinary door. By peering through its stout timbers, Barlow could see that a heavy wooden bar secured it from the inside. Inserting the blade of his saver between two of the timbers, he managed to lift the bar out of a bracket, which in turn allowed him to open the gate enough so that he could reach an arm inside and push the bar out of the bracket on the other side. Peering into the compound, he saw that the gate was obscured from the view of anyone in the fort by a broken-down wagon—a stroke of great good fortune. He motioned for Houston and the Cherokees to join him, and when they had done so, he opened the gate farther and led the way inside.

Crouched behind the wagon, Barlow turned to his companions. "Remember," he said, "to take out the sentries on the walls as quickly as you can."

The warriors nodded. Mondegah had selected men who both spoke and comprehended English very well.

Barlow turned to Houston. "Are you ready?"

"As ready as I'll ever be."

Barlow took a deep breath, trying to slow his racing
heart. Then he left the cover of the wagon and headed
across the compound at a dead run, aiming for the
gate in the eastern wall. The old Spanish fort's parade
ground was cluttered with huts and shanties made pri-
marily of wood, mud bricks and thatch. There were
men, women, children, dogs, pigs and chicken every-
where, all going about the business of their daily
lives—until one of the sentries, having seen the two
half-naked white men and recovering from his surprise, shouted the alarm. Then all heads turned.
Women screamed and scrambled to grab up their children. Some of the men grabbed their weapons. Two
of the lookouts brought their rifles to bear on the
intruders, but arrows fired straight and true by the
Cherokee warriors stationed at the broken wagon
killed them before they could fire, as well as a third
man on the wall. Others, though, did get off shots;
Barlow heard the reports, and saw dust kicked up by
a bullet a few feet in front of him. This just encouraged him to run faster. Before he could reach the
main gates, though, two men, one armed with a pistol
and the other with an ax, confronted him. The one
with the ax reared back and let go with a mighty swing
that would have decapitated Barlow, but for the fact
that he managed to duck underneath it. In the next
instant, he was driving his saber into the man's midsection, just as the second man triggered the pistol. The
pistol misfired and Barlow, withdrawing the saber
from the first man, kept running—straight into the second, who stood frozen in place, stunned by his monu-
mental bad luck. The impact sent the second man
sprawling, and before he could get back up, Houston,
who was following on Barlow's heels, ran him through
with his saber. As Houston raced by, the runaway
dropped to his knees, clutching at his belly, blood

leaking through his fingers. His companion lay on his side, writhing in his death throes.

Up ahead, three more men, two of them armed with rifles, were running toward the main gate; obviously, they had figured out what Barlow's intentions were, and were bent on stopping him. Barlow doubted he could count on another misfire—that would surpass good fortune and border on the miraculous. Yet he had no choice but to continue running for the gate, and a confrontation with better-armed adversaries. If he faltered now, it would mean certain death for himself and Houston. Then, as he drew within twenty paces of the gate and the three men—one of whom stopped to bring rifle to shoulder—the Cherokee warriors on the other side of the compound loosed more arrows. Two of the men—the ones with rifles—fell dying. The third, not at all interested in trying to defend the gate by himself, sought cover behind the nearest hut.

Reaching the gate, Barlow and Houston lifted the bar that secured it and swung open the portals.

They were greeted by the most welcome sight of Mondegah and nearly two hundred Cherokees racing across the open ground toward them. When they saw the gate opening, some of the warriors let loose exultant war cries. No guns spoke from the walls. All the lookouts had been killed.

A bullet slammed into the gate's timber, so close that a splinter of wood gashed Barlow's cheek, reminding him that there remained the task of keeping the gate open until Mondegah could reach it. Turning, he spotted a rifle on the ground—it had belonged to one of the men just slain by a Cherokee arrow. He picked up the weapon and threw a quick look around the fort, searching for a target. Pandemonium reigned. People and livestock were running in all directions.

But some of the runaways were recovering from their initial surprise. Rifles and pistols spoke from left and right, and the air fairly buzzed with bullets. Barlow was about to fire when, out of the corner of an eye, he saw Houston spin and then slump against the gate. As he turned instinctively toward his friend, Barlow was hit, too. The bullet struck him in the calf, knocking that leg out from under him. He fell, got up and lurched to Houston's side. Leaning heavily against the gate with the ensign, he asked, "Hurt bad?"

"Not yet," said Houston, through teeth clenched against the pain. "Here they come."

Sensing that they might have one last chance to close the gate and save themselves, a half dozen runaways were charging forward. The two wounded officers gripped their sabers and grimly prepared to meet this onslaught.

Only Mondegah and the Cherokees reached them first. Pouring through the open gate, they killed the six runaways on the spot and then proceeded to swarm through the compound like angry ants.

Mondegah paused to check on Barlow and Houston. "You will both live," he said. "Stay here. You have done enough. We will do the rest."

He barked an order in Cherokee, and four warriors formed a protective circle around Barlow and the ensign.

"I don't know about you," said Houston, "but if I keep getting shot to pieces in every little skirmish, I'm going to reconsider making the army a career."

That struck Barlow as funny, and he laughed. There was a hysterical edge to the sound, and he couldn't stop laughing. He thought it had to be due to the adrenaline coursing through his body, the adrenaline that was making his hands—so steady in battle—begin to tremble now that the fight, or at least his part of it, was over. The members of their Cherokee bodyguard looked at him, perplexed; this hardly seemed an appropriate time for joviality, with destruction all around them. The talked among themselves, and reached a quick consensus. Barlow had to be a very brave man to laugh in the face of death.

Once the Cherokees were inside Barracoon the fight was over in less than a quarter of an hour. A handful of diehard runaways holed up in a thick-walled storehouse, intent on making a last stand. At Mondegah's command, his Cherokees smoked them out by setting fire to the timbered roof; then they killed the ex-slaves as they came stumbling out. Mondegah reported to Barlow that about forty of Barracoon's men had been slain. A Creek woman, the wife of one of the runaways, had also died—she had chosen to fight to the death, and Mondegah speculated that she had found this fate preferable to becoming a slave to the Cherokees.

Barlow told Mondegah that all the blacks would be handed over to Sharp Knife. Jackson's intent was to return them to slavery. As for the handful of Indian women and children in Barracoon, they were to be set free. "We cannot bring them with us," he explained. "We have more fighting ahead." Mondegah said he understood. It was customary for the women and children of the enemy to be taken into slavery, but Barlow's wishes would be adhered to without question. As for the Cherokees, four warriors had lost their lives. A dozen more had been wounded. The latter would return to Tahlequah and carry the dead back with them. Barlow consented to this.

Mondegah turned next to the wounds suffered by Barlow and Houston. The ensign had been struck in the side, but the bullet had passed cleanly through the fleshy area above the hip, and though there was much bleeding, no serious internal damage had been done. Barlow's wound was potentially more dangerous, as the ball was lodged deep within his leg. Perhaps, said Mondegah, he should be taken back to Fort Scott.

"No," said Barlow curtly. "The bullet must come out now. I will not miss the rest of this campaign. And if I wait until I get back to the fort to have the bullet removed, the wound will poison, and they'll probably want to take my leg. Besides, if I go back to Fort Scott, what will the Cherokees do?"

Mondegah shrugged. "We have come to fight with you. If you will do no more fighting, then we will go home."

"And General Jackson would make you and your people pay dearly for what he would view as desertion," said Barlow. He shook his head. "The bullet must be removed now, Mondegah."

"I will do it," said the Cherokee.

Two warriors carried Barlow near a fire that was blazing in front of one of the Barracoon huts, built before the attack for cooking breakfast. Now Mondegah put it to another use. He heated the blades of two knives in the flames while another warrior cut open Barlow's trouser leg and cleansed the area around the wound with cold water. Mondegah gave Barlow a strip of rawhide—it looked to Barlow to have been cut from an old harness—to bite down on. Then the Cherokee cut deep into the wound, a three-inch lateral cut across the bullet hole, before using the tip of one of the heated blades to probe for the ball. The pain was worse than any Barlow had ever endured. He tried to keep his mind focused on an image of Sarah as a distraction, and managed to keep from passing out as Mondegah located the ball and deftly dug it out. He let the wound bleed clean for a moment before slap-

ping the other heated blade against it to staunch the
bleeding. The stench of his own flesh burning assailed
Barlow. Mondegah concluded by binding the wound
and removing the strip of rawhide from Barlow's
mouth. Barlow rubbed his jaws—they ached terribly
from clamping down hard on the rawhide. Now that
the ordeal was over, he wanted nothing more than to
sleep. The urge to do so was almost too great to resist.
Yet he did resist it. They had captured Barracoon, but
they were still deep in enemy country. There were
many things to do. The fort was his to hold until General Jackson arrived. This was not the time for sleep.

Jackson arrived several hours later, informed by a
Cherokee runner that Barracoon had fallen. When he
rode through the gates on a tall white horse, one of
the women who had been taken prisoner began to
wail. Instantly, others joined her. Barlow had ordered
all the prisoners placed in a corner of the compound,
posting guards on the walls above them as well as
around them on the ground. Annoyed by the terrible
sound issuing from the throats of the women, Jackson
cast a scowl in that direction as he stopped his horse
in front of Barlow and Houston.

"Why are they making such a racket?" asked Jackson.

"They know who you are, I suspect, sir," said Barlow.
"They probably expect you to have them hanged."

"I should do just that. We can't tolerate slaves turning against their masters. But those people are worth
a lot of money. I don't know that many of the gentlemen who own them would appreciate it if I hanged
the lot. I could, however, hang the leader. That might
discourage any of the others from causing problems."

"I don't think there was a leader, sir," said Houston.
"This was just a rabble."

Jackson looked the two young officers over. Their

uniforms were dirty and bloodstained. Wounded though he was, the ensign had to lend support to Barlow just so the latter could stand erect.

"I see you gentlemen had a hard fight on your hands. Why didn't you wait for my arrival before launching an attack?"

"It wasn't necessary to wait, General," said Barlow. "We devised a plan to take the fort, put it into action, and were successful. This way, you won't waste valuable time here and can proceed immediately to St. Marks."

Jackson peered at Barlow for a moment. "I see. Did any of these vermin escape?"

"I'm afraid one did, sir. We captured him before we took this place, but he killed the guard we placed over him and disappeared. His name is Joshua. He was the property of Captain Hatcher of the 39th, who lost his life at Horseshoe Bend."

"No matter," said Jackson. "I take it neither one of you wish to return to Fort Scott, despite your wounds."

"No, sir," said Barlow and Houston in unison.

"And I suppose these Cherokees would just head for home if I declared you unfit for duty, Lieutenant."

"I believe they would, sir."

"We will camp here for the night. In the morning, you shall proceed southward along the Apalachicola with your command, Mr. Barlow. I will take custody of the prisoners and have them sent under guard to Mobile. Then I shall put this place to the torch before following you."

"Yes, sir."

Jackson started to turn his horse to leave the fort, then thought of something and looked back.

"Oh—and well done, Lieutenant."

"Thank you, sir," said Barlow.

Chapter Nineteen

When returned from a day of hunting, a deer draped over his shoulder, Rook saw Amara step out of the house as he approached, giving him the impression that she had been watching for him. Korak stood beside her, and she was holding him close. There was nothing unusual in all of this—and yet Rook felt uneasy. And as he drew closer, he could see in a glance that something was wrong. The expression on his wife's face made that clear.

Dropping his kill on the ground, Rook was about to ask her what was wrong when he lost his nerve and decided against it. He had a feeling that he should delay, if only for a few seconds, hearing what she had to say.

"I was lucky today," he said, looking down at the deer. "Game has become more scarce."

"Tookla is gone."

"Gone? Where? To Tallahassee?"

Amara sadly shook her head. "To join Menawa and the others who fight the long hunters."

Rook nodded. Of course, he had known in his heart that it had to be about Tookla and the war. He had just refused to acknowledge that possibility.

"When did he go?"

"This morning, right after you left."

"Then I must catch up with him and bring him back."

Amara reached out to touch his arm as he started

to turn away. "You can't do that to him, my husband," she whispered, wincing as though the words themselves caused her physical anguish.

"I told him he could not go. He has disobeyed me."

"He is older than you were when you first went off to fight. You said so yourself."

"This is different."

"Not really. You had to prove yourself to the tribe. They had not accepted you because you had lived among the whites. You thought if you fought alongside them that would change."

"It didn't change. They never accepted me." Rook was surprised by how bitter he sounded. He had not intended to sound that way. He had always tried to pretend that what had happened to him as a child no longer mattered.

"But because you became a great warrior they tolerated you, at least."

"Tookla has nothing to prove."

"You know that's not so, Rook," she said, a gentle rebuke.

"Kinachi's daughter," he muttered.

"Her father has gone to war, and her older brother, too. Tookla is ashamed that he is still here."

"Has she asked him to go?"

"Of course not. She doesn't want him to, I'm sure. No, Rook, this is what Tookla feels he must do to be worthy of her love."

Rook shook his head, resisting the logic of what Amara was saying—resisting, too, the inevitable consequences of the truth.

"You don't want me to bring your son back to you?"

"He would resent us both," she said. "Perhaps forever. Don't you think I tried to talk him out of going? Believe me, I tried! But he had to go."

Rook gazed at her for a moment. "You know what that means, don't you?"

Amara nodded.

"If I cannot bring him back," said Rook, "then I must stay with him until the danger has passed."

She pulled Korak even closer. "Yes, I know."

Rook sighed. "I thought all along that there was no escape from war. You and Korak must go to Tallahassee. You can stay at Kinachi's home until I return."

"You don't need to worry about us. We will be safe."

"No one is safe as long as men like Menawa and Sharp Knife live. You must tell me that you will go, today, to Tallahassee."

Amara nodded. Then she stepped closer and put her arms around him and laid her head on his chest so that she could hear the beating of his strong heart. She did not want to let go of him, but after a moment she forced herself to do so, realizing that if she clung to him much longer she might not have the courage to say good-bye.

Rook tousled Korak's hair. "Take care of each other," he said, and turned quickly away. His heart was heavy. Many times circumstances had forced him to leave his family. But never before had he walked away knowing that the chances of his returning were virtually nonexistent.

Amara felt no great urgency in going to Tallahassee. While she knew Kinachi's wife would welcome her and her son with open arms, she was reluctant to leave her home. But she had told her husband that she would do so, and she always kept her word.

There were things to do first, however. The deer her husband had killed could not be allowed to go to waste, especially since, as Rook had said, game was

becoming increasingly scarce in the vicinity of Tallahassee. The only recourse was to butcher it out, which
she commenced to do. She skinned the deer and bundled the choice cuts of meat in the hide. Then she and
Korak dragged the remains away from the house, as
it would soon attract scavengers. Korak pointed out
that she was covered with the deer's blood, and
Amara decided to go down to the nearby creek and
wash herself, bidding her son to remain in the house
until she returned.

At the creek she shed her doeskin dress and moccasins and waded into the cold water, sitting on her heels
in the shallows and rinsing the blood from her arms
and face. She lingered there, enjoying the solitude and
dreading her stay in the Seminole town. At least she
would not show up at the door of Kinachi's wife
empty-handed; she would take along the venison, and
for a few days at least they would all eat well. But how
long would she have to stay in Tallahassee? Weeks?
Months? Being married to Rook, she had grown accustomed to living apart from others. At first she
hadn't cared for it; now she preferred to live that way.

Only when she stood to leave the creek did she see
the man standing on the bank. Amara gasped—she
had not heard anyone, and wondered how long the
man had been standing there, watching her. He was
partly obscured by brush.

"Who are you?" she asked, alarmed, but trying not
to sound like she was.

He stepped out into the open, and it was only then
that she recognized him.

"Joshua!"

"Didn't mean to scare you, Amara." He grinned.
"Your man around somewhere?"

"He . . . he will be back soon," she said, suddenly
compelled to lie. She wasn't sure why—perhaps it was

because of the way Joshua's gaze roamed over her glistening body.

"Good," said Joshua. "Y'see, I come to warn you folks. Andy Jackson's Cherokees attacked Barracoon a few days back. I think they killed just about everybody there, 'cept me. Women and children right along with the men. They showed no mercy. I was lucky to get away with my life. And I heard they was comin' here next."

"Here, to Tallahassee? Are you sure?"

"Oh, yessum, I'm sure. You all can't stay here. It ain't safe no more."

Amara moved to the spot on the bank where she had left her clothes. Joshua got there first. She noticed he was armed with a rifle, and had a bow and quiver of arrows slung across his back. He picked up the doeskin dress. She held out a hand—and for a moment it seemed that Joshua wasn't going to give the garment to her. Then, with reluctance, he surrendered it. Amara quickly covered herself. But she did not leave the shallows. Rook had never fully trusted this man, she recalled, and while Joshua had never done anything to warrant her mistrust, her instincts were warning her not to venture too close.

"Rook isn't here," she said. "He has gone after Tookla, who went to fight the long hunters. I will not leave Tallahassee until they return. But thank you for coming to warn us, all the same."

"Well," drawled Joshua, "seein' as how you decided to tell me the truth about Rook, I reckon the least I can do is tell you the truth, too. See, I didn't really come here to warn you. I come here for you, Amara."

"For me? What do you mean?"

"I've been wantin' you ever since I laid eyes on you, woman. All the time I been away, all I think about is you. Now, thanks to Andy Jackson, I gots to get out of Florida. And I decided you was comin' with me."

Amara stared at him for a moment—then turned and ran.

Bounding across the creek in two long strides, Joshua pursued her. She was quick and agile. She ran like a deer, and she would have left him far behind except for the fact that, as she threw a glance over her shoulder, she tripped over an exposed root and fell. She scrambled to her feet—and cried out in pain. She had twisted her ankle. Still, she didn't give up, but continued to run. Crippled as she was, however, she was slowed enough to allow Joshua to catch up. With one final lunge he tackled her. She rolled over and began to fight. Fending off her blows, Joshua laughed. But he stopped laughing when a fist connected with his jaw. Angered, he struck back, a blow that stunned her.

"Reckon I'll just make you mine right here and now, woman," said Joshua.

"I will *never* be yours!" she screamed.

He hit her again, and the fight went out of her. Too dazed to resist, she was vaguely aware of Joshua rolling her over on her belly, tearing at her dress, and then straddling her. She moaned as he took her, took her roughly, pinning her to the ground with his hands on her shoulders, and grunting like an animal as he had his way with her. Amara drifted in and out of consciousness. Belatedly, she became aware that he was no longer on top of her, no longer violating her. She tried to crawl away, but he kicked her viciously in the side, knocking the wind out of her.

"Now, that'll teach you," he said. "You try to run away from me again and you'll get worse. You hear me?"

She said nothing, and didn't move. Joshua picked

her up and slung her over a shoulder and set off into the forest. All Amara could think about was Korak, and a tear escaped her eye—before she slipped into unconsciousness and stayed there.

Three days after leaving Tallahassee, Rook found his son.

Tookla had made good time—and Rook surmised that he had done so in the knowledge that his father would be coming after him. In his haste, though, Tookla left a trail that Rook found easy to follow. On the second day, Tookla—and Rook, ten hours behind him—crossed the tracks made by a large group of Indians. Rook could tell that these were not the Cherokees who fought with Sharp Knife by the distinctive mark left by the stitching on Seminole moccasins. Whether Tookla had noticed this or not Rook could not say, but his son followed the sign southward.

On the third night, Rook spotted the flicker of cook fires in the woods ahead. He knew from past experience of being on the warpath with Menawa that the Great Warrior never failed to post lookouts all around his encampment. To locate and elude the lookouts in the dark would be virtually impossible. Rook's only recourse was to walk openly into the camp like a friend rather than lurk in the shadows like an enemy. And hope for the best.

This he proceeded to do. And he had not gone far before a Red Stick warrior dropped to the ground from the trees and blocked his path. An instant later, two more Indians, both of them Seminoles, flanked him.

"I know you," said the Red Stick. "I saw you at Cholocco Litabixee."

"I was there. I am Rook, of the Oakchay."

"What are you doing here?"

"I am looking for my son Tookla."

The Red Stick extended a hand. "Give me your rifle."

Rook complied.

"I will take him to Menawa," the Red Stick told his companions, and then ordered Rook to follow him.

Walking through the camp, Rook searched each knot of men gathered around every fire he passed, in hopes of spotting Tookla. Near the center of the camp Menawa sat at a fire with his Red Stick and Seminole subordinates. Among these was Toquay, who was the first to notice the approach of Rook and the lookout. Toquay leaped to his feet and came forward.

"Your son is safe," he said.

Rook nodded. "Thank you."

"What are you doing here? Have you come to take him home?"

"Toquay?" This was Menawa, calling from the circle of men around the fire. "Who is it?"

Toquay stepped aside so that Menawa could see that it was Rook. The Great Warrior got quickly to his feet.

"Why is he here?"

"His son came to join us. Rook has come to . . ."

"I have come to join you, as well, Menawa," said Rook.

Menawa came closer, peering coldly at Rook. "Why would you do that? You do not believe in our cause."

"No," said Rook bluntly. "Neither does my son. But he wants to fight, and I will fight beside him. And as long as we fight, you do not need to wonder why we are here."

"I do not trust your friend, Toquay," said the Great Warrior.

"I will vouch for him, Menawa," said Toquay.

This surprised both Menawa and Rook; they both

stared, surprised, at Toquay. Rook realized that his friend had effectively tied Menawa's hands; if the Great Warrior refused to let Rook stay at this point, it would be tantamount to saying he did not trust Toquay, who was one of his most trusted lieutenants. It would be a personal affront to Toquay.

"Then you are welcome," said Menawa, turning his back to Rook. His tone of voice belied the words he spoke. "If you want a fight, you have come just in time."

Saying no more, he returned to the fire.

"Come," said Toquay. "I will help you look for Tookla."

As they walked away from Menawa's fire, Rook asked what the Great Warrior had meant by his parting words.

"Sharp Knife is close by," said Toquay. "He marches down the Apalachicola with about seven hundred long hunters. Our scouts say he has no Cherokees or bluecoat soldiers with him. Menawa has decided to pursue him. We will not wait for the long hunters to attack us, this time. And we must strike before Sharp Knife joins up with the bluecoat soldiers, who we believe are along the coast."

Rook glanced around the camp. "There are only a few hundred warriors here. We are outnumbered."

"But we will have the element of surprise on our side."

"I see." Rook doubted that the element of surprise would be enough to balance the scales, but he saw no point in arguing about it.

"Besides," said Toquay, "Menawa believes Sharp Knife is heading for St. Marks. The redcoat, Ambrister, is there with guns and ammunition we need. If we don't stop the long hunters they will capture St. Marks. The Spaniards are few in number and they will not put up much of a fight. And if that happens, Sharp Knife will also capture the supplies the redcoat has promised to us."

"Father!"

Rook turned to see Tookla leave a group of warriors gathered around one of the fires and walk toward him.

"We will talk again later," said Toquay, and walked off.

"You are angry with me, I know," said Tookla, as he stood before his father. "You have come to take me home. But I will not go back. I want to stay and fight for our people."

"Our people?" Rook couldn't decide if he felt more relief or anger at the sight of his son. "Do you mean the Red Sticks? Or the Seminoles?"

"Does it matter? We are all brothers. The same blood flows in our veins. And we have a common enemy."

Rook sighed. "I am glad you think that way, Tookla."

"You are?" Tookla was surprised.

"Yes. I am glad you feel like you belong somewhere. I never did." Rook took another look around. "I never felt like they were my brothers. I do not want you to become an outcast, as I was. So I have not come here to take you home. Not right now, anyway. We will fight together, side by side."

Tookla beamed. "It is what I have always wanted. Then, when we have won a great victory against Sharp Knife, and driven the long hunters out of Florida forever, *then* we will go home."

"Of course." Rook could not bring himself to tell his son that he doubted any of that would come to pass.

Chapter Twenty

Departing from Barracoon, Barlow and the Cherokees proceeded down the Apalachicola River. They were more vigilant than ever; Joshua's escape left open the possibility that the Seminoles as well as the Spaniards were fully aware of their presence by now, or would soon become aware. Mondegah was of the opinion that the Red Sticks and the Seminoles would attack, and Barlow was inclined to agree, even though he was given to understand that the prevailing opinion among Jackson's officers was that the renegades would melt into the swamps instead, forcing their enemies to come in search of them.

Two days south of Barracoon they were met by a small flotilla of flatboats coming upriver—flatboats filled with supplies for Jackson's army. Barlow could scarcely believe his eyes. Until, that is, he learned that Jackson had sent a letter to the new Spanish governor, Colonel Jose Masot, warning the latter not to interfere with any attempt to provision his troops. Barlow had to laugh at the general's sheer gall. Amazingly, Masot had agreed, so long as the required duties were paid for the importation of such goods. Such, mused Barlow, were the often bizarre vagaries of war; the Spanish were collecting a tariff on the provisions of an invading army that, assuming Jackson had his way, would be the instrument of their downfall—and ultimate removal from Florida. Logic would dictate that the Spaniards' best interests would be met by seizing and destroying those supplies. Barlow appropriated some of the food from the flatboats for his command, even though the man in charge of the flotilla, a Texan named Everson, was reluctant to feed red savages regardless of whether they fought with Jackson or not. Barlow persuaded him by threatening to run him through with his saber, and, once the Cherokees had been supplied, dispatched the boats upriver.

On the third day, Barlow took his bearings and ordered his men to strike out due east from the river. St. Marks lay less than fifty miles in that direction, by his calculations. He sent a runner back to inform Jackson of his change in course. Early that same afternoon, the runner returned to inform Barlow that he had been unable to reach Sharp Knife. A large body of Red Sticks and Seminoles were moving westward toward the Apalachicola. He estimated there were between three hundred and four hundred of them, and that by now they would have reached the river.

"Which means that they'll soon be engaged in battle with Jackson's volunteers," Barlow told Houston, "if they aren't already."

"They've blundered into a trap then," said the ensign. "They couldn't know about us, else they would not have placed themselves between us and the general."

"Maybe. Or maybe they planned an attack on the general's column, and expected to strike and then withdraw before we could get there. Either way, we must make haste." He opened a map case tied to his saddle, extracted a chart he had acquired from Jackson at Fort Scott, and unrolled it. "My guess is that the general is right about here." He pointed at a spot along the line that represented the Apalachicola. "We have two options. We can retrace our steps to the river and then proceed northward, or we can cut across here, northwest, until we reach the river."

Houston peered at the map. "We don't know what lies to the northwest of us. Could be mile upon mile of swamp. And once we do reach the Apalachicola, we may be north or south of the army."

"But, with luck, we might shave hours off the time it takes us to reach the battle. And a few hours might make all the difference between victory and defeat."

Houston drew a long breath, and nodded. "It's a big gamble. But I say we take it."

Barlow smiled. "I agree. So be it."

In moments they were leading the Cherokees north by west, back toward the Apalachicola.

At midday, Menawa reached the river and prepared an ambush for Sharp Knife and the long hunters.

The key to success lay in locating and killing any advance scouts Jackson might have sent out. This the Great Warrior believed had been accomplished that morning with the deaths of three backwoodsmen and a Shawnee half-breed. He then positioned fifty Seminoles on a steep hill overlooking the river about five hundred yards north of the confluence of a fast-running, steep-banked creek with the Apalachicola. The rest of his warriors lay in wait deep in the forest about three hundred yards east of the river. As he explained it to his lieutenants, the long hunters, who were sticking close to the Apalachicola, would be allowed to file past the hill. The attack would take place when the head of Sharp Knife's column reached the creek. They would stop momentarily, and it was then that Menawa would lead his warriors against them. The long hunters would be trapped with the river at their backs. If they tried to flee north, past the hill, the fifty Seminoles would pick them off with their rifles. A few might try to get across the creek, but not many would have the time to do so.

Menawa made it plain that no mercy would be asked or given. No prisoners would be taken. And no retreat would take place. It would be victory or death.

Rook and Tookla were among those positioned in the forest. Spread out beneath the trees, Red Sticks and Seminoles alike stood or sat, seeing to their weapons or talking quietly, awaiting the arrival of the enemy. Rook watched his son. Tookla nervously checked his rifle a half dozen times before his father placed a hand on his shoulder.

"Do not dwell on what lies ahead," advised Rook. "Try to think of something else."

"I'll try," promised Tookla. "Father, were you afraid the first time you went into battle?"

"Yes. And the second time. And the third, as well. I'm afraid at this moment."

"You are? You don't look like you're afraid."

Rook smiled. He *was* scared, but not for himself. He was afraid he would fail to keep Tookla alive in the struggle that was about to occur.

"What is it like to kill a man?" asked Tookla.

"You will find out soon enough."

"I . . . I only hope I can do it when the time comes."

"You must do it. Or the long hunters will kill you. As bad as you will feel after having killed, you will know that you had no other choice."

"There is one other choice," murmured Tookla. "And that is not to fight."

Rook glanced at his son, surprised. "I have learned that there are some things worth fighting for."

Toquay joined them. "The long hunters are coming. When the fighting starts, the two of you stay back."

"Why?" asked Rook. "Is it because you don't think we have the courage to be Red Sticks?"

Toquay shook his head. Rook's words reminded him of their encounter in Tallahassee, when the Scotsman, Arbuthnot, had brought Ambrister to speak to the Seminoles of war, and when he and Menawa had confronted Rook.

"No," he replied. "Because once we were friends, and I would not want to see harm come to you or to your son."

"Neither would I," said Kinachi, appearing at Rook's shoulder.

"Is it not better to die for a just cause than to live in dishonor?" asked Rook.

"That depends on what you want in life," said Toquay. "You and Tookla should not be here."

"None of us should be here," replied Rook.

When the attack came, Andrew Jackson was at the head of the column of Tennessee volunteers. He had just finished cursing a fine blue streak at the stream that blocked his progress—after which he told one of his aides, Richard Keith Call, to take charge of a detail that was to cut down several of the trees that grew along the bank, felling them so that they would come down athwart the creek and provide makeshift bridges for his army.

A moment later, hundreds of warriors were coming at them through the woods. War cries and gunshots rent the air. Jackson spun his horse around and shouted at his men to form ranks and fire in volley. But the backwoodsmen weren't made for that. The loose column dissolved instantly into hundreds of buckskin- and homespun-clad men surging aggressively forward to meet the Indian onslaught. The battle immediately disintegrated into hundreds of man-to-man contests.

When Jackson's horse went down, dying from a bullet in the throat, his aides rushed to his side. Robert Butler and John Overton reached him first; Call was delayed momentarily by the necessity of killing a Red Stick who came at him with tomahawk raised. An instant later, Butler was hit in the fleshy part of the thigh by an arrow. "Stay down, General!" he gasped as he fell. Overton tried to push Jackson down behind the carcass of the horse, but Jackson would have none of it, and shook him off. He turned to Butler who, sprawled across the dead horse's withers, was trying to pull the arrow out—and accomplishing nothing more than inflicting more excruciating pain upon himself.

"By the Eternal!" roared Jackson. "Push the damned thing *through,* Robert!" He didn't wait for Butler to follow his instructions, but instead grabbed the arrow and thrust it deeper into his aide's leg, until the bloody head pierced the skin and emerged on the other side. Jackson then broke the shaft in two and pulled the front half out of Barlow's leg. Unbuckling his sword belt, Jackson untied the red sash around his waist and applied it to Butler's wound as a tight dressing to retard the flow of blood. As the general worked, Butler drew his pistol and shot down a warrior charging at them.

"Fine shot," remarked Jackson, with a quick glance to check Butler's handiwork. "I didn't know you were left-handed."

Butler grinned tautly. "I'm not, General."

Seeing that Jackson was exposed, Call summoned a half dozen backwoodsmen by shouting at them to rally 'round Old Hickory.

"By God, Richard," snapped Jackson, as Call arrived with the long hunters. "I don't need a damned bodyguard."

"Yes, you do, General," said Call. "Because otherwise you would go getting yourself killed, and then all would be lost. Besides"—he glanced at Overton and Butler—"we all promised Mrs. Jackson we'd do our best to keep you alive."

"Then take to the river, Richard, and go fetch Barlow and his Cherokees."

"They're at least a half day ahead of us, General! It would be morning before I could get back here with them."

"Then why are you wasting time?"

Call grimaced. He handed his pistol to Overton and, gripping his saber, waded into the Apalachicola until he could feel the pull of the main current, at which point he plunged into the swift, murky waters and was carried away.

When the shooting started and the warriors around them surged through the timber, Tookla seemed to lose his apprehension and made to run forward, into the thick of things. But Rook detained him.

"Don't be in such a hurry," said Rook. "You will get your chance."

"But we will miss the battle, Father."

"No, we won't. Stay with me."

Rook proceeded forward at a cautious pace, with Tookla to one side of him and Kinachi on the other. Toquay had gone ahead to lead the attack, as was to be expected from one of Menawa's lieutenants. The gunfire quickly intensified, becoming a constant din, like a rolling peal of thunder that never stopped. An acrid mist of powder smoke drifted through the trees, dense enough in places to completely obscure portions of the fighting.

As Rook had predicted, the long hunters did not panic. They did not try to flee, or run into the river to escape death. Their reaction was to strike back, to counterattack, and soon the forest was the scene of many individual battles. Not thirty paces ahead, a Seminole warrior fell, struck by a bullet; an instant later, he was set upon by a backwoodsman, who raised his rifle in order to slam the butt of the weapon into the wounded Indian's skull, crushing it. Kinachi quickly raised his rifle and fired, killing the long hunter. The shot drew the wrong kind of attention—a bullet buzzed past Rook's head seconds later. He whirled, saw the smoke-shrouded figure of another Tennessean to his left. The man was reloading his rifle. Rook did not hesitate, and shot him dead before he could finish.

Suddenly, a wave of long hunters was coming straight for them—five men moving shoulder to shoulder through the melée, cutting a swath of death. They saw Rook and his two companions and charged. Kinachi fired, wounding one, and then spun and fell. Rook could not spare even a second to look back and see how badly Kinachi was hurt. The Tennesseans were upon them. Tookla fired his rifle at almost point-blank range. One of the backwoodsmen clutched at his belly and fell heavily to his knees; staring in shocked surprise at Tookla, he opened his mouth to speak, but spewed blood instead, and then toppled forward onto his face. Tookla watched with mounting horror, frozen in place. He didn't seem to see the other long hunters, one of whom charged at him with a tomahawk raised.

Rook had not had time to reload his rifle; he was about to fend off another Tennessean by using the rifle as a club when he saw the danger Tookla was in. He switched targets in mid-swing, whirling to slam the

rifle's stock into the face of the man with the tomahawk, and doing so with such force that the stock
shattered. The long hunter fell backward, his face a
bloodied, mangled mess. In the next instant, Rook
found himself falling, too, clubbed from behind by a
Tennessean who used the butt of his own empty rifle
to do the damage. Before the long hunter could strike
again, however, Tookla, shaken out of his paralysis by
the gut-wrenching sight of his father falling, lunged at
him. Tookla thrust the blade of his hunting knife into
the man's belly. The impact of his lunge hurled the
backwoodsman to the ground. Tookla scrambled on
top of him and struck again and again and then again.
He looked up to see another long hunter standing
there, a snarl of hate on his bearded features as he
raised a pistol, drawing a bead. In that instant, Tookla
realized he was going to die.

But the long hunter never pulled the trigger. His
eyes suddenly widened and took on a faraway cast,
and he pitched forward to fall within a few feet of
Tookla. Tookla stared at the tomahawk imbedded between the man's shoulder blades. Then Toquay was
pulling him roughly to his feet. Tookla was covered
with blood, and for a moment Toquay thought he was
hurt. Once he was convinced that this was not the
case, that the blood belonged to the man Tookla had
killed with the knife, Toquay turned his attention to
Rook. The latter was trying to get up. Toquay helped
him—and held on to him as Rook, groggy, swayed
precariously.

"Toquay," mumbled Rook, straining to focus on his
friend's face. "What are you doing here?"

"You must go, Rook. Go now. The battle is lost."

Rook glanced beyond Toquay. The fighting still
raged, hand-to-hand. Nothing had changed.

"What do you mean?"

"Trust me!" said Toquay forcefully. "The ambush failed. The element of surprise was not enough. But then, you probably knew all along that it wouldn't be. This time Menawa will not withdraw. We will stand and fight until the last warrior breathes his last breath. That is why you must take Tookla away from this."

"You want me to run away?"

Toquay managed a wry smile. He had spoken those very words at Cholocco Litabixee when Rook had pleaded with him to join him in flight.

"Yes. You will live and I will die here. That way we both get what we want. Now go!"

Rook knew there was no time to argue. He turned to see Tookla kneeling beside Kinachi—just in time to watch, in shock, as Kinachi breathed one final, shuddering breath. Picking up the rifle of one of the slain long hunters, Rook grabbed Tookla by the arm, hauled him to his feet, and began walking away with long strides, reloading the rifle as he went.

He looked back only once. But Toquay was gone.

They had traveled but a few hundred yards when a Cherokee warrior stepped out from behind a tree to block their path. Rook pushed Tookla aside and began to raise the rifle—only to freeze when he felt a gun barrel nudge his spine. He looked over a shoulder to see a second Cherokee warrior. Why, he wondered, did they not shoot?

The answer came a few seconds later, when a young man with dark blue eyes and unruly black hair, clad in the blue coatee of an American officer, arrived on the scene astride a lanky dun horse.

"Tie them up and keep a close watch on them," said Barlow. "But under no circumstances are you to shoot." He listened a moment to the tumult of the nearby battle. "We must not let them know we're coming."

"Wait," said Rook desperately, as Barlow began to turn the horse away. "This is my son. He is just a boy. Let him go free."

Barlow glanced at Tookla. "He's covered with blood, and it's not his own."

Rook nodded. "It is true, he has fought against you. He killed a long hunter who was about to kill me."

Barlow looked away—and Rook followed his gaze, to see a line of Cherokee warriors moving as quietly as ghosts through the green late-afternoon shadows of the forest, moving resolutely in the direction of the battle.

"I don't have time for this," muttered Barlow. He looked bleakly at Rook. "Drop the rifle or you both will die."

Rook dropped the rifle. Barlow nodded and rode on, leaving the two Cherokees to tend to the prisoners.

As they drew closer to the fighting, Barlow and Houston dismounted and secured their horses to the limbs of a fallen tree.

"You sure you can maneuver well enough on that leg?" asked Houston.

Barlow untied a stout hickory stick from his saddle. Mondegah had given it to him several days before. Barlow's wound was still causing him considerable discomfort; the bullet had torn through muscle, and he could not yet put much weight on the leg. The hickory stick helped.

"I have this," he said, "and we'd be targets in the saddle."

They proceeded on foot, the Cherokee warriors arrayed on either side of them. Houston carried pistol and saber in hand. As per Barlow's orders, the Cherokees moved quietly; there would be no shooting until their presence was discovered by the enemy. When that happened, they would charge into the melée and, with luck, trap the Red Sticks and their Seminole allies between themselves and Jackson's Tennessee militia.

It was late in the afternoon; the sun was dropping below western hills, and the gloom beneath the forest canopy deepened. The fog of powder smoke further obscured things. Barlow and the Cherokees got within a hundred yards of the battle before they were spotted. Barlow saw long hunters as well as Indians, and suspected that some of the Tennesseans would mistake the Cherokees for enemy reinforcements. But there was no turning back. Bullets began to burn the air around him. Here and there along the line, warriors began to fall. Barlow could delay no longer.

"Let's go," he told Houston.

The ensign raised his saber and shouted: "Forward, Cherokees!"

The warriors charged, uttering their war cries. Barlow tried to keep up but couldn't; the Cherokees and Houston were soon well ahead of him. Trying to ignore the pain of his wound, he hobbled forward as fast as he was able.

A moment later he found himself in the thick of things. The fighting raged all around him. He leaned against the trunk of a tree, taking all the weight off his leg, amazed that no one seemed to be paying him any attention; everyone else appeared to be locked in a life-or-death struggle. And just then an arrow plowed into the tree trunk inches from his shoulder. He whirled, saw the Red Stick thirty paces away, fitting another arrow to his bow. Barlow dragged the pistol from his belt and fired. His aim was true, and the impact of the ball sent the Red Stick sprawling backward. Another Red Stick came charging out of the drifting powder smoke with tomahawk raised. Barlow drew his saber, blocked the downward sweep of the tomahawk with the hickory stick, and drove the saber into the Indian's belly. The Red Stick fell into him, knocking him off balance, and they both went sprawling. The saber, buried to the hilt, was wrenched from Barlow's grasp. As Barlow got up, he sensed rather than heard or saw the danger coming at him from behind. Turning, he saw a Seminole warrior running right for him, wielding a cane knife. The only thing Barlow had left with which to defend himself was the hickory stick. Crouching, he braced himself to meet the Seminole's onslaught without holding out much hope of prevailing against a better-armed adversary. But, not ten paces away, the Seminole stumbled and fell, virtually at Barlow's feet. Barlow looked up to see a backwoodsman lowering his rifle. It was Luther Wayne, the Clarksville volunteer Barlow had traveled with, years ago, from Fort William to Horseshoe Bend. Wayne came loping up, grinning like a wolf.

"Howdy, Lieutenant. Fancy meetin' you here."

"Hello, Wayne. Thanks. I think you saved my life."

"I figured it might come to that, someday, you bein' from Philadelphia and all." Wayne laughed—and then, brandishing a bloody knife, knelt to take the scalp of the Seminole he had just slain. He stuffed the scalp into a buckskin pouch. "That makes seven today. Maybe eight—I've lost count. Well, I'd love to stand around and chew the fat a while with you, Lieutenant, but there's more work to be done. So long!" And with that Luther Wayne loped away.

Barlow watched him go, and shook his head. Retrieving the saber, he proceeded in the direction of the river. The gunfire had suddenly diminished. He saw Houston coming across the field of dead and dying. Reaching Barlow, the ensign pointed to the north.

"What's left of the enemy is on a hill up that way. It's pretty much over."

Barlow nodded. "Sounds like it. We had better find General Jackson."

They went to the river. The first thing Barlow spotted was Jackson's white horse, stretched out dead on the ground. He was relieved to see Jackson standing near the water's edge, very much alive. The general was using a field glass to survey the hill, a few hundred yards upriver, where the hostiles were making their last stand. John Overton stood at his shoulder. Robert Butler, wounded in the leg, sat near the dead stallion. As Barlow and Houston approached, they were joined by Mondegah. Barlow and the Cherokee warrior exchanged nods; it was not necessary to put into words their relief at finding the other alive. Barlow's respect for Mondegah had grown by leaps and bounds in past weeks. The Cherokee had proven to be as fine a soldier as any Barlow had ever met. And he was a man of great integrity, besides.

Jackson lowered the field glass and saw them coming.

"Ah, Barlow! Your timing was exquisite. Your attack was the *coup de grâce.*"

"Thank you, sir."

"But how did you find out so quickly that we were under attack? I thought you were many hours ahead of us."

Barlow explained about the runner he had sent that morning, the one who had returned with word that Menawa's warriors were advancing on the Apalachicola.

"I dispatched Richard Call down the river to find you," said Jackson. He turned to Mondegah. "Send a couple of your men to find Call."

Mondegah looked at Barlow, who nodded. Only then did the Cherokee leave to carry out Jackson's wishes.

The general grimaced. "I forgot. The Cherokees only listen to you now, Lieutenant, isn't that right?"

Barlow considered telling Jackson that this was because he had never lied to the Cherokees, but wisely refrained from giving voice to a comment that, while undeniably true, was also inflammatory.

A group of seven Tennesseans approached. Four of them carried the body of a Red Stick as carelessly as they would the carcass of a game animal. They dropped the dead man on the ground at Jackson's feet.

"This here is Menawa," said one of long hunters. "The so-called Great Warrior. He don't look so great now, does he?"

"Are you certain it is he?" asked Jackson.

"Oh, yes, sir, I'm sure. This is him all right, no doubt about it. I met him myself, some years back, and more than once. That was when I used to trade some with the Upper Creeks' towns."

Jackson gazed with immense satisfaction at the dead Indian. "Well, my friends, we have achieved another great victory today. I think it's safe to say we've gone far toward ending the threat to our frontier settlements. But our task is not complete. To make certain that the threat never returns, we must drive the dons into the sea. Tonight we will bury our dead. Tomorrow we proceed to St. Marks." He looked at Barlow. "Lieutenant, you and your Cherokees will stay close from here on."

As he and Houston walked away, Barlow heard the ensign chuckle—a rare sound from one who was usually so serious.

"Coup de grâce?" murmured Houston. "I don't think it's an exaggeration to say we turned the tide of battle. But the general will never admit that the Cherokees saved his bacon."

"He probably would have prevailed without us."

"Maybe. But he would have lost a great many more men in the process. I'm thinking Menawa had Old Hickory worried there for a while. That's why he isn't going to send us far afield again."

"One thing," said Barlow. "We must keep our men away from the long hunters. There is no love lost between the Cherokees and the Tennesseans, not since the treaty at Fort Jackson. If we're not careful, we'll have another fight on our hands."

Houston nodded. "That would be a disastrous turn of events for me. Because I can't say which side I would take."

Barlow could have said the same about himself.

Chapter Twenty-one

Barlow had forgotten all about the two prisoners until, returning to the place where he had left his horse, he saw the two Cherokees bringing up Rook and Tookla. The guns were silent now, the battle over—Barlow assumed that the hill had been overrun. He wondered if these two Creeks were the sole survivors of Menawa's force.

"What are we going to do with them?" asked Houston.

Barlow shook his head. He noticed that the younger of the two, the son, looked both scared and defiant. The older merely looked resigned. He stepped up to the latter.

"You speak English very well," he said. "Where did you learn to do so?"

"In the white man's school, when I was a boy," replied Rook. "My father became a Christian, and took me to live among the whites for several years."

"Were you at Horseshoe Bend?"

Rook nodded. "I was fighting to protect my home."

"You wouldn't have needed to protect your home if the Creeks hadn't fallen under Tecumseh's spell and taken up arms against the United States," said Houston curtly.

"We would have taken their land anyway, Sam, sooner or later," said Barlow. "Just ask the Cherokees."

"Well, that's true, I suppose," allowed Houston.

"I was also at Horseshoe Bend," Barlow told Rook.

"We were enemies then, and now we're here and still enemies. Why shouldn't I kill you? The next time we meet we'll still be enemies, and you might try to take my life."

"Kill me if you wish. But let my son live. He is too young to die, but old enough to take care of his mother and his younger brother in my place."

"No!" said Tookla. "I will not leave you, Father!"

Thinking about all the dead and dying men beneath the trees not far away, Barlow realized he had no stomach for more killing today. And yet he knew that he could not be saddled with prisoners. There seemed to be but one option left open to him. He turned to the Cherokee guards. "Let them go free," he said.

The Cherokees clearly did not approve of his decision, but they said nothing, and lowered their rifles. Rook watched them and then looked in amazement at Barlow, as though he was having a difficult time believing what he was seeing.

"Go on," said Barlow brusquely. "Take your son and go home."

Rook nodded gratefully, and walked away with Tookla in tow.

As they melted into the forest, Houston shook his head.

"You better hope the general never gets wind of this," said the ensign. "He would skin us both alive."

"Well," said Barlow wryly, "I won't tell him if you won't."

In spite of what he had been told, Rook refused to believe that Amara was really gone—until he found the remnants of her dress in the woods not far from his now deserted home. Clutching at the torn doeskin garment, he looked bleakly up at Walker, who sat on his heels nearby, shaking his head slowly back and forth in an exaggerated motion.

"Reckon this mean Joshua gonna have to die," drawled Walker.

Rook was too distraught for words. He simply knelt there in the dirt for a while, feeling as though his heart had just been wrenched violently out of his chest.

Ever since his release by the bluecoat officer he had been living a nightmare. It had begun with the long trek back to Tallahassee, burdened with the knowledge that all the brave Seminole warriors who had followed Menawa on the warpath were dead. Including Kinachi. And he would be the one to deliver this terrible news to Tallahassee. His thoughts dwelled on Kinachi's wife—and all the other wives in the town who were widows and did not yet know it.

And the reaction to the bad tidings he carried was worse than he'd expected. The grieving began immediately upon his arrival—the wailing and self-mutilation of the stricken wives and mothers and sisters, the lost weeping of children who would never see their fathers again, the silent suffering of male relatives and friends who could not release their grief with tears.

Then, in the midst of all this anguish, the nightmare got worse. Kinachi's wife had been the one to tell him that Amara had been taken by force. Taken by a black man. Korak had seen it—he had disobeyed his mother's command to stay at home and had gone down to the creek to find her. He had seen her running, with the black man in pursuit. Frightened, Korak had raced to Tallahassee. But by the time Walker and several braves arrived back at the creek, she was nowhere to be found. The signs showed there had been a struggle. They showed, too, that the black man had been carrying her as he headed south; his tracks were deeper than normal, indicating he was burdened with more than his own weight.

Korak, of course, remembered Joshua, the black man who had accompanied him and his family on their journey south to Florida several years earlier. So there could be no doubt that Joshua was the one.

"You should have gone after him," Rook told Walker.

"I wanted to. But Hopaunee wouldn't permit it. He said he could not spare a single man. Said the long hunters was coming. Those were the rumors. Are the long hunters coming, Rook?"

Rook didn't answer. He didn't care about any of that. He only cared about one thing—getting Amara back.

"I reckon Joshua gone to Pensacola or maybe St. Marks," said Walker. "Reckon he's aiming to get out of Florida. Long as he stay, he's a marked man. Best way for him to go about doing that is on a ship. He sure can't go north. The slave catchers would get him for sure. They be thick as fleas along the border."

Rook stood up and started to walk away.

"Wait," said Walker, rising. "I'm going with you."

"No."

"You say Kinachi is dead. He told me was that to happen I was to belong to you."

"No," said Rook, more sternly than before. "I have no use for a slave. Go back and stay with Kinachi's family. They need you. I don't."

"Tookla can take care of things just fine till we get back."

"What about Hopaunee?"

"If I'm your slave, and you take me with you, then I ain't in no trouble with Hopaunee. And he ain't about to tell you you can't go after your woman."

"You're not my slave. You're free. I give you your

freedom. Now go back to Tallahassee." Rook started walking.

Walker started after him. "Reckon if I'm free, that mean I can go anywhere I want to. And I reckon you're wrong. You do need me."

Rook stopped and turned. "Why?"

"I know Pensacola and St. Marks both like the back of my hand. Before I lived with the Seminoles, I spent some years at sea." Walker grinned. "Well, there ain't no gettin' around it. They called me a pirate. If Joshua is anywhere on the coast, I can help you find him."

Rook stared at Walker for a moment, and then continued on his way without saying a word. Walker decided that since he hadn't been told he *couldn't* go along that he was being invited. So he fell in behind Rook as they followed Joshua's trail southward.

When Barlow first set eyes on St. Marks he was impressed by the size of the fortress that guarded the town and the harbor beyond. It was a formidable stronghold, with thick stone walls that fairly bristled with the snouts of big cannon protruding from embrasures. In the shadow of the walls, and the shelter of the guns, was a town built on the northern shore of a narrow bay, a natural harbor currently occupied by a British warship as well as a Spanish merchant brig.

As Jackson's army approached, a Spanish officer rode out to meet it under a flag of truce. The officer spoke English—it was the reason he had been chosen to act as courier.

"His Excellency, the Governor, Colonel Masot," said the officer when presented to Jackson, "respectfully requests the full disclosure of your intentions, and warns you that to proceed further will require him to defend property rightfully belonging to the King of Spain. As it is His Excellency's fervent hope to avoid bloodshed, he prays you will heed this warning, and wishes you to understand that while he has the utmost respect for you, he also has a duty to perform as a soldier and the loyal subject of his king."

Jackson listened impatiently. When the envoy had finished, he said, "Go back to Colonel Masot and tell him I have received his message."

The Spanish officer was momentarily nonplussed. He had expected a more detailed response.

"I will send my answer to the governor in my own good time," said Jackson curtly. "I will do so under a flag of truce, which I expect he will honor, as I have respected his own."

"Of course, General." The Spanish officer bowed stiffly, mounted his horse, and rode back to the fortress.

Jackson turned to his aides and subordinates, who had been summoned to witness the exchange. Barlow and Houston were among those present.

"Masot is bluffing," grunted Jackson. "I can feel it in these old bones. He wouldn't dare fire his guns at us, or try to resist our entrance into the town."

"A small but determined force could hold that fort for a quite a while," opined John Overton, warily gazing at the walls of the stronghold, clearly visible a half mile away across sandy lowlands spotted with palmettos. They stood on a narrow road that connected the port with several plantations—all of which had been found abandoned—located inland. The Tennesseans and Cherokees were arrayed on tree-covered hills behind them.

"The Spanish garrison is small," said Jackson, "but not determined, I'll wager. Masot doesn't have the stomach for battle. If he had, he would have intercepted our supplies going up the Apalachicola. No, gentlemen, he is hoping I will flinch from creating a diplomatic incident. But diplomacy be damned. We have come too far, and endured too much, to stop short of our ultimate objective. And unless the Spaniards are driven from Florida we can never guarantee the security of our frontier. Look there!" He stabbed a finger at the distant British warship, the Union Jack flying defiantly from its mizzenmast. "The bloody redcoats are still here, fomenting trouble, exciting the Indians and the runaway slaves against us. They signed the Treaty of Ghent, but they have not ceased to make war against us. And the dons are their willing accomplices. By the Eternal, such wicked subterfuge shall be stopped!"

"Even if it means war with Spain, General?" asked Overton.

"Even so. We've defeated the British army on the field of battle, John. The Spanish will be easy to vanquish compared to the redcoats, believe me. Not that it will come to this. Yes, Spain will complain. They will make threats. But in the end they will do nothing. Just like Colonel Masot."

They made camp on the spot. As had been the case for the last several days, Barlow made sure the Cherokees were bivouacked across the road from the Tennessee militia. So far there had been no incidents and he wanted to keep it that way.

He was waiting eagerly for coffee to brew when Richard Call appeared to inform him that the general was requesting his presence immediately.

"It would appear the honor will be yours, Barlow," said Call.

"The honor?"

"Of being the first one of us to step foot inside the fort. The general wants you to deliver his reply to Masot."

"I'll be right there."

As Call walked away, Houston, who was sitting on

his haunches by the fire they shared with Mondegah and several other Cherokees, shook his head.

"Honor?" asked the ensign. "If the general's reply is anything like what I expect it to be, Masot will probably clap you in irons, Timothy. If he doesn't decide to have you shot."

"I'll be under a flag of truce."

"Let's hope that will protect you." Houston stood up and drew Barlow aside, out of earshot of the warriors. "General Jackson hasn't been too happy with you, you know, on account of what's happened with the Cherokees."

"Surely you're not suggesting . . ."

Houston held up his hands. "I'm just suggesting that you watch yourself, my friend. That's all."

Mondegah approached them. "I will go with you," he told Barlow.

"No. You cannot. Don't worry, though. I'll be fine." Barlow glared at Houston.

"If you do not come out of that place," said Mondegah, "we will come to get you out."

Arriving at Jackson's tent a few minutes later, Barlow was ushered in immediately to find the general alone at his camp desk, putting the finishing touches on a letter, which he folded and sealed with wax. Rising, he presented the letter to Barlow.

"For Colonel Masot's eyes only, Lieutenant. I know I can rely on you. You did a fine job for me in Washington. Not only are you reliable, but you're attentive and tactful, as well. Mr. Overton is too cautious and Mr. Call is too reckless. Mr. Butler is incapacitated. So it falls to you."

"Yes, sir."

"I trust it's all right with your Cherokee friends that you do this for me."

"Just so long as I come out again, sir."

Jackson nodded. "Then don't forget this." He picked up a ramrod with a white cloth secured to it.

"As I recall," said Barlow wryly, taking the flag of truce, "the last time you sent a man into a Spanish fortification under one of these he was fired upon by British soldiers."

"That's true. So let us hope that in this instance history will not repeat itself. Good luck, Lieutenant."

Barlow was met at the fortress gate by a squad of green-coated Spanish fusiliers, who held him under their guns until an officer arrived. It turned out to be the same officer who had carried Colonel Masot's message to Jackson earlier that day. Barlow informed him that he carried a communique from Jackson to His Excellency, the Governor. The officer nodded and produced a blindfold.

"If you would be so kind," he said.

"By all means," said Barlow.

The officer placed the blindfold on him. Leaving his horse at the gate, Barlow allowed himself to be taken by the arm and led into the fortress. He heard the tramping of booted feet—men marching in formation. A moment later, he heard it again. And then he heard it a third time, just before he was taken indoors, up a flight of stone steps, and through a set of doors. The blindfold was then removed. He found himself in a long, high-ceilinged room. To his left was a massive stone hearth. To his right, were a row of arched windows set deep in a thick wall of stone. In front of him was a huge mahogany desk, with ornately carved lions rampant at the corners. The desk seemed to dwarf the short, slight man in a uniform heavy with braid and medals who stood behind it.

"His Excellency, the Governor," said Barlow's officer-escort.

Barlow snapped to attention and bowed, ever so slightly. "Your Excellency."

"And you are?"

"Timothy Barlow, Lieutenant, 39th Infantry Regiment, United States Army, at your service, sir."

Masot looked him up and down, taking note of Barlow's travel-worn and bloodstained uniform.

"I apologize for my appearance, Your Excellency," said Barlow hastily. "I have come a long way in a relatively short period of time, and have met with a mishap or two along the way."

Masot smiled. His were pale, patrician features—a wide, thin mouth, an aquiline nose, and dark eyes. Thinning black hair was plastered to his scalp, curling down onto his forehead in the Napoleonic style.

"I am pleased to see that General Jackson took my warning to heart," said Masot, "and proceeded no further. And I must apologize for the blindfold, Lieutenant. But I am sure you understand. Until we resolve the unfortunate misunderstandings that exist between us, I would be remiss if I permitted you a close scrutiny of these defenses."

"A sensible precaution, Your Excellency. May I present General Jackson's reply to your earlier communication?"

Masot snapped his fingers and the officer standing behind and to one side of Barlow came forward to take the sealed letter from Barlow's hand and deliver it to the colonel, who broke the seal and began to read.

"Are you privy to the contents of this communique, Lieutenant?"

"No, sir," said Barlow.

"Your general informs me that he has come to chastise the Indians and black brigands who make war against the United States. In order to do this, he is compelled to garrison this fortress with his own men. This, he claims, is justified on the grounds of self-defense. He expects that I will offer no argument on that score." An expression of amusement mixed with incredulity on his face, Masot glanced at the officer who stood near Barlow. "He goes on to promise that Spanish rights and property will be respected! My soldiers are to vacate this fort by sunrise tomorrow, leaving their weapons behind." Masot let the letter slip from his fingers and flutter to the desk. "Your general apparently harbors a dangerous illusion, Lieutenant Barlow. He seems to think we are not able to hold this fort against his army. He is quite mistaken. I can only hope that you will convey the truth in that regard to him. You will save many lives by doing so."

"The truth, Your Excellency? What is the truth, exactly? Does it have anything to do with the subterfuge of blindfolding me and then marching the same company of men past me three times? General Jackson may harbor an illusion, sir, but at least he is not in the habit of trying to manufacture one."

It was a bold bluff—all Barlow had were suspicions, and if he was wrong he would look like a fool, and Masot would have the upper hand. But the expression on the colonel's face immediately informed him that he *wasn't* wrong. To give himself a few valuable seconds in which to think of a response, Masot went to one of the windows and gazed out. Barlow sensed that the colonel was trying to decide whether to run his bluff to the end, or fold.

Masot sighed. "My most fervent wish is to prevent bloodshed. For that reason I will comply with General Jackson's demands. We will surrender the fort, on condition that we be allowed to leave St. Marks immediately, aboard the brig at anchor in the harbor—with all our arms."

"I am confident the general will agree to that condition. But we have one of our own. You will refrain from spiking the cannon or blowing up the magazine or committing any other sabotage that might render this place indefensible."

Masot nodded. "Of course. You have my word on it. We shall let our respective governments determine between themselves whether your general's actions amount to piracy. In my opinion, they do. And I fear the consequences will be grave."

Barlow made a mental note not to mention to Andrew Jackson that Masot had called him a pirate. *All we need,* he mused, *is for the commander of the southern military district of the United States and the governor of Spanish Florida to engage in a duel of honor.*

"As a demonstration of my good faith," said Masot, turning from the window, "I have a present for your general."

He nodded at the Spanish officer, who crossed the room to a single door, opposite the set of doors through which Barlow had entered. Opening the door, the officer spoke in Spanish to someone in an adjacent room. A moment later, two soldiers escorted two men who were shackled hand and foot through the door. One of the prisoners wore the uniform of a Royal Marine. The other, a white-haired and frail-looking older man, was dressed in civilian garments.

"May I introduce Lieutenant Robert Ambrister and Mr. Alexander Arbuthnot," said Masot, as cheerily as if they were all attending a soiree. "As I understand it, General Jackson has been vociferous in his insistence that the British have been encouraging the Indians to attack the southern frontier of the United States, and have gone so far as to provide them with weapons with which they carry out those attacks. I happen to know that these two have indeed been employed in that activity. I learned of this only recently, you understand, else I would have put a stop to it long before now. If I had but known."

"You unprincipled liar," said Ambrister, furious.

"Really, Masot," said Arbuthnot calmly. "You've outdone yourself this time."

Looking at Ambrister and Arbuthnot, Barlow knew they were dead men.

"I give them to you, Lieutenant," Masot told Barlow, with a grand gesture, "as a token of my willingness to cooperate with General Jackson's endeavors to bring a long-awaited peace to the region."

"I'm sure the general will be extremely grateful, Your Excellency."

"These two soldiers will accompany you back to your lines in order to assist you in transferring the prisoners—assuming you will personally vouch for their safe return."

"I will, Your Excellency."

Masot came forward and extended a hand. "I doubt we will meet again, Lieutenant, as by sunrise tomorrow I will have set sail for home." He leaned forward conspiratorially. "I can't say I'll be sorry to leave this mosquito-infested, disease-ridden land behind."

"And we won't be sorry to take it off your hands, Your Excellency."

Masot laughed. "How droll. I like you, Lieutenant. I like you."

Barlow wished he could say the same of His Excellency.

Chapter Twenty-two

As Barlow had suspected would be the case, Andrew Jackson's first order of business upon taking possession of the fort at St. Marks was to convene a military court to hear evidence against the two British prisoners, Ambrister and Arbuthnot. As luck would have it, General Gaines arrived with the 39th Infantry on the same day the Spanish sailed out of the bay. This permitted Jackson to fill the court with twelve regular army officers, presumably giving the proceedings the flavor of greater legitimacy.

The charges against Arbuthnot were that he had been actively involved in a conspiracy to supply arms to the Indians waging war on the United States, and that he had acted as an agent for those Indians in correspondence with the British government, said government having as its policy aiding and abetting those tribes hostile to the republic. He was, in short, an agent provocateur. A spy.

As for Ambrister, he was charged with aiding the enemy as well. Among the pieces of evidence against him was a letter he had written only hours prior to his arrest by Masot's soldiers, a letter in which he had given specifics as to the number of guns and amount of powder and shot provided to the Indians thus far. He had intended to send this letter to his superior, Major Nicholls, via the captain of the British frigate. Jackson's sudden arrival had prompted him to change his plans, and he had been intent on escaping with

Arbuthnot aboard the warship when Masot's soldiers placed them under arrest. The frigate had sailed away the moment its captain learned that Masot had surrendered St. Marks.

For his part, Barlow was glad he had been passed over when the twelve offices of the court had been selected. He did, however, sit in as a spectator to the trial, and was present when Arbuthnot was allowed to speak in his own defense.

"May it please the court," said the Scotsman, "if I say only that I have never encouraged the Seminoles to war against the United States. The Seminoles have long been my friends, and I would not advise them to pursue a course that would guarantee their destruction. However, once they had made their decision, I did participate in seeing to it that food and blankets provided by the Crown reached the towns. With so many men gone to war, there were women and children in dire need of such provisions. Not that I expect the court to differentiate between aiding those Seminoles who remained in their towns with aid to those on the warpath. The United States made no distinction between friendly Creeks and Red Sticks at Fort Jackson. I make the point only to set the record straight."

After a swift deliberation, nine of the twelve officers agreed that Arbuthnot was guilty of the charges made against him, and sentenced him to hang.

Then it was Ambrister's turn. Standing ramrod straight and defiant before the court, the Royal Marine denied only that he was a spy. He was, he said, a soldier doing his duty, obeying orders, and serving his country. For this he was quite ready to die. He had but one request—that he be executed by firing squad and not by the gallows.

This time the court's deliberations took a good deal

longer. When they reconvened, Barlow was startled by their judgment. While Ambrister was found guilty as charged, he was sentenced only to fifty lashes, followed by confinement at hard labor for a period of twelve months. Barlow almost laughed out loud. Jackson had been undone by his insistence on placing regular army officers on the court. Arbuthnot was one thing—a civilian living among hostiles could not expect any sympathy from military men. But Ambrister was something else entirely—a fellow officer, albeit one who wore a different uniform, but also one who lived by the officer's code of honor and commitment to duty. This the court *could* sympathize with.

Barlow concurred wholeheartedly. While he did not think Arbuthnot deserved to die, the Scotsman had understood the risks involved in what he had been doing, and by providing comfort to Seminole women and children he made it possible for Seminole warriors to go on the warpath. Besides, Barlow had a hunch that the old trader was ready to die, and he surmised this was the case because Arbuthnot did not want to live to see the destruction he knew would soon be visited upon the people he loved. Ambrister, on the other hand, was certainly no spy. He wore his uniform proudly.

It came as a surprise to nearly everyone when General Jackson put aside Ambrister's sentence and declared another—death by firing squad.

As soon as he heard the news, Barlow hurried to the 39th's camp on the outskirts of St. Marks and found Colonel Williams in his tent. Though he had been detached from the regiment for several years now, Barlow felt no less comfortable now than he had in the past in going to the colonel with a concern or complaint. Williams encouraged openness from his junior officers, and was thought of as a mentor by many of them, Barlow included.

"You've got to do something, sir," said Barlow. "Lieutenant Ambrister doesn't deserve the sentence he has been given."

"I agree. Neither does Arbuthnot, in my opinion. But you're too late, Lieutenant. I've already made my feelings known to the general, and I think it's safe to say my sentiments are shared by most of the regiment's officers. Yet, as I suspected at the outset, it didn't make any difference. Jackson hates the British. Ever since one of them slashed his face with a saber, when he was just a lad. And don't forget, his brother perished on a British prison ship during the War for Independence. Ambrister is doomed, and there's nothing we can do about it, I'm afraid. We'll just have to sit back and watch the drama unfold."

"I'm not sure I follow you, sir."

"I mean the general's actions will antagonize both the Spanish and the British governments. There will be a diplomatic furor. Our government may find it necessary to use Jackson as a scapegoat. They may sack him to appease Britain and Spain. I don't think anyone can deny that he has gone too far this time."

Barlow thought about it—and shook his head. "They may try to ruin Jackson, sir, but somehow I doubt they'll succeed."

"Time will tell. At any rate, I'm glad you've come to see me. I just received this." Williams brandished a letter. "It's from the general, dated yesterday, informing me that he has put his signature on a field commission bestowing upon you the rank of captain. I heartily approve of the promotion, and I'm sure the War Department will concur. You have served the republic with distinction. I understand you're married?"

"Yes, sir," said Barlow, trying to recover from his shock.

"Then you should be able to provide nicely for your wife on a captain's pay. You may even see fit to start a family now that your financial situation will be substantially improved."

Barlow felt a sharp pang of regret. The colonel, of course, could not know that Sarah was no longer able to bear children.

"At the general's suggestion," continued Williams, "I have issued you a six-month leave of absence, with pay, effective immediately."

"Thank you, sir. May I make a recommendation of my own?"

Williams smiled. "Houston?"

"Yes, sir."

"I will take it under consideration." The colonel stepped forward and shook Barlow's hand. "Congratulations, Captain. May I suggest you not linger here?"

"What about the Cherokees?"

"It seems Jackson knows they won't linger, either, once you're gone. They are free to return home. I understand they will be given an official letter of thanks that will express the gratitude of the country for their service."

Back in the Cherokee encampment, Barlow told Houston and Mondegah what had transpired.

"*Captain* Timothy Barlow, is it?" asked Houston, pleased. "Well, I suppose you deserve it. And I thank you for recommending me for a promotion. But if this little war is well and truly over, I'm going to hand in my resignation and go live with the Cherokees."

"The army will be losing a fine soldier." Barlow turned to Mondegah. "I'm going home to see my wife.

And then I'm going to Washington, to do what I can for your people."

Mondegah nodded, obviously pleased. "You are a good man. They will listen to what you have to say."

"Don't get your hopes up," said Barlow. "I think there's a chance of undoing what was done at Fort Jackson. But it's an awfully slim chance."

"I know one thing," said Houston. "Old Hickory won't be too happy when he finds out what you're up to."

Barlow nodded pensively. "I know I'm doing the right thing, and that he was wrong to take Cherokee land, but I still regret going against him. It's hard to explain."

"I understand," said Houston. "Believe me, I do. I still don't know quite what to make of Andrew Jackson. At times I think he's a hero, and at others I see him as a ruthless villain."

"Perhaps he's both. After all, he *is* only human."

Houston nodded. "When are you leaving?"

"In the morning, first thing."

"You'll miss the executions."

Barlow grimaced. "That's the idea."

"Then at least go into town with me tonight. We'll have a drink and make a toast to the future."

Barlow accepted the invitation.

When they arrived at St. Marks and saw the Stars and Stripes flying over the fort, Rook's heart sank. Joshua's trail had led them here, but the presence of the Americans made following him into town that much more dangerous. Still, he had no choice, and was prepared to make the attempt in broad daylight. But Walker stopped him.

"They will think you're a Red Stick," said Walker.

"And they'll either throw you in irons or shoot you. And they'll probably shoot me, too, if they don't haul me away to die a slave on some plantation."

"I am not going back without Amara."

"I know. We wait until night, then we cross the bay to get to town."

"How do we do that?"

"You just leave it to me," said Walker, confidently.

When night fell, they made their way to the northern tip of the bay. Walker dove into tall reeds and in a matter of minutes located a small rowboat.

"Whose boat is this?" asked Rook.

Grinning, Walker just shrugged. "Who knows? Smuggler's, maybe. Lots of smuggling goes on here, or used to anyhow, on account of the Spanish duties. Get in."

Rook climbed into the boat. Walker pushed off and took up the oars, bending his muscular back to the task of rowing them across the inky black surface of the bay. There was a wind blowing in from the sea, but the tide was on its way out, and the waters were not all that rough. They made good time, and it was apparent to Rook that Walker had a lot of experience handling small craft. Across the bay, lights along the shore marked the location of St. Marks, the forbidding walls of the fortress looming above town and silhouetted against the indigo sky.

It took them nearly an hour to traverse the bay. As they drew near the town, Rook surveyed a row of clapboard buildings lining a wharf. Walker rowed them right under a pier that jutted out from the wharf, and told Rook to secure the bowline to one of the pilings.

"You wait here," said Walker. "I know some folks to ask about Joshua. If he's here, they'll know about it. If I ain't back in an hour, I ain't coming back at all."

Rook nodded. Walker stood up in the boat, grabbed the edge of the pier and swung his body up onto it.

Ten minutes later Rook heard footsteps—two men coming down to the end of the pier. As they passed overhead, Rook caught a glimpse of them as he peered up through the planking. They were American soldiers. The night was clear, the moon nearly full, and he could clearly make them out. They paused at the end of the pier to survey the empty bay for a moment before turning whence they had come.

A half hour later, Walker reappeared, swinging down off the pier into the boat with the agility of a circus performer.

"He's here," he whispered.

"And Amara?"

Walker nodded. "Got here a few days back, right before Jackson and his long hunters showed up. The Spaniards are all gone. Joshua tried to get aboard their ship but they turned him away. Now he's holed up in town."

"Where?"

"Close by. Come on. Reckon we can get your woman back and then get out of here without anybody being the wiser—if we're lucky."

They climbed up onto the pier, ran to the wharf and paused, leaning against the back of a building. Rook could hear voices through the wall, and the sound of a fiddle. Light blazed from a nearby window. Walker in the lead, they ran to an adjacent building, and then to the next. Walker took his bearings and said, "This is the one. Joshua and Amara, they should be inside this here warehouse."

Rook saw that there were several sets of heavy timbered doors along the wharf side of the warehouse.

He took a step toward the nearest, but Walker grabbed him by the arm.

"No. Them doors'll be barred from the inside. This way."

He led Rook around the corner of the building, into a narrow alley to a smaller door. Walker tried the latch. The door gave a little, but would not open all the way. Walker pushed harder, but to no avail. Impatient, Rook pushed him aside and rammed a shoulder into the door. It swung inward with a splintering of wood—a sound followed instantly by the report of a pistol close by. Rook was momentarily blinded by the muzzle flash. He heard Walker cry out behind him as he stumbled sideways, bringing up the rifle he carried. But he couldn't shoot. Not until he knew Amara's location. He heard someone moving, and then a body struck him full on, knocking him down. He rolled, throwing Joshua off, and groping for the knife sheathed at his side. His sight was slowly returning. The warehouse was dark, but some moonlight leaked in through narrow windows above the wharf-side doors. He could see Joshua leaping to his feet and whirling. A cane knife lay atop a barrel within his reach. He swept it up and dropped into a crouch, grinning at Rook.

"I figured you'd come, was you still alive," said Joshua.

He lunged, swinging the cane knife. Rook barely avoided the blade. Joshua kept coming, slashing again and again in mighty, lateral strokes, backing Rook up until he found himself trapped against a stack of crates. With a shout, Joshua lunged, bringing the cane knife down. Rook ducked under and slashed the runaway's belly open with the knife. Joshua roared with pain, turned and swung the cane knife again, but he was off balance, and Rook was able to cut his arm to the bone. Joshua dropped the cane knife. Clutching at his belly, he stared at Rook in disbelief.

"You killed me," he gasped.

"I should have done it a long time ago," muttered Rook—and lunged, turning the blade of his knife so that it slid between Joshua's ribs and ruptured his heart.

He found Amara in a corner of the warehouse, covered with a blanket and tied hand and foot. He wiped Joshua's blood from the knife onto his leggings before cutting her bonds. As soon as her hands were free, she threw her arms around him.

"Come," he said. "We must hurry."

At the door he knelt beside Walker's body to check for a pulse. There was none. He stood and took Amara's hand and led her out. They could hear men running on the wharf. Peering around the corner of the building across the alley from the warehouse, Rook saw the two soldiers he had spotted earlier on the pier. They were coming toward the warehouse, drawn by the gunshot. Rook pushed Amara up against the wall and stood beside her, knife at the ready. But the soldiers ran past the mouth of the alley. Rook didn't hesitate. Leading Amara, he left the alley and began to run for the pier. They were nearly there when two more soldiers appeared in front of them, coming around the building from which Rook had heard the fiddle and the voices. He recognized them both as the officers who had been with the Cherokees at the battle of the Apalachicola. Rook glanced over his shoulder. The two soldiers were in hot pursuit.

"We're trapped," gasped Amara.

Tightly gripping her hand, Rook turned and leaped off the edge of the wharf into the waters of the bay.

As the soldiers reached the spot where Rook and Amara had disappeared, they raised their rifles, preparing to fire when their prey surfaced. Barlow arrived an instant later, and knocked the rifle held by the nearest soldier aside.

"No shooting," he said curtly.

"Looked like a Red Stick Creek to me, sir," said one of the soldiers.

"Maybe so." Barlow glanced at the water below. "But they're gone now."

"They couldn't have gotten far," protested the soldier.

Barlow looked at him. "They're gone. Continue on your rounds."

As the soldiers walked away, Houston said, "That Indian looked familiar."

Barlow nodded. "It was the one I set free at Apalachicola."

"He had a woman with him. Wonder who she was?"

"I suppose we'll never know. Come on, we were about to have that drink."

They headed back for the tavern from whence they had come. Barlow lingered at the corner of the building. He could hear the fiddler sawing up a storm inside.

"You go along," he told Houston. "I'll be along in a minute."

"Try to stay out of trouble, Captain." Houston smiled and went inside.

Barlow waited in the shadows until he saw the small rowboat emerge from beneath the pier. In a moment it was lost from sight against the black surface of the bay.

"Well, General," he murmured. "It looks like two of them got away."

With a satisfied smile, he turned and entered the tavern.

SIGNET BOOKS (0451)

JUDSON GRAY

RANSOM RIDERS 20418-2

When Penn and McCutcheon are ambushed on their way to rescue a millionaire's kidnapped niece, they start to fear that the kidnapping was an inside job.

DOWN TO MARROWBONE 20158-2

Jim McCutcheon had squandered his Southern family's fortune and had to find a way to rebuild it among the boomtowns.

Jake Penn had escaped the bonds of slavery and had to find his long-lost sister...

Together, they're an unlikely team—but with danger down every trail, nothing's worth more than a friend you can count on...

To order call: 1-800-788-6262

Classic John Jakes...

The New York Times *bestselling*
Crown Family Saga

California Gold   0-451-20397-6

James Macklin Chase was a poor Pennsylvanian who
dreamed of making it rich in California. But at the turn of
the century, the money to be made was in oil, citrus,
water rights, and the railroads. Mack would have it all, if
he had his way. And along the way, the men and women
he met, the passion he found, the enemies he made, and
the great historical figures like William Randolph Hearst,
Leland Stanford, and Theodore Roosevelt, he encountered,
helped bring glory to the extraordinary century.

The Bold Frontier   0-451- 20419-0

These tales capture the glory and suffering of the men and
women of the American West. From a strange saloon
shootout and a trapper seeking vengeance against a fur
company to double-crossing outlaws and a duel between
medicine men, John Jakes's thrilling stories span the legacy
and fuel the imagination—of the American frontier.

To order call: 1-800-788-6262

SIGNET

Charles G. West

Medicine Creek   0-451-19955-3

The white-born, Cheyenne-raised warrior Little Wolf has left
the warpath behind to create a prosperous life with his wife
Rain Song. But when a renegade army slaughters his tribe
and takes Rain Song captive, Little Wolf's dreams for peace
are overrun by the need for bloody vengeance.

Mountain Hawk   0-451-20215-5

Mountain man Trace McCall must rescue his beloved from a
kidnapper without getting caught in a growing conflict
between white homesteaders and Indians.

Son of the Hawk   0-451-20457-3

When a war party of renegade Sioux slaughters his Shoshoni
tribe, the young brave White Eagle has no choice but to
venture into the world of the white man to find mountain man
Trace McCall—the father he never knew.

To order call: 1-800-788-6262